Murder of a Medium

A Redmond and Haze Mystery

Book 15

By Irina Shapiro

Copyright

© 2024 by Irina Shapiro

All rights reserved. No part of this book may be reproduced in any form, except for quotations in printed reviews, without permission in writing from the author.

All characters are fictional. Any resemblances to actual people (except those who are actual historical figures) are purely coincidental.

Cover created by MiblArt.

Table of Contents

Prologue..5
Chapter 1 6
Chapter 2 12
Chapter 3 14
Chapter 4 18
Chapter 5 23
Chapter 6 33
Chapter 7 43
Chapter 8 50
Chapter 9 54
Chapter 10 62
Chapter 11 71
Chapter 12 77
Chapter 13 83
Chapter 14 92
Chapter 15 103
Chapter 16 111
Chapter 17 115
Chapter 18 120
Chapter 19 124
Chapter 20 129
Chapter 21 135
Chapter 22 142
Chapter 23 146
Chapter 24 152
Chapter 25 158
Chapter 26 161

Chapter 27 166

Chapter 28 174

Chapter 29 177

Chapter 30 184

Chapter 31 189

Chapter 32 192

Chapter 33 199

Chapter 34 213

Chapter 35 216

Epilogue..221

Prologue...224

Chapter 1 227

Chapter 2 231

Chapter 3 237

Prologue

It had been a pleasant evening, warm and fragrant with the scents of flowers and cut grass, but tendrils of thick yellow fog had begun to drift from the river after the sun had set, turning the air thick and soupy, and very cold. Neil Lacky couldn't wait to return to Bermondsey and leave his hansom at the cab yard so he could finally go home, rest by a warm fire, and enjoy a good supper and a pint of lager. Maybe two.

He had just dropped off his previous fare in North Audley Street and had turned into Upper Brook Street when he saw her. The woman emerged out of the fog like a vengeful apparition, all swirls of black silk and wild hair. Her face was bone-white, and her eyes resembled dark caves. Pale lips were compressed into a thin line as if she were making a supreme effort to contain a scream.

The woman raised a quivering hand to get Neil's attention, but he wasn't interested in picking up some drunken doxy. The last time he'd made that mistake, his hansom had reeked of vomit for a week. But something about the woman gave him pause as she stumbled into a pool of shimmering light cast by a streetlamp. Now that he could see her more clearly, Neil realized she was no streetwalker. Her silk gown was fashionable and well made, a jeweled brooch was pinned to the high lace collar, and she wore earbobs that sparkled like diamonds in the gaslight. The woman carried a beaded reticule, and the ring she wore over her black glove looked like the real thing, not a paste bauble.

"Please, stop," the woman moaned, and Neil took pity on her.

She had difficulty getting into the hansom, so Neil climbed off his perch and gave her a hand. The woman gripped his wrist and stared into his eyes. Her gaze was unfocused, and her speech was slurred, but she didn't smell of spirits, nor did the folds of her gown release the sickly-sweet aroma of opium. The woman let go of his wrist and held up one finger, then unclasped her reticule and fumbled inside until she found what she was looking for. She pushed a card into his hand and slumped back against the seat, closing her eyes, and resting her head against the side.

Neil looked at the address on the card, then pushed it into his pocket. One last fare, and then he was off home.

Chapter 1

Friday, June 18, 1869

Inspector Daniel Haze hurried up the steps and pushed open the heavy door. The duty room at Scotland Yard was pleasantly quiet in the morning, when most miscreants were still abed. The action picked up throughout the day and built to a crescendo after sunset, when the constables hauled in brawling drunks, weeping prostitutes, and underage pickpockets, who loudly proclaimed their innocence despite their bulging pockets.

Sergeant Meadows sat behind the desk, perusing the morning edition of *The Illustrated London News*. The *News* was a favorite with the men, not only because they enjoyed the pictorials but also because sometimes their names were mentioned and their likenesses captured in the drawings that depicted violent criminals being arrested by the brave and dedicated constables of the Metropolitan Police. Sergeant Meadows set the newspaper aside and smiled in greeting.

"Good morning, Inspector Haze. Beautiful day."

"So it is," Daniel agreed.

"Might take the missus out for a stroll once I go off duty."

"I'm sure she'd like that."

"The superintendent is expecting you," Sergeant Meadows said, now that the pleasantries were out of the way and they could move on to the business at hand.

Although Daniel wasn't quite sure what that business was. He had been summoned by Superintendent Ransome, but the message had been cryptic at best, and Daniel wasn't quite sure if a crime had taken place, and neither was Constable Putney, who'd come to fetch him. The constable had assured Daniel that Jason Redmond had also been sent for, which usually implied that a postmortem was required, but the constable had said that there was no body, which was puzzling in the extreme.

"Do you know anything about the case, Sergeant?" Daniel asked before moving along to Ransome's office.

"Nah. He's playing it close to the chest with this one," Sergeant Meadows said. "And you know what that means."

Daniel nodded. If Ransome was keeping the details from his men, then whoever was involved was an important personage whose name was best kept out of the mouths of the constables, whose penchant for a good gossip could rival that of any fishwife. Taking off his bowler, Daniel crossed the duty room and strode down the corridor toward Ransome's office. Ransome had been in a good mood these past few weeks, but Daniel had a feeling that was about to change and this case would bring out his less amiable qualities. The door was firmly shut, so Daniel knocked and waited until he was bidden to enter.

Ransome sat behind his desk, but whereas he was usually applying himself to a never-diminishing pile of paperwork, the desk was clean, the pot of ink, blotter, and pen neatly arranged in the right corner. Ransome appeared to be staring into space, his shoulders drooping with either resignation or fatigue, despite the early hour.

"Good morning, sir," Daniel said.

"Nothing good about it," Ransome snapped. "Shut the door and take a seat, Haze."

Daniel settled in one of the guest chairs and waited for Ransome to explain himself. Asking questions would only irritate the superintendent, and he would share the details with Daniel in his own time. Ransome sighed so heavily, Daniel felt a gust of warm air hit his face.

"What's happened, sir?" he couldn't help but ask.

"Constantine Moore was waiting for me when I arrived this morning. Remember him, do you?"

Daniel nodded. Constantine Moore was the assistant and paramour of Alicia Lysander, the famed medium, whose ability to commune with the dead had reached mythical proportions in recent years. Members of the ton were willing to pay any amount, no matter how exorbitant, to lure Alicia to their homes, where she conducted private séances and somehow managed never to disappoint those who were desperate to contact their dearly departed.

Daniel had been skeptical of Alicia Lysander's ability and had believed her to be a charlatan of the highest order until Alicia had helped him locate his missing daughter at Jason's behest. If not for Alicia, Daniel might have never seen his darling Charlotte again, and Daniel's gratitude was boundless. He would move heaven and earth to help Alicia if she were in trouble, and by extension Constantine Moore, who had to have come to see Ransome on Alicia's behalf.

"What did Moore want?" Daniel asked.

"He was worried about Mrs. Lysander," Ransome replied. "She had been invited to conduct a séance at the home of the Earl of Ongar last night. They had agreed that Mr. Moore would collect her at ten o'clock, once the séance had finished, but when he arrived, Mr. Moore was informed by the earl's butler that Mrs. Lysander had already departed." Ransome sighed again. "This was unusual, but not overly alarming. Mr. Moore thought that perhaps the séance had not gone as planned, or that maybe someone had become distressed and wished to call an end to the proceedings. He assumed that he would meet Mrs. Lysander at home. When he arrived, there was no sign of her, and as of this morning, she had not returned."

"I see," Daniel said, but he was certain he wasn't looking at the whole picture.

It was concerning that Alicia Lysander had not returned, but as of now, there was no indication that anything untoward had befallen her. And why the secrecy and such obvious concern on Ransome's part? If Alicia Lysander had left the séance of her own free will, what possible reason would Ransome have to worry about the earl's involvement?

"The Earl of Ongar is a very important man, Haze," Ransome said, as if he had read Daniel's thoughts. "He's quite close with the commissioner and has the ear of the prime minister. His Grace and Mr. Gladstone dine together at least once a month, and I hear Mrs. Gladstone has taken Ongar's young countess under her wing. The earl has a reputation for having a short temper and a long memory. If we handle this incident in a manner he finds offensive, he could ruin all our careers and begin a campaign of attrition that could affect the police service as a whole."

"You mean he can ensure that our budget is cut?" Daniel asked.

Despite the stellar work of the Metropolitan Police and the superhuman efforts the public seemed to expect of the thinly stretched and underpaid policemen, there were always those who advocated to defund the police or at the very least cut the funding significantly since they believed the Met's efforts to be useless and a waste of valuable resources. The commissioner was always fighting their cause, and Ransome, who had been an experienced copper before his promotion, spent most of his time trying to figure out how to stretch the budget to pay the men a decent wage and hire enough bobbies to patrol the more turbulent areas of London, where one man with a truncheon and a whistle was about as effective as a slingshot against a cannon.

"Among other things," Ransome said. "We need to manage this very carefully."

"Do you think the earl is somehow involved in Mrs. Lysander's disappearance?"

"I don't know, but she was last seen leaving his house in Grosvenor Square, so that is where we need to begin our inquiries."

"I see no need to involve the earl," Daniel said. "I can question the staff, then try to ascertain which way Mrs. Lysander went after leaving the earl's residence."

"Good man," Ransome said. "I have sent for Lord Redmond. He's on good terms with Mrs. Lysander and has the trust of Mr. Moore. Perhaps this is a case of domestic discord and Mrs. Lysander and Mr. Moore have simply had a falling out."

Ransome looked like he hoped for just such an outcome, but if Alicia Lysander did not appear unharmed within the next twenty-four hours, they would have no choice but to involve the earl and his family, since they had been the ones to host the séance and the earl's servants had been the last people to see Alicia Lysander alive.

"Do you know who was present at the séance, sir?"

"I don't have the names of the attendees, but I'm sure anyone the earl associates with will not appreciate being interrogated by the police."

Daniel was about to ask another question when there was a knock at the door.

"Come," Ransome called.

Daniel was pleased to see Jason, who nodded silently to both men as he walked in and sank into a vacant chair with the relief of a man who'd been on his feet for hours. Jason looked unusually tired for so early in the morning and wore an expression that was too grave to be explained away by carriage traffic or some minor domestic incident.

"Thank you for coming, my lord," Ransome said. "I was just explaining to Inspector Haze that we have a rather delicate situation on our hands. Yesterday evening, Alicia Lysander conducted a séance at the home of the Earl of Ongar. She left the earl's residence before ten o'clock but never returned home. I expect she and Mr. Moore had a lovers' tiff, and she simply decided to put some space between them, but until we can be certain that no one in the earl's household was involved in the lady's disappearance, we must tread very, very carefully. With any luck, Mrs. Lysander will turn up today and we'll say no more about it."

"Mrs. Lysander has turned up already," Jason replied gruffly. He did not look like a bearer of happy news, but his somber expression seemed to be lost on Ransome.

"Splendid," Ransome exclaimed. "I'd rather deal with ten run-of-the-mill murders than investigate a case where a high-ranking member of the nobility is involved, especially someone as highly esteemed as the Earl of Ongar."

Jason's expression became even grimmer, and Daniel strongly suspected that he was about to deliver a blow that would thoroughly ruin Ransome's day.

"Superintendent, last night, around half past ten, Alicia Lysander hailed a cab in Upper Brook Street. She gave the driver my address. By the time she arrived in Kensington, Alicia Lysander was dead."

"Dead?" Ransome sputtered. "Where is she now?"

"Downstairs, in the mortuary."

"You brought her with you?"

10

"I don't have the means or the inclination to perform a postmortem at my home."

"Yes. Of course," Ransome said under his breath. "What was the cause of death?"

"I cannot say for certain until I open her up, but I think she was attacked."

"That's it," Ransome said. "She must have been set upon in the street. A random mugging."

"Mrs. Lysander still had her reticule and was wearing several pieces of jewelry. As far as I could tell, nothing was taken."

Ransome nodded. "Then I suggest we hold off questioning the earl's staff until we're sure about the cause of death."

"I agree," Jason said. "Shall we reconvene in say three hours?"

Ransome checked his watch. "I'll see you at one o'clock."

Chapter 2

Shutting the door to the mortuary behind him, Jason stood still, his gaze on the woman laid out on the table. Alicia was fully dressed, her hair, which had come free of its pins, rippling down the sides like the dark water of the Atlantic on a stormy day. Her skin was chalky, her lips parted in what must have been a final cry. Jason had closed Alicia's eyes, but they had been open when he'd come out to fetch her from the cab, her pupils dilated with either pain or a drug she might have taken shortly before death, her skin still warm. Her body had felt light in his arms, even though a dead body always weighed more than a living one, and her limbs had been pliable, rigor mortis not having set in.

Some part of Jason had hoped that Alicia was still alive, and he would be able to bring her around despite the lack of a pulse or the absence of breath, but deep down he had known it was too late. Alicia had passed away on her way to him. Perhaps she'd had something she'd needed to tell him, a final message she couldn't take to her grave, or the more likely answer was that she had hoped he'd be able to save her. Jason hadn't noticed any wounds when he'd laid her down on the settee and had gone through the ritual of confirming death, but Alicia must have known that she was dying, and her final living act had been to give the cabbie Jason's address.

The cabbie had looked shocked as he stood with his hat in his hands, watching Jason lift Alicia out of the cab and carry her inside. He had been able to answer a few basic questions and had shown Jason the card Alicia had given him, but didn't seem to know anything else, only that the woman had been alone and unsteady on her feet, clearly unwell but still alive. The cabbie had fled before Jason could ask for his address or fetch money to pay him. He had been understandably terrified that he would be accused of hurting a passenger, but Jason was certain that the man had had nothing to do with Alicia's death. Whatever had occurred had happened shortly before Alicia had got into his cab.

Worried that someone would come downstairs and see the dead woman in the drawing room, Jason had asked his surly butler to guard the body while he roused his coachman, who preferred to sleep in a loft above the carriage house. Together, Jason and Joe had hidden the body in Jason's brougham until he could deliver it to Scotland Yard in the morning. Joe had gone back to bed, but Jason had remained in the carriage house, watching over Alicia until the first rays of the morning sun painted the sky salmon pink and Alicia's still face emerged out of the darkness.

Only then had Jason returned to the house. He'd washed and dressed, explained what had happened to a sleepy Katherine, and returned to the carriage house. As he sat next to Alicia in the brougham, he'd reached for her hand, and even though he knew she was gone and couldn't hear him, he had promised that he would discover what had happened to her. He wasn't a religious man. He had lost his faith after the horrors he'd witnessed during the American Civil War, but he now believed that a person's spirit lived on, some kernel of consciousness surviving death and decay and passing to some other realm, where it dwelled for eternity. Alicia had been able to tell him about his parents' final moments, and more important, she had been instrumental in getting Charlotte back after she had been abducted. Jason wouldn't call Alicia a friend, but he had liked and respected her, and he owed her this one last service.

Approaching the table, Jason studied Alicia's frozen features. Had she known what was going to happen to her? Had she foreseen her own death? Was that why she had carried his card in her reticule when they hadn't been in contact for months? Jason's arms felt leaden as he removed his coat and hung it on a hook, then put on the leather apron and tied the strings behind his back. He pushed his hair beneath the linen cap and set out the instruments he would need for the dissection. Ready at last, he took a deep breath and laid a gentle hand on Alicia's cheek.

"Forgive me," he said.

Jason didn't expect an answer, but something in the air shifted, and although no sound had passed Alicia's lips, not even an exhalation of gas that was already beginning to build up in the lungs, Jason could have sworn he heard Alicia's voice in his mind.

"I trust you, Jason."

"I won't fail you," Jason said, and carefully turned the body over, ready to undo the buttons that ran down the back of Alicia's gown and begin the postmortem.

Chapter 3

Normally, Jason needed to eat after a postmortem, since he never breakfasted before starting on a body, but today he had no appetite. He felt worn out and nauseated as he ascended the steps and paused before the door to Ransome's office. He didn't want to talk about Alicia as if she were nothing more than a body. To him, she was still a person, an intelligent, vibrant woman who had been like no one he'd ever met, but the tang of her blood was still in Jason's nostrils, and even though he'd scrubbed with carbolic soap, his hands didn't feel clean, reminding him that she was now a cadaver. Sadness tugged at his heart, and his limbs felt heavy and sluggish. He wished he could take a short rest, but given what he'd learned, he realized that his day was just beginning, and he had to find a way to tap into his reserves of energy if he were to be useful.

"Come in," Ransome called once Jason knocked. "Where's Haze?"

"Right here," Daniel said as he strode down the corridor.

The two men resumed their seats, as if the hours in between had not happened. Daniel looked expectant, but Ransome's expression was strained, his lips compressed into a thin line as he studied Jason across the expanse of his desk. He probably hoped Jason would tell him that Alicia Lysander had died of natural causes and there was no need for an inquiry. Jason wished that were the case. He would be sad and angry that Alicia's life had been cut short, but he would accept her passing and hold on to the memory of the woman she had been. The only thing he would remember now was her eviscerated body, the glistening organs, and the weight of her brain in his bloodstained hands.

"Well?" Ransome asked when Jason failed to speak. "What's the cause of death?"

"Alicia Lysander died of a cerebral hemorrhage that was the direct result of blunt force trauma that fractured her skull."

"And yet she still managed to find a cab and get to your house," Ransome said confusedly.

"Death is rarely instantaneous when there's a slow bleed on the brain," Jason explained. "The person might have a headache and suffer from disorientation, blurry vision, and slurred speech, but they're still able to formulate thoughts and move about, although their coordination might be impaired. Had Alicia lived another few minutes, she might have been able to tell me what had happened to her, but she slipped away shortly before she arrived. I would like to think that her passing was peaceful, but given that someone had fractured her skull, she was likely in great pain."

"She may have fallen and hit her head," Ransome offered.

Jason shook his head. "I don't think that's likely."

"Based on what?"

"Based on my examination of the contusion. The fracture is at the top of the parietal lobe." Jason pointed to the top of his head for the benefit of Daniel and Ransome. "If Alicia had fallen, the fracture would be lower, whether she fell backward and landed on the ground or hit her head against something hard while still upright. No debris was caught in the hair or had adhered to the skin. Had she fallen to the ground, there would be dirt and grit, and if her head was smashed against the wall, there would be residue from the bricks. However, there was mud on her skirts and dirt on her palms. I think she went down on her knees after she was struck and balanced herself on her hands before pushing to her feet."

"Can you tell anything about the object used to hit her?" Daniel asked.

"I think it was heavy, round, and made of metal, since there were no splinters or bits of stone."

"Would she have seen her attacker?" Ransome asked.

Jason shook his head. "There are no defensive wounds. It is my belief that someone came up behind her and hit her hard."

"Would the person have to be taller than the victim to strike her at that angle?" Ransome asked.

"Not necessarily taller, but they would have to be of at least average height, since Alicia was tall for a woman."

"And were there any health concerns that would have hastened her demise?"

"Alicia Lysander was in good health at the time of her death," Jason said.

"Was she hit repeatedly?" Daniel asked.

"I saw no evidence of multiple blows," Jason said. "Perhaps her assailant saw her go down, assumed she was dead, and ran. Had they looked back, they might have seen her rise, but the darkness and the thick fog would have hidden her from view as soon as her assailant was a few feet away. I don't know how long she was down, but eventually, she rose and was able to stumble to the road, where she stopped a cab."

"So attempted murder, then?" Ransome asked, now all business.

"Attempted and accomplished," Jason replied. "Alicia died of her injuries, which makes her attacker guilty of murder."

"Are you able to estimate the time of the attack?" Ransome inquired.

"If Alicia was due to leave the séance at ten but departed early and was delivered to my door just before eleven, then she was probably attacked between nine thirty and ten thirty, after she had left the earl's house."

"Grosvenor Square is not known for violent attacks on respectable women," Daniel pointed out.

"Mrs. Lysander's respectability was questionable at best, but you're right, Haze. This sounds premeditated. We need to fill in that missing hour if we're to find out what happened," Ransome said.

"Which means we must start with the earl and his household," Daniel replied.

Ransome glared at him. "Well, get to it, then. And remember, kid gloves, Haze."

"Yes, sir," Daniel replied, and pushed to his feet.

Jason stood as well. The sleepless night and lack of food had finally caught up with him, and he swayed on his feet, but he quickly caught himself on the back of the chair and followed Daniel out of Ransome's office. He had every intention of accompanying Daniel to Grosvenor Square.

Chapter 4

"Jason, have you eaten?" Daniel asked as soon as he and Jason stepped outside.

It had started to rain while Jason had been working in the mortuary, but the rain had stopped, leaving the air chilly and damp. A dank wind tugged at their coats and hats, and carried with it all the unpleasant smells of London in June, the miasma all the more dangerous since cases of cholera were mounting and the sickness had already claimed a number of victims in the seedier parts of London, where people lived cheek by jowl.

"Not yet," Jason replied tiredly.

Daniel peered at him. Jason looked pale, and his movements seemed slower than usual, but Daniel didn't think Jason was ill, just tired after a sleepless night and an emotional few hours spent working on Alicia. Jason had to eat every few hours in order to stave off bouts of hypoglycemia that came on quickly and left him feeling shaky and faint, the symptoms worsening if he didn't eat something right away. Daniel could understand Jason's distress at what had happened and felt his weariness as if it were catching, but despite their personal connection to the victim, they had to treat this like any other case if they were to understand what had happened to Alicia. Jason had said much the same thing when Charlotte had been taken, and although all Daniel had wanted to do was to crawl into some dark cave and not come out until Charlotte was safely back, he had overcome his debility and had participated in the investigation spearheaded by Jason.

"Let's get you something to eat before you have one of your turns," Daniel said, and was relieved that Jason didn't argue or proclaim that he was fine when he clearly wasn't.

Daniel steered Jason toward a chophouse they frequented when in Westminster, and they placed their usual order with the usual waiter, who seemed inclined to chat but then quickly left when he must have sensed their grim mood and a need for privacy.

"Are you all right?" Daniel asked once the waiter had brought them half pints of ale and hurried off to the kitchen to check on their order.

Jason took a few sips of ale, which would begin to restore his equilibrium once it hit the bloodstream, and nodded.

"I'm just sad," he said. "Alicia was so young and vibrant. She was like no one I had ever met. The world seems a darker place without her in it."

"Yes, it does." As far as Daniel was concerned, the world had been plenty dark already, but he had to admit that he felt the loss almost as keenly as Jason. "What are your thoughts?"

"Alicia came to me because she needed a doctor, but she also wanted me to find whoever did this to her. Had she lived a few minutes longer, she could have told me."

"Would you have been able to save her?" Daniel asked.

Jason shook his head slowly. "I doubt it. I would have had to drill a hole in her skull to relieve the pressure on the brain, but I don't think it would have helped, and if performed without the benefit of anesthesia, the procedure would probably have sent her into shock. Even if Alicia had still been alive when she arrived, it would have already been too late."

"Then you did everything you could," Daniel replied. "And you will continue to fight her corner until you get to the truth."

"I can only do that if this wasn't a random attack."

"Do you think it was?"

"No," Jason said, his answer immediate and firm. "Someone had a motive to want Alicia dead, or at least seriously injured. If she had survived the attack, she might have been cognitively impaired for the rest of her days. And even if she wasn't, a brain injury could be used to discredit any evidence she was asked to give."

"I agree with your assessment, and I would like to start by speaking to Constantine Moore," Daniel said. "Just because he reported Alicia missing doesn't mean he's not responsible. He might have met her after the séance, and then perhaps they quarreled. Would a smooth stone be consistent with your conclusions regarding the murder weapon?"

"It might be," Jason replied hesitantly.

"So, unbalanced by the argument and driven by rage, Constantine could have picked up a stone and hit Alicia over the head when she turned away from him. Believing she was dead, he reported her missing early the following morning in order to cover his tracks."

"Constantine loved Alicia, which is not to say that he couldn't have murdered her," Jason mused. "When passions run high, human beings are capable of untold savagery."

"Perhaps she had been unfaithful to him, or maybe she had decided to leave him. They weren't married, so she wasn't legally bound to him. And she was the breadwinner in that relationship. Without her, Constantine would be left without a partner, both personally and professionally."

Jason nodded. "And he would appropriate Alicia's assets, since she had no family to challenge his claim."

Daniel sighed heavily. "I will need to speak to the Earl of Ongar."

The prospect worried him. Not only had Ransome made the earl sound just this side of rational, but a man in his position had the power to destroy Daniel's prospects and rob him of his livelihood just for his temerity to question the earl as if he were a suspect. One word to the commissioner, and Daniel would be finished, his career with the police service cut short, leaving him without a means to support himself. He supposed he could always return to Birch Hill. Squire Talbot had never appointed a permanent parish constable after Daniel had left, so the position would be his for the taking, but the idea of returning to that life scared Daniel more than the possibility of losing his place at the Yard. CI Coleridge of the Brentwood Constabulary would probably have him back, but Daniel hated the thought of coming back to the station with his tail between his legs.

"I'll speak to the earl," Jason offered. He looked considerably better now that he'd had something to drink and was halfway through his fillet of beef.

Daniel admired the fact that Jason didn't hide his emotions and wasn't ashamed to show his feelings to those beyond his family circle. Daniel would never share his true self with Ransome or anyone at Scotland Yard, but Jason was also a man who didn't give in to his melancholy and dealt with feelings of grief and loss by losing himself in work. The most meaningful thing he could do for Alicia was to discover what had happened last night, and he would conduct the most difficult interview, both because his noble rank placed him in the same social class as the earl, which gave him leverage, and because he cared enough about Daniel to shield him from what could turn out to be career suicide.

"I will question the servants," Daniel offered. "Several members of the household staff would have been present for the séance, and they would have seen the guests to the door once the evening came to an end. They would know precisely who left, who stayed, and who had escorted whom." Daniel paused, considering. "Is there anything more to be learned from the cabbie?"

"I don't think so. The man told me everything he knew, which wasn't very much, but I did get his name, if you'd like to speak to him yourself."

Daniel nodded. "Let's start with the individuals who were the last to see Alicia before the attack and then decide if we need to track down the cabbie. I expect he's employed with one of the cab yards in Bermondsey so will not be too difficult to find."

"Given the earl's connections, I can only assume that Ransome will try to keep the story under wraps until he knows more," Jason speculated.

"Wouldn't you?" Daniel replied. "Ransome is no fool. To even mention the earl's name in connection with Alicia's death could result in an accusation of slander, especially if the earl's connection to the victim makes it into the papers."

"Is it really slander if the information is verifiable fact?"

"No, but as of now, the only fact we're in possession of is that Alicia Lysander attended a séance at the earl's home. And at this time, there's nothing to suggest that the earl is even aware of what happened."

"We only have the butler's word that Alicia was unharmed when she left," Jason pointed out.

"Are you suggesting that she was attacked inside the earl's residence?" Daniel exclaimed.

"I'm only saying that we can't rule out the earl's family or his staff until we know more." Jason pushed away his plate and took a sip of his ale. "I propose we start with Constantine. I have several questions to put to him before I speak to the earl."

"Let's go," Daniel said, and placed several coins on the table. "My treat this time."

"Thank you," Jason said.

He looked more like his usual self, and Daniel was gratified to see the determination in his eyes. His partner was back, and the investigation was about to begin in earnest.

Chapter 5

Constantine Moore and Alicia Lysander resided in a three-story house in Greek Street. Given Alicia's occupation and moral flexibility, Daniel thought the area strangely appropriate to her needs. It was a street known for its history of libertines and philanderers, some of its more famous occupants having been Giacomo Casanova and Thomas de Quincy, the author of *Confessions of an English Opium-Eater*, which to Daniel's thinking said it all. Daniel supposed the residents of Greek Street took no issue with having an unmarried medium and her lover as neighbors since their standards clearly weren't very high. Perhaps this estimation of Alicia wasn't quite fair, given the service she had rendered him in the past, but Daniel liked to call a spade a spade, and this spade hadn't much cared about the opinion of others, a trait he secretly admired and aspired to.

The two men were admitted by a young, fresh-faced maidservant who appeared relieved to see them.

"Mr. Moore will surely be glad to see you, sirs," she prattled as she took their things and showed them to the parlor. "He's been in a state since last night. Didn't know what to do. He was about to go prowling the streets at midnight, but I talked him out of it. He wasn't likely to find the mistress, I said. He'd only get his pockets picked for his trouble. 'She'll be back when she's ready,' I told him, and he finally fell asleep around two, the poor lamb. Then he was up at eight and on his way to Scotland Yard as soon as he was dressed."

"How do you know what time he fell asleep?" Daniel asked, hoping to catch the maid in an admission of guilt if she and Constantine had been together, but she stared at him blankly, as if he'd asked her a very foolish question.

"Well, I sat up with him, didn't I?" the maid answered. "How could I leave him on his own when he was beside himself with worry? I made him coffee and tried to get him to eat something, but he refused. Just sat there staring at the door like a devoted labrador."

"Where's he now?" Jason interjected when the woman came up for air.

22

"Locked himself in the bedroom and hasn't eaten a morsel all day. 'You'll make yourself ill, sir,' I keep telling him, but he won't listen. I can hear him pacing the bedroom floor like a caged animal. Mr. Moore does love Mrs. Lysander so. Devoted to her as if they were married in the eyes of God and man."

"What time did Mr. Moore go out last night?" Daniel asked.

"He left at half past six, and I didn't see him again until half past ten. He said he'd gone to collect the mistress from the séance, but she'd finished early and left without him. Imagine his dismay when I told him she never came home. He was going to go right back to Grosvenor Square, but she wasn't going to be there, was she? Maybe you can talk some sense into him. The poor man is distraught. If you would just make yourselves comfortable while I fetch him," the maidservant said once she'd seen them to the parlor.

The room reflected Alicia's personality and heritage and was like nothing Daniel had ever seen in London. He supposed Alicia's childhood spent in India had left more of an imprint than he had expected and outweighed the Britishness that had been imposed on her by her father and late husband. Those formative years shaped people in ways they never realized and at times left them with a sense of nostalgia for something they couldn't name. Perhaps it was simply the innocence of being a child, but Daniel didn't think Alicia's childhood had been uncomplicated, not when her mother had been a native and could never have taken her place next to a British diplomat, at least not in the legal sense. But her spirit had to be right here in this room, since no Englishwoman would decorate a room as Alicia had.

The parlor was painted saffron yellow, and the furniture was upholstered in silver-and-gold-embroidered maroon brocade. The velvet curtains matched the upholstery, the folds held back with gold braided cords. The carpet was yellow and red with cobalt blue accents. A pale blue statue of a man with the head of an elephant was displayed on an intricately carved wooden pedestal, and there were several other statues that depicted strange, otherworldly creatures scattered about the room. Daniel found one such statue particularly unsettling. It was of a fierce-looking bronze woman who wore a strange headdress and not much else to cover her voluptuous curves. She had ten arms, every wrist adorned with several bracelets and each hand holding an object that could only be described as threatening. The woman's expression was utterly terrifying, and Daniel backed away, inwardly recoiling from these foreign objects.

He had assumed that Alicia had been raised in the Church of England, but now he wasn't so sure. She had clearly retained emotional ties to her native India and might have worshipped heathen deities.

Jason didn't seem perturbed by this shocking glimpse into Alicia's inner life. He wasn't someone who'd judge another person for having beliefs different from his own and probably admired the pagan idols, treating them as pieces of art rather than the religious objects they clearly were. Perhaps it was Alicia's unchristian beliefs that had enabled her to commune with the dead since she had been able to access another realm in which no one ever truly died.

Daniel sat down on the settee, while Jason walked around the room, studying the objects as if he were on a visit to the museum.

"There are no photographs on display," he said as he came to sit across from Daniel.

"So?"

"No reminders of the people gone from her life."

"Perhaps she doesn't miss them, or maybe they're always hanging about, in spirit form."

"I wonder," Jason said slowly.

"What about?"

"Indians believe in reincarnation, and not only from human to human but sometimes from a human into an animal. I'm curious if Alicia could still contact a spirit that had been assigned a new body."

"What utter nonsense," Daniel exploded, then lowered his voice. "Surely you don't believe in all that codswallop."

Jason shrugged. "Who's to say what really happens to a soul once a person dies?"

"It goes to Heaven or Hell," Daniel hissed. "As you well know."

"I know no such thing," Jason replied calmly. "I only know that it makes me feel more hopeful to think that I might one day see people that I had loved and lost."

"You're not likely to see them if they've been turned into cockroaches or fish."

Their discussion was interrupted by the arrival of Constantine, who looked absolutely terrible. His face was the color of whey, he hadn't bothered to shave, and his chestnut-colored hair looked like he'd run his hand through it a dozen times and maybe even backwards. His eyes were bloodshot, the redness a stark contrast to the dark blue irises that encircled his dilated pupils. Although seemingly clean, Constantine's clothes lacked their usual flair since he had chosen a simple black waistcoat, a black tie, and black trousers. When he folded himself into a chair and faced his visitors, he had the look of a terrified child who wanted to be reassured that all would be well. Ignoring Daniel, Constantine turned to Jason, whose expression had become pained.

"I've been so worried," Constantine wailed. "Please, you have to find her. Alicia is never late, and she always tells me where she's going to be. I just don't understand." His eyes glittered with tears. "Where could she be?" he whispered.

Jason stood and walked over to Constantine. He laid a hand on the man's shoulder and waited for Constantine to look him in the eye. Constantine looked at his folded hands and shook his head, as if he sensed what was coming and could chase the terrible news away and pretend that Alicia was still alive and would be coming home.

"Constantine, I'm very sorry, but Alicia died last night while on her way to my home."

"Died of what?" Constantine cried. "People don't just die."

"She died of a cerebral hemorrhage, which in layman's terms is a brain bleed."

"I don't understand," Constantine wailed again. "How does someone get a brain bleed? Alicia was fine when I saw her yesterday. She was healthy and strong. And why was she going to your house?"

"We believe someone attacked her and fractured her skull."

Constantine stared at Jason, his mouth going slack with shock. "So, someone fractured Alicia's skull, and she set off for your house? That doesn't make any sense."

"She would not have realized the severity of the injury right away," Jason said. "It would have taken some time for the situation to become critical. She did, however, know that she needed my help."

"Help to do what?" Constantine asked, still staring up at Jason as if he were speaking in a foreign tongue.

"Help to discover who wanted her dead."

"She was supposed to wait for me. Why did she leave? Where did she go?" Constantine asked. He looked so lost, Daniel felt a pang of pity for the man.

"We're going to find out what happened, but first, we need to ask you a few questions," Jason explained gently.

Constantine nodded. "I'm sorry, but I must have a drink. Would you care to join me in a glass of Indian whisky?"

"Thank you, no," Jason replied for both Daniel and himself.

Constantine stood and walked over to an inlaid cabinet, from which he extracted a decanter and a cut crystal glass. His hand shook as he poured himself a very large drink, then he walked back to the chair he'd vacated, his gait unsteady, as if he were drunk already. He raised the glass in a toast but didn't say anything, instead taking a large gulp and setting the glass down.

"I'm ready," he announced.

Daniel had questions to put to the man, but he gave Jason the floor, since Constantine clearly respected him and saw Jason as a friend to both him and Alicia.

"Did Alicia have any reservations about attending last night's séance?" Jason asked.

"Not that I know of."

"Would she have sensed danger?"

Constantine made a show of thinking. "Well, I suppose she would if the danger was immediate, but I don't think she would know someone meant her harm before she was in their presence."

"Would the spirits not warn her?" Daniel asked.

"That's not how it works."

"How does it work?"

"Alicia sensed the energy in the room and projected that energy into the spirit world. If the spirit that had an emotional connection to someone present wished to pass on a message, they came through. At least that's how I understand it."

"Do you know who was going to be in attendance?" Jason asked.

"Rex Long, the 13th Earl of Ongar, and his lady, his sister Jane and her husband Lord Percival Guilford, and His Grace's widowed sister, Lady Amelia."

"Do you know anything about the family?" Jason asked.

As Alicia's assistant, Constantine made it his business to vet Alicia's clients in order to ensure her safety when she went to their homes, but as far as Daniel knew, Constantine did not dig into the attendees' past for fear of tainting Alicia's reputation as a medium or somehow influencing the outcome of the séance by telling Alicia too much about the people she was about to meet.

"Not very much," Constantine said once he'd taken another sip of his whisky. "Only that the earl is immensely wealthy and moves in rather exalted circles. His sisters devote their time to philanthropic pursuits, as noble ladies tend to do. And Lord Guilford likes to gamble but always pays his debts and has a reputation for being a good sport."

"Who were the family hoping to contact?" Jason asked.

"Alicia never asked beforehand," Constantine explained. "It gave the hosts a chance to test her veracity and see if she would bring forth the right person. That was the first step in gaining their trust."

"Did the wrong person ever come through?" Daniel asked.

"Sometimes. Not every spirit wishes to make contact with those they left behind."

"Why is that?"

Constantine shrugged. "I suppose because they have moved on."

"Moved on?"

"Didn't leave any unfinished business," Constantine explained. "Their souls are at peace."

"Even if those they left behind aren't?" Daniel asked. He genuinely wanted to understand how the process worked.

"Every person has their own truth, Inspector, and it doesn't always align with the truth of others, be they living or dead."

That sounded like a load of psychic claptrap, but Daniel decided not to pursue the inquiry. He didn't suppose it really mattered to the investigation how Alicia's process had worked, only how those in attendance had responded.

"Did you meet the earl, Mr. Moore?" Daniel asked instead.

"Very briefly, when I called for Alicia last night. He seemed an affable enough fellow and reassured me that Alicia had left."

"Was there anyone who held a grudge or threatened Alicia recently or in the past?" Jason asked.

"No!" Constantine exclaimed, agitated once more. "Clients were always grateful to her. She brought them comfort and helped them to make sense of their grief. Alicia was a conduit, nothing more. She did not express any opinions of her own or judge anyone for their part in the spirit's passing. All she did was ferry the messages from the great beyond."

"Someone might have seen such a message as a threat or a judgment," Daniel pointed out.

"Yes, they could have, but Alicia always made sure to explain that she was a medium and not in control of what anyone said or did. She was a tool and had no opinion on what took place. If the clients weren't emotionally prepared to receive a message, they could change their mind and cancel the séance. Alicia always returned the fee when that happened, so she didn't profit from their fears."

"And did that happen often?" Jason inquired. "Did many clients cancel a séance once it had been scheduled?"

"No, but once in a while someone lost their nerve."

"And how were things between you two?" Daniel asked. He'd thought that would be the first thing Jason asked, but he seemed to be holding back on the really personal questions.

Jason shot Daniel a look that warned him to back off, but Daniel needed an answer.

"Things were good. We were happy," Constantine replied.

"You weren't married," Daniel said. "Why was that?"

"Alicia did not want to marry again. I would have married her without hesitation, and I told her that again and again."

"Why did she not want to get married? Was she afraid that everything she had earned would revert to you?"

Constantine's eyes flashed with anger. "Are you suggesting I was only with her for the money?"

"I'm not suggesting anything," Daniel replied calmly. "I'm asking you a question."

"Alicia felt nothing but disdain for convention. She didn't think marriage was necessary when two people were devoted to each other on a spiritual plane. And we shared everything, Inspector. There was no such thing as hers or mine. It was ours."

"Do you own this house, Mr. Moore?" Daniel asked.

"No. We signed a three-year leasehold when we settled in London."

"And would you have been able to afford the rent on your own?"

"I would not," Constantine replied, his eyes radiating his dislike of Daniel.

"Will you now have to move into more affordable lodgings, or will you use the savings Alicia accumulated through her work to support your lifestyle?" Daniel pressed.

"I was Alicia's assistant. That was my work. I never pretended to be anything else, and Alicia was satisfied with that. And yes, I will look for smaller lodgings because I can't bear to remain here without Alicia. She was my life, Inspector, and now she's gone. No amount of money can make up for such loss."

"So, what will you do now that Alicia is gone?" Jason asked.

"I don't know," Constantine said, and his sorrowful expression said it all. He was heartbroken and lost, and he would need time to come to terms with his grief.

"Don't leave town, Mr. Moore," Daniel said as he stood to leave.

"When can I collect Alicia's remains?"

"Whenever you're ready," Jason replied. "You can have an undertaker collect the body from Scotland Yard today or tomorrow. After that, Alicia's remains will be moved to City Mortuary to make room for incoming victims."

Constantine looked taken aback. "I'm really not sure what sort of burial she would have wanted. We never talked about it."

"A Christian burial sounds right to me," Daniel interjected. "Her father was British, after all."

"Yes, I suppose, although she may have liked to be cremated, her ashes immersed in holy water so that her soul could rise to Heaven."

"I doubt any vicar would allow you to desecrate the holy water with ashes."

"Not *that* holy water," Constantine replied. "I would have to take Alicia's ashes to India."

"Seems an awfully long way to go to dispose of some ashes," Daniel replied, and silently acknowledged that he was being an arse.

It was only natural that Constantine would want to honor Alicia's beliefs when it came to her funeral, and if he wanted to have her cremated and her ashes scattered in India, who was Daniel to pass judgment?

An awkward silence ensued, which was broken by Jason.

"I'm deeply sorry for your loss, Constantine. If there's anything you need, please don't hesitate to ask."

"Thank you, my lord. Alicia held you in high regard in life, and she would be glad to know that you were the one to look after her in death."

That was a euphemism if Daniel had ever heard one, but he didn't think any man wanted to imagine what happened to the body he'd loved when it met with a surgeon's scalpel.

"Get some rest," Jason said. "We'll apprise you of any developments."

"Will we?" Daniel asked once he and Jason had stepped outside. "He's still a suspect as far as I'm concerned."

"Yes, he is, but we still owe him the respect he deserves as the victim's domestic partner."

"Domestic partner?" Daniel scoffed and was surprised to see a smile tug at Jason's lips. "What?" Daniel asked sulkily.

"I could think of someone else who has a domestic partner," Jason said, and began to walk.

"Flora Tarrant is not my *domestic* partner. She's Charlotte's nursemaid," Daniel cried as he fell into step.

"I didn't name any names," Jason replied, and Daniel nearly kicked himself for falling into Jason's effortlessly laid trap.

Chapter 6

By the time Jason and Daniel arrived in Grosvenor Square, it was nearly three o'clock. The sky had cleared, but the air was still thick with moisture, and it had grown considerably warmer. The fragrance of freshly cut grass wafted from the sizable expanse of open parkland at the center of the square, and the birds sang their hearts out, the peaceful scene a balm to the soul after the grim events of the morning. Grosvenor Square was one of the most prestigious addresses in London. The houses that flanked the well-tended park were palaces in their own right and belonged to the most wealthy and influential members of London society.

Several fine carriages could be seen coming, going, or waiting at the curb as this was the time for morning calls, and the visitors would continue to arrive until close to five o'clock since visiting hours were extended by an hour during the summer months. *If one stays in bed until noon, then this is morning,* Jason thought tiredly as they approached the earl's residence, which was one of the grandest houses in the square, even by Grosvenor Square standards. Jason hoped it wasn't a wasted journey and the earl and his wife would be at home to receive them. If they were out paying calls, Daniel would have to contend with speaking to the servants while Jason walked from the earl's front door toward Upper Brook Street, where Alicia had materialized before Neil Lacky's cab. He very much doubted he would find any physical trace of last night's attack, but he was curious to see how long it would take him to get there in order to narrow down the window he and Daniel were working with.

The earl's residence was located on the north side of the square and was enormous, with three floors punctuated by at least two dozen windows, a grandiose entrance, and a carriage house that was connected to the main building by means of a covered walkway and was large enough to accommodate several vehicles. The servants' quarters had to be a warren of rooms dedicated to various chores, storage areas, and accommodation for the staff. It was strange to think that so much space and that many people were required to see to the comfort of two young, healthy individuals.

The butler gave the two men a once-over, his eyebrows lifting just enough to express his surprise at finding them on the earl's doorstep. He was an imposing individual in his late forties or early fifties and had the demeanor of a mythical dragon that guarded a cave filled with treasure. "His Grace is not receiving today," he intoned.

Daniel showed the man his warrant card. "I am Inspector Haze of Scotland Yard, and this is my associate, Lord Redmond. Your name, please?"

"Jones."

Like most men in his position, the butler went by his surname and wasn't given the respect of being called mister, whereas the housekeeper, who was below him in the hierarchy of the staff, always went by the title of Mrs., even if she had never married. Similarly, a surgeon wasn't granted the title of doctor because he was considered inferior to a physician, whose knowledge came strictly from texts rather than hands-on experience of the human body. Jason found all these rules ludicrous and heeded them only when it served his purpose.

"What is your business with His Grace, Inspector?" Jones asked. He tried to appear indifferent, but a note of anxiety had crept into his voice. A visit from the police never boded well, even if the residents were as innocent as newborn lambs. Police inquiries were synonymous with scandal, and no one wanted to be associated with anything that had the potential to turn sordid.

"Mrs. Lysander, who conducted a séance here last night, was assaulted and died as a result of her injuries," Daniel said. "I need to speak to the staff, starting with you, Mr. Jones. His lordship would like a word with His Grace."

"Assaulted?" Jones asked, doing his best to look affronted. "Surely you don't mean that she was set upon in this house."

"I don't know precisely when she was attacked, which is why I must retrace her movements from the time she arrived at the earl's residence until she passed," Daniel explained.

Jones looked set to argue, but to conduct a conversation on the doorstep could lead to undue speculation from the neighbors, especially if they were aware that the earl was not receiving that afternoon.

"Come in," Jones said grudgingly. "Please wait while I consult with His Grace."

Jones left the two men in the foyer and returned a few minutes later, followed by a crisply uniformed young maidservant, who took their things.

"His Grace will receive you in the library, my lord," Jones said in a tone that was now deferential. "Malva will show you to the servants' hall, Inspector," he added, and turned his back on Daniel.

Jason watched Daniel follow the maidservant through the green baize door that separated the house proper from the servants' domain, then followed the butler to the library. They walked down a wide corridor before finally reaching the door to the library, which had to face the back of the house. The butler knocked timidly and was bid to enter.

"Lord Redmond," Jones announced pompously.

The library was a magnificent room, paneled in maple-colored wood and filled with beautiful cabinets that held an assortment of volumes. Stained-glass windows cast colorful rays onto the studded leather armchairs that were separated by an occasional table topped with an ornate reading lamp. A carved sideboard held several decanters and crystal glasses of various sizes as well as a silver bowl filled to the brim with exotic fruit. It seemed the earl spent enough time in the library to enjoy this oasis of peace and comfort.

Rex Long, 6th Duke of Epping and 13th Earl of Ongar, got to his feet and came forward to greet Jason as if they were old friends. He was slim, a few inches shorter than Jason, and around the same age. His thick fair hair wasn't doused in pomade and curled gently around an angular face, and his sideburns angled sharply towards a full mouth. Slightly slanted brown eyes shone with curiosity as the earl took Jason's measure. The earl was elegantly dressed in a suit of dove gray and wore a claret-colored waistcoat embroidered with a pattern of silver leaves and a matching puff tie.

"Your Grace," Jason said, and bowed from the neck.

"My dear Lord Redmond, what a pleasure it is to make your acquaintance. Please, make yourself comfortable. Can I offer you a drink?"

Jason tried not to show his surprise at the earl's bonhomie. He accepted the offer of a drink and settled in one of the leather chairs, his hand sliding along the buttery armrest. The earl poured them both generous measures of brandy and handed Jason his glass as if he were a butler rather than the lord of the manor. Long settled in the other chair and raised the glass in a toast.

"To new friends."

Jason toasted him and took a sip. It was exceptionally good brandy, probably French. The earl took a sip as well, but his gaze never wavered from Jason's face. Although he hated to draw conclusions based on a first impression, Jason sensed that behind the open smile and the friendly manner was a will of steel and the earl would do anything in his power to get what he wanted. Perhaps Jason's perception of the earl had been colored by Ransome's opinion of the man's character, but Jason trusted Ransome's instincts and thought that he should tread carefully, no matter how welcoming Rex Long appeared to be.

"I had the honor of knowing your grandfather. Fearsome fellow," Rex Long said with a shake of his head. "You must have been terrified of him as a child."

"Unfortunately, I never met my grandfather," Jason replied. "He and my father were estranged, and I was born and raised in the United States."

Jason thought Long was fully aware of his history, given that Jason's name appeared in the papers with irritating frequency and the articles never failed to mention his American upbringing and military rank, neither of which had anything to do with his volunteer work at the hospital or the cases he investigated for Scotland Yard. He supposed his background, ungentlemanly activities, and noble rank made for an eccentric character that was sure to capture the interest of the public.

"Forgive me," the earl said. "I did know that your father lived abroad, but I wasn't aware there had been an ongoing rift. It's not the sort of thing one discusses in public, you understand."

Jason wasn't sure if this was a dig at his perceived lack of breeding or simply an explanation for Rex Long's ignorance of the situation.

"But to grow up in America," Long exclaimed. "How I envy you, my dear man. I have never been, but I long to go. When I imagine your homeland, it's all endless plains, soaring mountains, and merciless outlaws galloping through frontier towns and whooping with glee as they shoot up the townsfolk."

Jason chose not to point out that he had grown up in New York City, which had neither plains, mountains, nor whooping outlaws, even though there were plenty of criminals who came from every walk of life. "For someone who's never been, you certainly have a very vivid picture of what America is like," he said instead.

Rex smiled. "I have it from my wife's brother, who spent a year in the territories, that it is a vast and rugged place, full of natural wonders. He was particularly fond of Montana and Colorado. Bernard said the sky stretched as far as the eye could see without a man-made structure to mar the horizon. Have you been out West, Jason?"

Jason had not invited the earl to call him by his given name, but he wasn't about to call the man out over his rudeness.

"I have not, Rex," he replied with a discourtesy of his own, and was gratified to notice the shock in the man's eyes. "I spent most of my time on the East Coast and fought in the South during the American Civil War."

"Ah, the South," Rex Long said, his eyes twinkling with amusement. "I expect it's still as unruly as our North."

Jason assumed that he was referring to Scotland and Ireland and their centuries-long discontent with British rule, but he wasn't about to engage in political discourse. For one, he was sure that he and the earl would vehemently disagree on every aspect of the ongoing conflict, and for another, he found that he didn't care for the man and wanted only to ask his questions and leave.

"I thank you for your hospitality, Rex, but this is not really a social call."

Rex Long's eyes widened in surprise, as if he had assumed all along that Jason had decided to call on him out of the blue and he had been cruelly deceived. Jones was sure to have told his employer that Jason's companion was a detective with Scotland Yard and the reason for their visit, making Jason question the real reason behind the earl's duplicity.

"Then why are you here, Jason?" Rex Long exclaimed. The man looked confused and also a little offended, as if Jason had abused his hospitality under false pretenses.

"I'm here on a police matter."

"Police matter? Is this some sort of joke?"

"A suspicious death is never a joking matter, Rex," Jason said. He was certain that Rex Long already knew what had happened and was intentionally putting Jason in a position where he had to explain himself in order to justify his intrusion into the earl's peaceful afternoon. "Alicia Lysander, who was your guest just last night, died shortly after leaving your house."

"My dear man, why didn't you say so right away? I daresay Jones tried to spare me any unpleasantness and didn't explain the reason for your call," Rex Long exclaimed. He looked horrified, his hand gripping the armrest in distress. "I am so very sorry to hear it. Delightful woman. And so beautiful. What on earth happened?"

"It would appear that Mrs. Lysander was assaulted, an attack that left her with a fractured skull."

"Good Lord," Rex Long exclaimed. "How ghastly. I offered her the use of my carriage, but she insisted on finding her own way home."

"Her assistant was due to meet her after the séance but was told that she had already gone."

"Yes, I met him last night. Charming fellow. He seemed awfully concerned. I now see he had good reason to be."

"Can you tell me about what happened at the séance?"

"Of course, but what possible relevance could our little séance have to Mrs. Lysander's death?"

"Mrs. Lysander was not robbed, which leads me to believe that this was a targeted attack rather than a random mugging that turned violent."

The earl studied Jason with obvious consternation. "What is your interest in this, if you don't mind me asking, Jason?"

37

"I lend my services to Scotland Yard on a pro bono basis. And Alicia Lysander was also a friend."

"Was she, indeed?" Rex's gaze turned sly. "Well, I must say, you are full of surprises. Working for Scotland Yard and associating with mediums. I'm not sure your grandfather would have approved."

"Given that he's long gone, I'm not overly concerned with gaining his approval," Jason replied.

"So, Alicia Lysander was your friend. How good a friend, if you don't mind me asking?"

Jason pushed down his annoyance. The man was clearly trying to goad him, not because the earl was guilty of murder but because he could. Jason got the impression that this was his way of dealing with anyone he thought was inferior and could be intimidated and bullied into doing the earl's bidding. To rise to the bait would play right into Rex Long's hands.

"Lady Redmond and I were very fond of Alicia," Jason said, making certain the earl understood that there was nothing underhanded in his dealings with Alicia.

"I see," Rex Long said. "Well, I'm afraid there isn't very much I can tell you. The séance was arranged by my sister Jane at my wife's request. She's young and impressionable and was taken with the idea of contacting the dead. Since we were informed that a séance usually works best with six people, I asked several family members to participate. They were happy to join us and hoped for an entertaining evening."

"Whom did Her Grace hope to contact?"

"Cynthia was desperate to contact her cousin, Caroline. The poor girl passed quite recently. It was a dreadful shock. She came home from her morning ride, and said she felt unwell and needed to lie down. By the time her maid came in to check on her an hour later, she had slipped away."

"Was the cause of death ever determined?"

"The family physician thought it was a blood clot in the brain."

"An aneurism," Jason said.

"Yes, I believe that was the term that was used. It was very sad. Caroline was just twenty-one and had recently become engaged to a very worthy young man."

"I'm sorry for your loss," Jason said.

"And I'm sorry for yours. To think that dear lady is gone when last night she was so wonderfully alive. Is there anything I can do, Jason? I would be happy to cover the funeral expenses if she had no family to make the arrangements."

"Mrs. Lysander's associate will see to the funeral."

Rex Long nodded. "You must let me know when the sad event is to take place. I would like to send my condolences. And maybe a wreath."

"That's kind of you, but can you tell me more about the séance? Who was present? Did anything unexpected happen that might have upset one of the participants? Why did the séance end early?"

"Are you actually investigating Mrs. Lysander's death?" Rex Long scoffed. "I assumed your interest was from a purely medical standpoint."

"Yes, I have been charged with investigating what happened to Alicia Lysander," Jason replied, which was true enough as far as the earl was concerned.

"Is this a hobby of yours, or are you genuinely passionate about the pursuit of justice? I daresay, it's rather common, Jason. Must be your American upbringing. Democracy for all, eh?"

"The names, if you don't mind," Jason pressed.

The earl's insolent manner was beginning to grate on Jason, and he could see why Daniel had dreaded the interview. Rex Long would have ground Daniel into the dirt since Daniel would have no recourse and would have had to accept whatever crumbs of information he was given before he was shown the door. Jason had no intention of leaving until he got what he had come for. Rex Long's obstructive manner was either a symptom of his privilege or an attempt to distract Jason from what had really happened last night. Jason didn't think the earl would tell him the whole truth, but sometimes, it was enough to evaluate a suspect's body language to see if they might be holding something back.

"If you insist," Long said. "My sisters Jane and Amelia, and Jane's husband Percy Guilford."

"How long have Jane and Percy been married?" Jason asked.

"I really don't see how that's relevant, but they have been married for nearly two years. I've known Percy since our days at Eton and had always hoped that he and Jane would make a match of it. It's a friendship that has survived adolescence, adulthood, and his marriage to my sister, who can be rather a handful, if I say so myself," the earl added with a chuckle.

"And were you able to contact Caroline?"

"Yes, but very briefly. Cynthia became distressed when she heard Caroline's voice and fled. Once the connection was broken, Mrs. Lysander was unable to continue and ended the séance early."

"Did Caroline say something that upset your wife?"

Rex Long assumed an expression of infinite sadness. "She did. She said she was cold and lonely in her grave. That's enough to upset anyone, wouldn't you say? Cynthia and Caroline were close from a young age, and Cynthia mourns her deeply."

"Was that all?" Jason asked.

"What more do you want?" the earl snapped. "It was distressing for everyone since we all knew Caroline very well."

"So, Mrs. Lysander was alive and well when she left last night?"

Rex Long tried to contain his irritation, but his tone was brusque, his patience with Jason's questions running thin. "Yes, she was. A little put out with the way things ended, but quite well aside from that. And she received her fee in full, so I imagine that went a long way toward calming her."

"Did she explain why she had refused your offer of a ride home?"

"She did not, and I saw no reason to press her."

"What did you do after Mrs. Lysander had left?" Jason asked.

"We adjourned to the drawing room and had a well-deserved drink. Everyone left by eleven."

"May I have a word with Lady Cynthia?"

The earl stared at Jason in shock. "You wish to question Cynthia? Why?"

"Because she might have something to add to your account."

"That is quite out of the question. Cynthia is still upset, which is why we're not at home to visitors today. She had no wish to see anyone until she felt more herself. I assure you, there's nothing more Cynthia can tell you. It was all very brief."

"In that case, thank you for your time, Your Grace. It was a pleasure to meet you."

Rex Long fixed Jason with a sardonic smile. "You are a Redmond through and through; I'll give you that."

"I'll take that as a compliment," Jason replied, and he stood.

"If you enjoy being regarded as unconventional, stubborn, and outspoken to a fault, then I suppose it is."

"Thank you," Jason said, and smiled. He bowed stiffly and took his leave.

Daniel was still speaking to members of the earl's household staff, so Jason asked for his things to be brought and stepped outside. He was going to undertake a brief reconnaissance mission.

Chapter 7

Daniel spent more than an hour in the butler's pantry, questioning the staff. No one besides Jones and Malva, the parlormaid, had come in contact with Alicia Lysander, who had requested that the staff be dismissed for the duration of the séance, in case they should unwittingly turn on the light or make a noise that would scare off a skittish spirit. Jones had already said that Alicia had been absolutely fine when she'd left, and Malva swore on all that was holy that madam had been in good spirits when Malva had delivered her bonnet and cape, and had wished Malva a good evening before disappearing into the night.

"Did she seem at all nervous?" Daniel asked the girl, who leaned forward in her eagerness to help, her brown eyes wide with disbelief that the woman she had helped only last night was now dead.

"No, sir. But she was anxious to leave, I could see that."

"I believe His Grace offered her the use of his carriage."

"Yes, but Mrs. Lysander declined."

Daniel nodded. This was getting him nowhere. "Malva, did you hear anything during the séance?"

"No, sir. I was told to return to the servants' hall and not to come up again until I was summoned."

"And what time was that?"

"Nine thirty or thereabouts," Malva replied.

"And did you see any of the others as they came out of the room?"

Malva nodded. "They were a bit quiet, but I suppose that's natural when you've just been offered a glimpse of the afterlife, isn't it?"

"Yes, I expect it is."

"If there's nothing else, sir," Malva chirped. "I have chores I need to be getting on with."

"Of course. Thank you, Malva."

"I hope you find out what happened, Inspector. She seemed a nice lady."

"She was."

Malva hurried off, leaving Daniel to ponder what to do next. He left the butler's pantry and came face to face with Mrs. Ascot, the housekeeper.

"I'd like a word with her ladyship," Daniel said.

Mrs. Ascot, a plump woman of middle years, shook her head so hard, the ribbons of her lace cap danced about her neck as if it were a maypole.

"I'm afraid that's not possible, Inspector. Her ladyship has taken to her bed. She needs her rest, the poor dear."

"Is she ill?"

"I think she was just frightened. Imagine coming face to face with a cousin you'd lost nearly a year ago. It would give anyone the collywobbles. If we were meant to speak to the dead, then everyone would be able to do it," Mrs. Ascot declared. "It's unnatural, these séances. Some think it's just a silly diversion, but if you ask me, it's a sin against God."

"They seem to be all the rage," Daniel replied noncommittally.

"They're wicked and unchristian, and should not be undertaken by decent folk," Mrs. Ascot said. "It's black magic is what it is, but if His Grace feels it's appropriate, then who am I to question my betters?" Mrs. Ascot backtracked when Jones appeared in the doorway, his eyebrows lifting in obvious censure and reminding Mrs. Ascot that she was speaking out of turn.

"Has anyone spoken to her ladyship since the séance?" Daniel asked.

"Only her lady's maid, Crumlish. She brought her breakfast and has been checking on her regularly."

"I'd like to speak to Miss Crumlish, if I may."

"I don't know what you hope to learn, but she's just there."

The housekeeper jutted her chin toward the servants' hall, where a young woman sat at the long table, a sewing box before her as she bent over a lace collar.

Daniel thanked Mrs. Ascot and walked toward Miss Crumlish, waiting until she looked up from her work to introduce himself. The maid was in her early twenties, a dark-haired, round-faced young woman with wide blue eyes and overplucked eyebrows. She had a snub nose and rosy cheeks, and looked at Daniel with apprehension, her mouth opening slightly when she realized he was waiting to speak to her.

"Good afternoon, Miss Crumlish. I'm Inspector Haze of Scotland Yard. May I have a word?"

Miss Crumlish looked uncomfortable and would probably have said no if she'd thought she was permitted to refuse to speak to an inspector of the police. She nodded and indicated a chair across from her, then laid down the collar she had been mending on the table, giving Daniel her full attention.

"Perhaps we can speak somewhere more private," Daniel said when a footman passed by and purposely slowed his step in order to eavesdrop on the conversation.

"Go on with you, Zachary," Miss Crumlish admonished him. "This is not a conversation for your ears. Nosy bugger," the maid said under her breath once Zachary had passed. "Always creeping about."

"Let's step into the butler's pantry. I don't believe Mr. Jones has reclaimed it yet," Daniel said.

Miss Crumlish gathered up her things and followed Daniel to the butler's office, which was still vacant since Jones was now berating Zachary loudly enough for everyone to hear.

"I expect you've heard that Mrs. Lysander, who was here last night, has died in suspicious circumstances," Daniel said once he'd shut the door, and they'd settled in the only two chairs in the room.

"Yes, but I don't know anything about that."

"Miss Crumlish, where were you during the séance?" Daniel asked.

44

"I was in my lady's bedroom, putting away clean laundry and turning down her ladyship's bed. When His Grace and Lady Cynthia are not out in the evening, she likes to retire before eleven, so I wanted to make sure everything was ready for her."

"I imagine it's a very long day for you, Miss Crumlish."

The young woman smiled sadly. "Such is the life of a lady's maid, Inspector, but I do like my job. Lady Cynthia has been good to me."

"And His Grace? Has he been kind to you as well?"

If Miss Crumlish was surprised by the question, she hid it well. She shook her head. "Our paths rarely cross."

"Did they cross yesterday?" Daniel asked.

"I don't quite know what you mean, Inspector."

"Did you see His Grace after the séance?"

Miss Crumlish nodded. "He came up to see her ladyship, but she locked the door against him."

"Why?"

"She was terribly upset. She burst into the room, slammed the door shut, and threw herself on the bed. She was beside herself. I have worked for Lady Cynthia since she married His Grace, and I have never seen her so distraught. She was downright hysterical." Crumlish whispered that last word, probably mindful of commenting on her mistress's mental state.

"Did Lady Cynthia tell you why she was so distressed?" Daniel asked.

"No, she refused to speak of it. I thought Caroline—that is the Honorable Miss Coleman—had come through. She was her ladyship's cousin and dearest friend. Lady Cynthia was devastated when Caroline died, but I think she was prepared for Caroline and would have welcomed the chance to say goodbye."

"So, who was it that came through during the séance?" Daniel asked.

Miss Crumlish looked conflicted and glanced fearfully toward the door. Daniel listened intently, wondering if she had heard someone, but the corridor beyond the pantry was quiet.

"I don't know if I should say, Inspector. It can't be relevant to what happened to Mrs. Lysander and can get me in trouble with Mrs. Ascot."

"Anything you tell me is strictly confidential, Miss Crumlish. I assure you."

"Well, I don't suppose it can do any harm if I tell you," she conceded, but failed to speak.

"Please, go on," Daniel prompted.

Miss Crumlish sighed, her shoulders drooping with resignation. "Lady Cynthia was so frightened, she asked me to stay with her until she fell asleep. I was dead on my feet and longed for my own bed, but what could I do? I pulled up a chair and sat next to the bed for nearly an hour while Lady Cynthia twisted and turned and moaned about how terrified she was. I asked several times what had scared her so. Sometimes it helps to talk things through, I said. Face one's demons, so to speak, but she wouldn't say a word."

Miss Crumlish sighed again. "I thought she'd be up all night, but finally she dozed off, and I thought I could leave. It was as I was creeping toward the door that I heard it, clear as a bell."

"What did you hear?" Daniel asked. The woman certainly had a flair for the dramatic and was drawing out her account when one sentence would have done.

"She said, "Daphne, please leave us in peace.""

"Does that name mean something to you?"

Miss Crumlish appeared shocked by Daniel's question. Evidently the name should have meant something to him as well, but he had never heard of this family until today, and Daphne could have been anyone, from Cynthia's friend to her favorite spaniel.

Miss Crumlish leaned forward and lowered her voice to a whisper. "Lady Daphne was His Grace's first wife."

"So, you think the apparition that came through during the séance was Lady Daphne?" Daniel asked.

"I'm certain of it," Miss Crumlish said with a nod. "And I think she made some sort of threat."

Daniel waited, hoping there was more. Surely Lady Cynthia had been aware that her husband had been married before, and what sort of threat could the lady make from beyond the grave that would frighten the current countess out of her wits?

Or perhaps Lady Cynthia was just an emotional young woman who had been frightened by an apparition. Daniel had never believed in parting the veil or communing with the dead, as Alicia had referred to her talents, but he no longer doubted her ability and could imagine how terrifying it would be to come face to face with one's long-deceased predecessor, especially if the spirit did not come in peace.

If he were honest, he would find it frightening as well, which was probably why he had never considered attending a séance, even though he'd spent many a night lying awake and thinking of all the things he would say to his late wife Sarah if he had one more chance to speak to her. To imagine seeing her ghostly form floating in the darkness and hearing her voice sent a shiver of fear racing down his spine. Perhaps it was for the best that people couldn't talk to the dead because it was never really about saying goodbye. It was about fear, guilt, and anger with the departed for leaving their loved ones behind, a desire for answers, and sometimes just raw, visceral pain that had nowhere to go, and that the deceased could never take away, no matter what they said.

Why did you leave me? Why wasn't I enough? Why did you choose a dead child over a living one? Why didn't you try harder? Daniel didn't need to attend a séance to hear the answers. He knew them already. Sarah had not loved him and Charlotte enough to fight. She had given in to melancholia and had thrown away the most precious gift of all—life. There was nothing she could say, and the only thing he could do was move on and let her go rather than try to summon her back to a place she'd needed to leave.

"Inspector Haze, are you all right?" Miss Crumlish asked when something of his inner dialogue must have shown itself on his face.

"Yes. Forgive me. Erm, how did Lady Daphne die?"

Miss Crumlish's eyes shimmered with unshed tears. "She died abroad, Inspector. Of cholera," she whispered. "His Grace said her last days were…" She couldn't finish the sentence, but Daniel could imagine all too well what the lady's end must have been like, especially in a foreign country where the level of care had to be substandard to England.

Silent tears slid down the young woman's face, and Daniel wondered why she was so affected by the death of someone she wouldn't have known if she had joined the earl's household when he'd married Lady Cynthia.

"Did you know Lady Daphne?" Daniel asked.

Miss Crumlish nodded. "I grew up in this house, Inspector. Lady Daphne was…" Miss Crumlish paused as she searched for the right word. "A saint," she said at last. She was crying in earnest now, clearly still grieving for a woman she had admired from afar. "May I go now?" she choked out.

"Of course. Thank you, Miss Crumlish."

Miss Crumlish nodded and fled. Daniel didn't really expect to learn anything more from the staff, and Jason had to have finished upstairs by now. Leaving by the tradesmen's exit, Daniel went in search of Jason and hoped he'd had better luck with the family.

Chapter 8

Daniel found Jason in Upper Brook Street, walking slowly as he studied the stately homes and made note of the late afternoon traffic. A residence in Upper Brook Street did not come close to the prestige of an address in Grosvenor Square, but it was a fashionable area inhabited by the wealthy and titled. It wasn't the sort of place where residents had to fear for their lives when walking after dark or had to look over their shoulders for fear that some thug might be hiding in a dark alleyway. The houses were attached, a narrow road that led to the mews the only way to access the rear of the buildings. Several carriages were moving down the street, the vehicles sleek and expensive.

Jason stopped walking when Daniel approached, and Daniel could sense his sadness and frustration. Alicia Lysander's death had affected him deeply, and even though Jason was always logical and thorough, he had the look of a man who wanted answers, and he wanted them now.

"What was Alicia doing here?" Jason asked. "Why would she leave the earl's house on foot on a foggy night and walk to Upper Brook Street? It doesn't make any sense."

"The sensible thing to do would have been to either accept the ride that had been offered or to wait for Constantine."

Jason nodded. "Perhaps she became disoriented. The fog can do that."

"Yes, but why did she set off on foot in the first place?"

"Perhaps she felt threatened and wanted to put some distance between herself and the earl's residence."

"But why? Did you speak to the earl?" Daniel asked.

"Yes, but I didn't learn anything that would explain what happened to Alicia. Rex Long said the séance went much as expected, with the exception of Lady Cynthia becoming upset when her cousin Caroline made an appearance and said she was cold and lonely in her grave."

"Caroline?"

"Yes. That's whom they were trying to contact. Did you have any luck with the servants?"

"No. Everyone except Jones and the parlormaid, Malva, was in the servants' hall during the séance since they had been asked to remain belowstairs. Both Jones and Malva confirmed that Alicia left around nine-thirty and appeared to be unharmed. Miss Crumlish, Lady Cynthia's maid, said that Caroline did not come through, but shared with me in confidence that Lady Cynthia was hysterical when she came upstairs and too frightened to remain on her own. Miss Crumlish heard her mistress call out to Lady Daphne in her sleep, asking Daphne to leave them all in peace."

"Who's Lady Daphne?" Jason asked, his gaze more alert now that he'd been presented with a new name.

"The earl's first wife. Did Long mention her?"

"No. Were you able to learn anything about her?"

"Only that she died while abroad. Cholera. And Miss Crumlish, who knew the lady, called her a saint. Is there something in it?" Daniel asked.

Jason shook his head. "Outbreaks of cholera are not uncommon during the summer months, when most Brits travel abroad. In fact, cases are on the rise right here in London. If measures are not taken to check the spread, we might have an epidemic on our hands this year."

"Is it as bad as that?" Daniel balked.

"It will be unless a public health warning is issued, and people are instructed on how to prevent the spread of contagion."

"And is that likely to happen?"

"It is not," Jason replied. "Most medical professionals are too short-sighted to see the benefits of improved hygiene and masking. They will swear that those precautions make little difference to the outcome, which, in my opinion, is a grave mistake."

"I will instruct Flora to keep away from crowded public spaces and wash her own and Charlotte's hands whenever they come home from the park."

"Good man," Jason said. "I have already issued instructions to my own household."

"So, what now?" Daniel asked, his mind returning to the problem at hand. "We don't have a single lead."

"We need to speak to the other attendees before they have a chance to confer with each other and close ranks," Jason said, already moving purposefully down the street.

"You think something happened at the séance that led to the attack on Alicia?"

"Alicia was a calm, practical woman, Daniel. Given the hour and the inclement weather, she would have accepted the offered ride or waited for Constantine to arrive. Something prompted Alicia to leave, and I don't think it was a desire for a nighttime walk in the fog, especially not when she had just been paid for her services and was wearing expensive jewelry."

"Are you suggesting that she fled the earl's house because she was afraid?"

"I think it's a distinct possibility."

"Jason, Alicia Lysander was a medium. She was gifted enough to convince you that her ability was genuine, which is a feat in itself. Would she not have foreseen whatever was going to happen before she arrived in Grosvenor Square?"

"Constantine said that's not how it works."

"So, how does it work? He didn't seem to fully understand."

Jason stopped walking and turned to face Daniel. "I have no clue. All I know for certain is that Alicia was attacked sometime after she left the earl's house and before she hailed the cab. Whether the attack was a result of something that had come out during the séance or because she had made a foolhardy decision is what we need to determine, and the only thing that's in our power to do is to discover what exactly was said."

"Whom should we speak to first?" Daniel asked.

"We should start with Lady Amelia. She's the earl's older sister and therefore more likely to try to shield her brother if she believes he might be in any way responsible. We need to get to her before she finds out that Alicia was attacked."

"All right," Daniel agreed. "Let's go, then."

Chapter 9

Lady Amelia lived in Knightsbridge, not far from Jason, and was fortunately at home and happy to receive them. Her home was identical to its neighbors on the outside, but inside, it was a world unto itself, an exotic paradise of potted plants, twittering birds, and eclectic pieces of furniture. The lady herself was as unusual as her abode. She was significantly older than her brother, close to fifty, if Jason had to guess. The large gap in age was frequently indicative of children who had either died in utero or had passed away in the intervening years.

Short and plump, Lady Amelia reclined on a velvet chaise and wore a colorful turban decorated with a large ruby and a garment that was more a flowing robe than a gown, the entire ensemble reminiscent of a Turkish pasha. Jason was fairly certain that she wasn't wearing a corset beneath the colorful swathes of fabric and admired her audacity. Few ladies would dare to receive callers in such unconventional attire.

"Do sit down, gentlemen," Lady Amelia invited once her maidservant had announced them and departed. "Will you take a dish of tea, or perhaps something stronger?"

"Tea, please," Jason said.

Lady Amelia pulled on a bellpull conveniently located near her chaise and faced the men, her glittering dark eyes taking in every detail of their appearance.

"I've seen your photograph in the papers," she said to Jason. "It didn't do you justice. You are much more striking in person."

"Thank you, my lady," Jason said, and smiled at their hostess.

"I don't know your wife, but from what I heard, I daresay your grandfather is spinning in his grave," Lady Amelia continued. "He was an unyielding old stick, but I expect you don't give a fig. Good man," she said with feeling, then turned to Daniel. "And you're an inspector with the police?"

"Scotland Yard."

"I'm well acquainted with Sir David. Knew him long before he became commissioner," Lady Amelia announced. "His wife is dowdy and plain, but I hear they're happily married, despite her shortcomings," she said, evidently surprised that such an outcome could be possible. "So, why are you here? I've come by my treasures honestly, I swear," she said with a chuckle, and made a vague gesture meant to encompass her surroundings. "And no Indian shrine was violated to acquire this jewel," she quipped, and pointed to the ruby in her turban. She was clearly referring to the diamond that was stolen in *The Moonstone*, which had been published last year and had kept Jason up half the night until he finally got to the end.

"Alicia Lysander was attacked last night and died of her injuries," Jason replied. "We are trying to piece together what happened."

"And how do you think I can help?" Lady Amelia asked, her eyebrows disappearing into her turban as she looked to Jason for an explanation. It was obvious that she was shocked by the news but chose to respond with insouciance.

"She was set upon shortly after leaving your brother's house. We wanted to recreate the final hours of her life."

Lady Amelia shook her head, her gaze reflecting her sadness. "She was a strange one, that Alicia. Something of a modern-day Cassandra. Always foretelling doom and gloom. I knew her father when my husband was viceroy to India. Oh, the times we had," Lady Amelia said with a dreamy smile. "I would have been happy to remain in Simla forever, but good times never last, do they? At least for people like us."

Jason wasn't sure what sort of people she thought they were or why she imagined that good times lasted for others, but those were questions that didn't require an answer since they had no bearing on the case.

"Did Mrs. Lysander recognize you when you all gathered for the séance, my lady?" Daniel asked.

"I imagine she did, but she didn't acknowledge me, and I saw no good reason to acknowledge her. I have read about her, of course, but I had not seen her in person since she was a girl."

"Can you tell us what happened at the séance?" Jason asked.

Lady Amelia stared into the distance, as if the events of yesterday evening were replaying in her mind. "It was strange," she said at last. "I've been to a number of séances over the years. They are entertaining at best, disappointing at worst, but I had never been invited to a séance conducted by Alicia Lysander. To be frank, I'm not sure I would have gone if I had been."

"Why was that?" Daniel asked.

Lady Amelia sighed. "Perhaps because I had heard from enough people that Alicia had a true gift. I suppose there was no one I wanted to contact for fear that they would have nothing but reproachful things to say to me."

"Who did you think would come through for you?" Jason asked.

"My parents. My late husband. It is my firm belief that sometimes it's for the best to leave something unsaid, since the things one really wants to say are not words of love."

Daniel nodded, clearly in agreement with Lady Amelia.

Jason still grieved his parents' untimely deaths, but he had no unresolved issues or anything he needed to say to them, other than that he missed them and wished they could meet his family. Alicia had assured him that his parents had known that he had loved and respected them, and they had been immensely proud of him.

"So why did you agree to attend last night's séance?" Jason asked.

"I only went as a favor to Rex. And I didn't think it would have anything to do with me. It was Cynthia who had expressed her desire to contact dear Caroline, and Jane who had helped her to secure Alicia's services."

"Did your sister know Alicia?"

"I don't believe so."

"And was the séance different from the ones you have attended in the past?" Jason asked.

"It was. I suppose what struck me right away was the austerity of Alicia's format. Most mediums use tarot cards or crystal balls, and some even bring runes. One charlatan had a bag of human finger bones that bore pagan markings. It was deliciously morbid, but the mystic was a fake through and through, which became evident as soon as she began. Alicia had nothing but a candle."

"Did anyone come through, your ladyship?" Daniel asked.

Lady Amelia nodded. "A young woman. At first, we all thought it was Caroline, but it quickly became obvious that it wasn't."

"How did you know it wasn't Caroline?" Jason asked. "Did the spirit introduce herself?"

"No, but it was something she said. Something odd, yet entirely in keeping with the sort of nonsense she used to spew in life."

"Who do you believe she was?" Daniel asked, leaning forward in his eagerness to hear the answer.

Jason thought it was entirely possible that Miss Crumlish had got it wrong and Lady Cynthia's dream, or nightmare, had nothing to do with the séance, but Lady Amelia immediately disproved that theory.

"It was Daphne, my brother's first wife. Either that or it was a clever trick meant to destabilize Rex. The poor man went white to the roots of his hair. We could see his reaction even in the light of a single candle. And it really frightened Cynthia. She yanked her hands out of mine and Rex's and ran from the room."

"What was it that Lady Daphne said?" Jason asked.

Lady Amelia made a show of remembering, then said, "'In death, you have anchored me to eternal life.'"

"What does that mean?" Daniel asked.

"I don't know, but it obviously meant something to my brother."

"Why do you believe that this was in keeping with Lady Daphne's character?" Jason inquired.

"I hate to speak ill of the dead, I really do, and Daphne died such an awful death, but the girl was always a bit odd. I told Rex as much, but he was besotted and thought he could win Daphne over if he tried hard enough."

"Did she not love him?" Daniel asked.

Lady Amelia shook her head. "Do you believe you were born to be a doctor and could never be anything else, Lord Redmond?" she asked.

The question took Jason by surprise, but he answered as truthfully as he could. "I don't think a person is born to be anything, but we all have certain interests and aptitudes that shape us into the individuals we become."

"Daphne had no interests beyond faith. She was very devout and endlessly fascinated by medieval saints and martyrs. I honestly think she was born to be a nun, but her father, Lord Burrows, would never have stood for it even if there were still cloistered monasteries left in England. Daphne was his eldest daughter, and he was determined to see her advantageously married. She had several offers before a proposal from Rex, but the old man held out for an earl. Lord Salter, who'd proposed to Daphne, married her younger sister, Imogen. I always thought he got the better bargain."

"Why do you say that?" Jason asked.

He'd never encountered Lord Salter, but Katherine had mentioned Imogen Salter, whom she'd met through one of her charitable committees. They weren't friends, but Katherine had spoken well of the woman and seemed to hold her in high regard.

"Imogen was nothing like her sister, even though they were quite devoted to each other," Lady Amelia said. "She wasn't as beautiful or as accomplished, but she had other qualities that I have always found more desirable in a woman. She was clever and pragmatic, and had her feet firmly planted on the ground. She would have made Rex a much better wife, in my opinion, and she would have learned to be happy with the arrangement and make the most of her position and wealth."

"Was Lady Daphne unhappy in her marriage?" Daniel asked.

"We never spoke of such things, but she greatly admired women of faith who refused to be bullied into marriage. Christina of Markyate, Saint Agatha, and Saint Frances of Rome. Daphne was heard to praise Saint Etheldreda, who was wed twice but remained pure and eventually threw off the bonds of marriage and became an abbess."

"Did His Grace and Lady Daphne have children?" Jason inquired.

"They had a son," Lady Amelia said, and her eyes misted with tears. "The poor mite didn't live to see his first birthday."

"What was the cause of death?"

"The child developed an inflammation of the bowels and could not hold down any nourishment. Rex blamed the wetnurse and had her replaced, but the situation grew even more dire with the new nurse. Bertie essentially starved to death."

"Dear God," Daniel exclaimed. "Jason, have you ever heard of such a thing?"

Jason nodded. "It sounds like a gastrointestinal infection that can be caused by contaminated milk."

"So, Rex was right to blame the wetnurse," Lady Amelia exclaimed. "It's a wonder none of her own children suffered the same fate."

"How many children did she have?" Daniel asked.

"At the time she nursed Bertie, she had three children under the age of three," Lady Amelia said.

Jason nodded. "It's possible that she didn't have enough milk to feed so many children, and rather than lose the wages she earned from nursing an earl's son, she supplemented Bertie's food supply with cow's milk. The older children were probably able to digest it, but an infant is not meant to drink cow's milk."

"Bertie's death nearly undid Daphne, and she was in the grip of melancholia for nearly two years. We didn't think she would ever recover, but Rex came up with an idea that seemed to lift her out of her bottomless despair."

"What was it?" Daniel asked.

"He offered to take her to Italy. Daphne had always dreamed of going and had a long list of sites she wanted to visit."

"And that trip proved fatal," Daniel said.

"Yes. Daphne contracted cholera while in Venice. I always did say that those canals were no better than sewage drains," Lady Amelia scoffed. "And now look what's happening right here, in London. Contagion spreading unchecked. I wager anyone who's anyone will be leaving the city in the next few weeks. Oh, and Crumlish, Daphne's maid, died too," she added as an afterthought. "Thank the good Lord Rex was spared."

Lady Amelia dabbed at her eyes. "One of Rex's greatest regrets is that he was forced to bury Daphne in Italy. He wanted to bring her home, but it wasn't safe to transport the remains of a woman who'd died of an infectious disease. Daphne and Crumlish are buried on Isola di San Michele. There's a Protestant section," Lady Amelia explained when she saw Daniel's horrified expression. She sighed deeply. "Jane and Percy had planned to announce their betrothal when Rex and Daphne returned from Italy, but as you might imagine, their life had to be put on hold until the mourning period was at an end. Poor Jane was devastated. She adored Daphne and saw her as another sister, but Jane had been in love with Percy since she first met him at the tender age of twelve, and having to wait so long to marry came as quite a blow."

"Is Miss Crumlish the daughter of the woman who died in Italy?" Jason asked.

"Yes. Bernice Crumlish stayed on and became Cynthia's lady's maid after Rex and Cynthia married."

"Did Lady Cynthia not have her own lady's maid?"

"She must have had, but Rex could hardly dismiss Crumlish when he felt responsible for her mother's death. Perhaps Cynthia's maid remained to look after Cynthia's sister."

"I met Crumlish this afternoon," Daniel said.

Lady Amelia shrugged. A lady's maid was clearly of no interest to her beyond what her presence signified for her brother.

"Lady Amelia, how did Alicia seem when the séance came to an end?" Jason asked.

"She was a little taken aback, but Cynthia can't be the first person to run screaming from the room," Lady Amelia said. "Alicia blew out the candle as soon as the gas lamps were lit, collected her things, and made her way to the foyer. Rex offered to have his man take her home, but she refused."

"Did she give a reason?" Daniel asked.

"No."

"Did she seem frightened?" Jason asked.

Lady Amelia looked to the ceiling, then turned her dark gaze back on Jason. "Now that you mention it, perhaps a little. She seemed in a hurry to leave."

"What time was this?" Jason asked, to see if Lady Amelia's answer would align with that of the servants.

"I don't know exactly, but probably half past nine."

"Thank you," Jason said, and stood.

"I'm sorry Alicia is dead," Lady Amelia said. "She had a hard life, and now it seems she's had a hard death. Some women are born to suffer."

"Or are made to suffer by others," Jason replied. "Good day, my lady."

"Good day. I do hope we meet again but under happier circumstances."

"No doubt we will," Jason said before he bowed to Lady Amelia and strode from the room, followed by Daniel.

60

Chapter 10

"Go home, Jason," Daniel said once they had stepped outside into the still-bright light of the summer evening. "You look exhausted."

"I don't think I'll be able to rest," Jason protested.

"Jason, we're not going to solve this murder today. Or tomorrow. These things take time, and you need to look after yourself."

Jason nodded. "You're right. Shall I call for you tomorrow at nine?"

"Yes, thank you," Daniel replied. "Goodnight."

Daniel watched Jason until he melted into the crowd and disappeared from view. He supposed he should go home too. He longed to spend some time with Charlotte before Flora put her to bed and then enjoy a peaceful dinner, but he had one more stop to make before he could allow himself the luxury of rest.

Jason was right. It was imperative to interview everyone who had attended the séance before they had a chance to talk amongst themselves and come up with a palatable version of events that reconciled the two versions Jason and Daniel had been presented with so far. The earl had claimed that Caroline had made an appearance and had said that she was cold and lonely in her grave, while Lady Amelia believed that the apparition had been Lady Daphne and had said something quite different. Bernice Crumlish also thought that the attendees had been visited by Lady Daphne, and Daniel was curious to see what Lord and Lady Guilford had to say.

It was too late in the day to pay a call on members of the nobility, but Daniel decided that the worst thing that could happen was that he would be refused entrance and have to return tomorrow with Jason. On his own, he lacked the legitimacy Jason's noble rank provided. Not for the first time, Daniel reflected on the unfairness of the class system and how some names opened every door even if the person who bore said name was a scoundrel or, worse yet, an unrepentant criminal. Daniel had arrested his share of noble men and women, and although the noose was the great equalizer when it came to meting out justice, some still received preferential treatment while in prison or at their trials. Even their deaths were easier.

Daniel had not known much about the logistics of an execution, but he had learned more than he'd ever hoped to know about the coordination of a hanging when he'd investigated the murder of Phillip Hobart, Newgate's principal executioner. It seemed that the condemned or their loved ones could pay to guarantee that the neck snapped during the hanging, ensuring a quick and almost painless death, while those who didn't have coin to spare could wind up suffocating for up to an hour before finally meeting their Maker. There was little fairness in the world, even when it came to the administration of justice, but Daniel knew that neither he nor Jason would be able to rest until Alicia's senseless death had been avenged.

The Guilfords lived nearby in Hanover Square, and although their residence wasn't as ludicrously palatial as that of the earl, it could still comfortably house several families and their servants. The Guilfords' butler was surprisingly young and nodded gravely while Daniel explained the purpose of his visit. A more experienced man would have turned him away, but the butler asked Daniel to wait while he conferred with the lord and lady of the house, then escorted him to a well-appointed drawing room.

Although Percy Guilford had to be the same age as the earl, since they had met at school, he looked no older than thirty and clearly took pride in his appearance. He had the lean physique of someone who took regular exercise, along with exquisitely tailored clothes and the neatly pomaded dark hair and carefully trimmed moustache of a man who spent a considerable amount of time before the mirror. His wife, Lady Jane, was quite attractive as well. She had the large brown eyes and the sable-colored hair of a baby deer, and her heart-shaped face was framed by bouncy curls. Lady Jane's bronze taffeta gown complemented her coloring beautifully and shimmered in the soft light pouring through the tall window.

Lord Guilford peered at Daniel through a gold-rimmed monocle, then lowered the lens and studied him with both eyes.

"What's this all about, Inspector?" he asked. Daniel couldn't tell if Lord Guilford was curious or mildly irritated. "We don't normally welcome policemen into our home, but Perkins said it was quite urgent that you speak with us. Naturally, we agreed."

Lady Jane nodded and gave Daniel a tiny smile. Daniel assumed Perkins was the butler and inwardly thanked the man for championing his cause with the Guilfords.

"Forgive the intrusion, my lord," Daniel said. He had not been invited to sit and stood awkwardly before his hosts. "Alicia Lysander, the medium who conducted the séance at the home of the Earl of Ongar last night, was set upon and died as a result."

Jane Guilford's hand flew to her mouth as she let out a strangled cry.

"It's quite all right, my dear," Percy Guilford said soothingly. "It's got nothing to do with us."

Jane gave her husband a look of reproach, and he instantly rearranged his features into a bland mask of civility. It seemed his wife held sway over him, and if Daniel wanted answers, he had to appeal to her.

"Mrs. Lysander's death was neither quick nor peaceful," Daniel added for Jane's benefit. "And I have been charged with investigating what happened."

"That's dreadful, and we're very sorry," Percy said in a tone laced with false sorrow. "Do go on and ask your questions, Inspector. We will assist in any way we can."

"Thank you."

Daniel wished he could sit, partly because he felt foolish standing there like a schoolboy and partly because he was tired, but it would have been the height of rudeness to sit down without being invited to do so.

"Please, sit down, Inspector," Jane said, sensing Daniel's discomfort.

"Thank you, my lady." Daniel lowered himself into a hardback chair and faced his hostess. "Your ladyship, I was informed that you were the one to engage the services of Mrs. Lysander for last night's séance. Can you tell me how that came about?"

"And how's that relevant?" Percy bristled.

63

"I'm simply trying to gather the facts and establish a timeline," Daniel replied, hoping the banal explanation would pacify Percy Guilford, but the man wasn't so easily duped.

"A timeline of what?" he demanded. "The woman, God rest her soul," he added hastily when he looked at his wife, "was attacked after she left Rex's house. What possible bearing can Jane's involvement have on her death?"

"I don't believe the attack on Mrs. Lysander was random," Daniel explained. "She was wearing jewelry, and there was a considerable amount of money in her purse, but nothing was taken. Someone hit her from the back and fled."

"So, you think she was assaulted by someone who knew her?" Jane exclaimed.

"I do, my lady."

"Well, I for one am happy to tell you everything I know, Inspector," Jane said. "Which isn't very much."

"Anything you can share with me will be immensely helpful."

Lady Jane clasped her hands in her lap and fixed Daniel with that fawn-like gaze. "Dear Cynthia was distraught when Caroline died so suddenly. You know about that, do you?"

"I do," Daniel assured her.

"A séance is not the sort of thing one normally gives as a gift, but Cynthia had expressed a desire to contact Caroline, and I thought that to say a proper goodbye to Caroline would bring her peace of mind."

Percy harrumphed but refrained from commenting.

"Anyway," Jane went on, "I had heard that Lady Denby had hosted a séance last month and was very pleased with the result. She had lost her youngest son, who was on his grand tour and took ill while in Athens. Lady Denby was desperate to contact the poor boy, and from what I had heard, he'd come through and had assured his mother that he was happy and well and she should not grieve for him."

Daniel was about to ask what any of this had to do with Alicia Lysander when Jane forestalled him. "I had never met Lady Denby, since she was in mourning for her husband and then her son when I came out into Society, but I do know Lady Blackney, who knows Lady Shrewsberry, who's said to be close with Lady Denby, and was present at the séance."

"My love, do get to the point," Percy said mildly. "I'd like to dine at some point this evening."

"Sorry, dear. As I was saying, I was able to get Lady Shrewsberry to secure an invitation to Lady Blackney's bridge party, and then once there, I begged an introduction to Lady Denby. Lady Blackney said that Lady Denby had retreated to her country estate and would not return to London until September at the earliest, but it turned out that Lady Blackney knew Sadie Goodall, who was quite close to Alicia Lysander and could facilitate an introduction. And that was how I was able to secure Mrs. Lysander for our séance."

"I see," Daniel said. "So, did you meet with Mrs. Lysander before the séance?"

"I did, yes. She was rather standoffish, I might add. Acted like she was doing me a favor. I mean, if not for people like us, she wouldn't be able to make a living, would she?" Jane asked indignantly. "It's members of the ton that are her bread and butter."

"Did Mrs. Lysander seem reluctant to accept your invitation?" Daniel asked, wondering once again if Alicia might have sensed that something was off and feared the coming engagement.

"Yes, I suppose so." Jane's mouth opened slightly, and her eyes widened. "Do you think she knew?"

"Knew what, Jane?" Percy asked.

"That she was going to die. She was psychic, Percy."

"She was a fraud," Percy erupted. "What was all that guff about anchoring the dead to life? And the spirit that was cold and lonely in her grave. I mean really, Jane!"

"Yes, I suppose that was unnecessarily dramatic," Jane admitted.

"Dramatic?" Percy cried. "It was a parlor trick, nothing more. Every corpse is cold and lonely in their grave. And that... that thing... wasn't Caroline."

"Lady Amelia said it was Daphne, His Grace's late wife," Jane added for Daniel's benefit. "She passed three years ago. Terrible business. Daphne died in Italy, and poor Rex has never been the same since. Well, until he met Cynthia. She brought him back to life. Didn't she, Percy?"

Percy ignored his wife's question, his mind clearly still on the séance. "And what was Daphne doing there, I ask you?" Percy demanded. "No one summoned her. We all clearly said we wanted to speak to Caroline."

"Maybe Daphne had something to say," Jane replied. "You can't control the spirit world, my dear. We must accept whatever comes and be grateful. It's so reassuring to receive a message from the dead, even if it's not quite what one expected."

"The whole charade was nothing more than a cruel prank. Cynthia is fragile as it is after Caroline's death. Rex should have never agreed to it," Percy exclaimed. "I told you it was a bad idea."

"I couldn't have known that Daphne would make an appearance," Jane replied petulantly.

"How do we even know that it was Daphne? It was a shimmering sphere that sounded like a woman. Any woman!" Percy reiterated. "Or more likely the woman who had orchestrated the whole thing."

"You always were cynical, my love, but some of us believe in the eternal life of the soul."

"And some of us believe in money, and that woman was fleecing people who were grieving for their loved ones."

Jane gave Percy a look that clearly said she hadn't asked for nor was she interested in his opinion of Alicia Lysander.

"A woman is dead, Percy," Jane rebuked him. "A young, beautiful woman who hadn't done anything wrong. I came to her, remember? She didn't approach me."

"She didn't have to," Percy retorted. "There are plenty of gullible fools who will pay any amount of money to see their dearly departed one more time. What they see is a fabrication."

"It makes people feel better," Jane said. "Lady Denby felt lighter after speaking to her son. Lady Blackney said so."

"She felt so light that she has sequestered herself at her country house?"

"She hasn't sequestered herself. She simply left London for the summer, as many people do. In fact, I wouldn't mind a few weeks in the country myself, what with cholera raging in the seamier parts of London. No one is immune, Percy. It's not as if we don't come in contact with the lower orders."

She glanced at Daniel, no doubt intending to remind her husband that he was within sneezing distance of a representative of the lower orders at that very moment.

"Then let's go. We can spend July and August at Waverly," Percy said. "I could do with the peace and quiet for a few weeks."

"I'll inform Mrs. Lucas, and she can start to make preparations tomorrow morning," Jane said happily.

"Do," Percy snapped.

"If I may," Daniel interjected, and the Guilfords stared at him as if they had quite forgotten he was there. "Can you tell me what happened after the apparition appeared?"

"Cynthia became upset, the apparition vanished, and we all went home," Percy replied.

"My lady, did you speak to Mrs. Lysander after the séance came to an end?"

"I did, yes," Jane replied, drawing out the words. "She wasn't upset exactly, just a bit surprised that the séance had ended so abruptly."

"Then what happened?" Daniel asked.

"She asked for her things and left."

"I was told that His Grace offered her the use of his carriage."

"He did, and damn chivalrous it was too," Percy said. "But Mrs. Lysander refused. Rather churlishly, I might add."

"What did she say?"

"She said she would prefer to walk. And that was the last any of us saw of her," Percy concluded.

"Was there anything at all that seemed odd to you?" Daniel asked, directing the question to Lady Jane.

"All of it was odd," Percy said.

"Not odd, but very sad," Jane replied, as if her husband hadn't spoken. "There was such a sense of sorrow. It was no wonder Cynthia became upset. We all know we will die someday, but such a stark reminder is difficult to bear, especially when one is—"

"Jane." Percy's tone held a note of warning.

"When one is what?" Daniel asked, even though he didn't think he would get an answer.

"When one is a replacement," Jane said. "She doesn't think Rex is quite over Daphne. She was the love of his life."

"Really, Jane," Percy growled.

"Cynthia told me so herself just last week. To have Daphne suddenly appear…"

Jane didn't finish the sentence, but she didn't really need to. Any young bride who wasn't secure in the affections of her husband would be rattled by a visit from his first wife.

"This remains between us, Inspector," Percy said.

"Of course, my lord," Daniel replied.

Daniel didn't think he would learn anything more from the Guilfords, so he thanked them for taking the time to speak to him and took his leave. There was nothing more he could do tonight, and although he was as frustrated as Jason had been by the lack of progress, he was more than ready to leave the investigation until tomorrow and devote the remainder of the evening to Charlotte and Flora.

Chapter 11

The house was unusually quiet when Jason let himself in. He peeked into the drawing room, but it was empty, and there was no sign of Dodson or Fanny, who always came to greet him as soon as he got home. Jason experienced a moment of panic, then admonished himself for jumping to unwarranted conclusions. If someone was ill or if something had happened, his household would be in an uproar. His fear was due more to his feelings than anything that might have occurred in his absence.

Heading downstairs to the kitchen, he was relieved to hear Mrs. Dodson's familiar voice. She said something to Kitty, Kitty replied, and the two women laughed, the sound of their merriment allowing Jason to breathe easier.

"My lord," Kitty exclaimed when she saw him. She had worked for the Redmonds for several years now but still treated Jason as if he were a member of the royal family.

"Good evening," Jason said. "Where is everyone?"

Kitty returned to chopping vegetables, correctly assuming that Mrs. Dodson would take the question.

"Mary is upstairs with the children, Dodson has a touch of indigestion, and Henley and Fanny are in the garden," Mrs. Dodson said with an amused smile. It was an open secret that Fanny and Henley had been spending time together of late. In the past, Jason would have warned Fanny about becoming involved with his valet, who had a drinking problem, but Henley had been as good as gold and seemed to have turned over a new, teetotaling leaf.

"What about Katherine?" Jason asked.

"She's upstairs," Mrs. Dodson said. Her explanation was woefully incomplete, but Jason didn't detect anything in her demeanor that gave him cause to worry.

"Should I check on Dodson? I can give him a solution of potassium permanganate. It will help to cleanse the bowels."

Mrs. Dodson chuckled. "No need, sir. He's feeling much better now. Can I get you anything?"

"I'll wait," Jason replied. "What's for dinner?"

"Baked salmon with roasted potatoes and asparagus, and fresh fruit for dessert."

"Sounds wonderful," Jason replied, glad that Mrs. Dodson wasn't preparing a heavy meal. He didn't think he had the stomach for it after the day he'd had.

He left Mrs. Dodson and Kitty to it and hurried upstairs. He found Katherine sitting in a chair by the window, her gaze dreamy as she looked into space.

"Katie, are you all right?" Jason asked as he walked into the bedroom and shut the door.

Startled out of her reverie, Katherine sprang to her feet and rushed toward Jason, wrapping her arms about his neck. "Oh, Jason," she whispered. "I'm so sorry." She pulled back a little and looked at him in that way she did when she thought Lily might be running a temperature. "You look dreadful."

Jason felt dreadful. His muscles groaned in protest with every step, and his mind was frustratingly sluggish, the thoughts forming at a slower rate and a pressure caused by fatigue building behind his eyes. It had been a long time since he'd had a sleepless night or been on his feet all day, as he had been during the war years when he'd sometimes operated through the night only to receive a wagonload of new patients in the morning. But he had been young then and driven by urgency and purpose. He was still driven by purpose, but now there was no urgency. There was no one to save. Alicia was gone, and all he could do was make certain that justice was served posthumously.

"Come sit down and tell me everything," Katherine urged.

Jason nodded and settled on the bed, Katherine sitting next to him. There was no use pretending he didn't know what she was talking about since she clearly knew everything, and Jason had no need to ask how. Dodson had told Mrs. Dodson, who had told Henley, who had told Fanny, who'd had a bit of a gossip with Mary, who had never met Alicia Lysander but knew all about her and had been the subject of the medium's warning. Mary had told Katherine, and here they were, with Jason's wife looking at him as if he were made of glass and about to shatter.

Jason wanted to reassure her that he was absolutely fine and there was nothing to worry about, then realized that having someone to worry about you was one of the nicest things about being married, and he wasn't about to belittle Katie's feelings by pretending he had no need of her. He did need her, and he needed to understand what had happened, but for now, he would settle for the pleasure of being at home among people who cared about him.

"Were you able to discover anything?" Katherine asked once Jason had explained what had happened to Alicia.

Had Jason been married to any other woman, he would have spared her the more disturbing details, but Katherine was strong, intelligent, and compassionate. She did not scare easily, nor did she like to be coddled.

"And nothing was taken?" Katherine asked, her brow creased with confusion.

"It doesn't seem that way. If theft was the motive, I can't imagine that her assailant would leave behind money and jewelry."

"No, they wouldn't," Katherine agreed. She looked away for a moment, then turned back to Jason, her gaze resolute. "Was Alicia raped, Jason?"

"I saw no evidence of sexual assault," Jason replied truthfully.

"What sort of animal would hit a defenseless woman over the head and leave her to bleed to death in the street?"

"The sort that had something to gain by her passing."

"But who would benefit from her death?"

Jason shrugged tiredly. "Alicia touched many lives, Katie. She went into people's homes and sometimes delivered messages they weren't prepared to hear. Perhaps she had unwittingly made someone feel threatened."

"How?" Katherine cried.

The thought hadn't occurred to Jason before, but now that it had, he realized it had merit. "Perhaps a spirit had leveled an accusation of wrongdoing from beyond the grave or said something to threaten an attendee's inheritance or livelihood. Others might not take the accusation seriously or even credit it, but a person who's guilty of a crime would not be too quick to dismiss the implications."

"But wouldn't murdering Alicia bring attention to their actions?"

"Not if the crime was never solved. We have no way of finding out what Alicia knew."

"Surely she confided in Constantine."

"Constantine was not privy to the details. That was one of Alicia's tenets. Anything revealed during a séance remained completely private. So, if she had unwittingly learned something, the information would die with her unless the other individuals present chose to disclose it."

"Was there anyone Alicia was close with, besides Constantine, I mean?" Katherine asked.

"I don't know."

If Jason were to describe Alicia Lysander in one word, it would be opaque. She did not like to talk about herself or reveal the details of her private life. She had probably told him more than she had any of the other clients, because she had trusted him, but Jason was under the impression that even her lover had known little of the woman he had shared his life with.

"Do you think she was in contact with her family in India?"

"Alicia's father sent her mother away when Alicia was a child, then eventually brought her to England, where she married Captain Lysander. Her mother died when she was small, so I highly doubt that she maintained ties with her mother's family. Why do you ask?"

"Perhaps the person who attacked her was someone who'd recently come over," Katherine said.

"But what reason would they have to attack Alicia?"

"Maybe they blamed her for something."

73

"Such as?"

Katherine shrugged. "I don't know. I'm just speculating. We know so little about the private lives of others, don't we?"

"It's better that way. Knowledge can be a dangerous thing."

"Whatever do you mean, Jason?"

"Knowing other people's secrets can make one a target, and Alicia knew more than her share of people's private affairs."

"I suppose," Katherine said thoughtfully. "I don't think we should tell Micah."

Jason nodded. Alicia Lysander had broken his ward's fragile heart by delivering a message from his mother, but in some strange way, she had also given him leave to move on. *A stór*, his mother had called Micah from beyond the grave. My treasure. An Irish endearment that only Micah would understand and recall from his days as a small boy, when the Donovan family had still been intact, and Micah had enjoyed the love of his parents and two older siblings. Everyone except Mary was gone now, Micah's mother buried in Maryland, and his father and brother sleeping in a mass grave in Andersonville, Georgia. That brief message from beyond was the closest Micah had come to being able to say goodbye to the mammy he'd loved, and his heart seemed a little lighter for it, especially now that Mary and her son Liam were with him once again.

"Micah has a right to know," Jason said. "He can handle it. He's almost a man."

"I still think of him as that flame-haired little boy I met when you two first arrived in Birch Hill," Katherine said with a wistful smile. "How life has changed since then."

Her expression turned dreamy, and when their eyes met, Jason thought he knew what Katie wanted to tell him but wasn't sure if this was the right time to talk of happy things. Being a doctor, he had guessed, but he hadn't said anything, allowing Katie to share her news when she was ready. But already there was a new softness in her gaze and changes to her body. She experienced an aversion to certain foods and was easily brought to tears, her eyes brimming when she gazed upon their daughter or read something that upset her.

It was early days, and much could go wrong, so it was wise not to share the news, but Jason could see that Katherine was desperate for him know, especially in view of the day's events. They moved at the same time, and when Katherine walked into his arms and pressed her cheek against his chest, Jason pulled her close and couldn't keep from asking, "When?"

"End of December."

"I can't wait."

"I hope it's a boy this time," Katherine said into his chest.

"Another daughter would be a blessing," Jason said, and meant it. He would like to have a son, but he couldn't imagine loving a child more than he loved Lily. A girl would be just as welcome, and just as adored.

"It would," Katherine agreed. "It seems wrong to say it when Alicia lies dead, but I'm so happy."

"That's life, Katie. Every minute of every day, people die, and new people are born. It's the cycle of life, and we're all a part of it."

As a vicar's daughter, Katherine understood more than most about life and loss, but when it came to one's own family, no amount of understanding could assuage the fears that were born along with the children, who had the power to rip one's heart out if anything were to befall them. To love was to be made vulnerable, and to be vulnerable was to be afraid.

"All will be well, my love," Jason said into Katherine's hair. "All will be well."

And he prayed that it would be.

Chapter 12

By the time Daniel returned to St. John's Wood, Flora had already gone upstairs to the nursery to put Charlotte to bed. He was sorry to have missed spending a few minutes with Charlotte, but it had been a long and difficult day, and all he really wanted was a few moments of quiet to enjoy a tot of brandy while he considered what he had learned. Daniel got the brandy, but not the quiet.

"Sleeping like an angel," Flora announced as she walked into the parlor. "How was your day, Daniel?"

They had long since dispensed with *Inspector Haze* and *Miss Tarrant*, and although Daniel and Flora were not married, nor did they share a bed, they were as much a couple as he had once been with Sarah—if not more so, since Sarah had withdrawn from him in the final years of her life and had left him as emotionally isolated as if she had been gone already.

"That bad?" Flora asked as she topped up his drink and poured one for herself.

That was another thing about Flora. She was neither timid nor conventional, and Daniel found that he loved that about her. After years of loneliness and bitter regret, Daniel felt not only cared for but supported. Flora was there to share his trials and offered the kind of no-nonsense pragmatism that Katherine provided for Jason. Had she not been born a woman, Flora Tarrant might have been anything or anyone she wanted, and she openly chafed against the limitations placed on her by a society that wanted women to know their place. Daniel could see how this angered and frustrated Flora's parents, who weren't happy with this unorthodox arrangement and were too embarrassed to tell their friends that Flora was now a nursemaid rather than the wife of some stodgy business associate of her father's. Flora relished the freedom, however, and did not hold back when it came to offering her opinions.

Years ago, Daniel would have recoiled from a woman who was so outspoken and sure of herself. He would have thought her a hoyden at best, unnatural at worst, but he found that he liked Flora's directness and her refusal to bow down to convention. It took courage to be different, and even more courage to act on one's principles. Most women would have succumbed to the pressure and acquiesced to their parents' wishes, but not Flora. Daniel was certain that if he made a decisive move, Flora would not bat an eyelash and not only follow him to the bedroom but lead the way. Daniel had to admit that these changes in his attitude were probably due to Jason's influence and realized that some people would think less of him for adopting a more liberal view of the world, but he found that he felt freer and happier, and for the first time in years, he felt like he finally had choices.

"Daniel, are you even listening to me?" Flora asked, interrupting his internal monologue. She didn't sound annoyed, just amused, and smiled at him, her hazel eyes warm with affection.. "You were a million miles away."

"I'm sorry. I was just thinking."

"Clearly. But what were you thinking about? It was probably the case, but I can't help but hope you were thinking about me," Flora said with a coy grin.

Daniel smiled back. She was so completely unselfconscious, he sometimes wished he had the courage to just blurt out what was on his mind.

"It *was* you," Daniel admitted. "And the case. This one is close to home, Flora."

"How so?" Flora asked, instantly alert.

Flora knew all about Charlotte's abduction and Alicia's part in bringing her home, and her eyes filled with tears when Daniel told her what had happened and how he had spent his day.

"Oh, my dear," Flora said. She set down her drink and came toward him, cupping his cheek and kissing him on the forehead as if he were a child who needed to be comforted.

And it was comforting. Daniel didn't have to pretend to be unmoved by Alicia's death or carry on like he was an infallible detective who unfailingly solved every crime. He could be himself and show Flora his insecurity without fear of judgment or rejection. She understood and liked him regardless, accepting him as a flawed man who sometimes needed the guidance of a woman, even if he didn't always realize it.

"It was Constantine. It had to be," Flora said once Daniel had relayed all the details of the case.

"What would be his motive?" Daniel asked, amused despite the grim nature of the subject. Flora had the look of a hound on the trail of a fox.

"There could be several," Flora said. "Perhaps Alicia had met someone else. She and Constantine weren't married, so she could simply ask him to leave. Likewise, she might have discovered that Constantine had been unfaithful and wanted nothing more to do with him. Perhaps she had decided to draw up or change an existing will and he was not to be her beneficiary."

"What?" Daniel asked, setting his empty glass down with a thump.

"If Constantine thought he would get the entirety of Alicia's estate in the event of her death, that would come as quite a shock, don't you think?"

"Her estate?"

Daniel and Jason had considered the ways in which Constantine would benefit if he were to appropriate Alicia's savings, but they had never considered an estate.

"Well, yes," Flora said. "Alicia must have inherited something from her father, and she had been married to Captain Lysander. He must have left her adequately provided for if she was able to live comfortably on her own and shun the possibility of another marriage. Most women don't have that luxury if they know their savings will run out within a year or two. They have to either remarry or find suitable employment."

"But Alicia was employed," Daniel pointed out. "I'm sure she made a comfortable living."

"She made a comfortable living recently, but what about when she was first widowed? She was twenty, was she not?" Flora asked. "She was on her own and completely unknown. It would have taken years to build up a reputation and get to the point where she could afford to turn away prospective clients. And she did turn clients away," Flora said. "She was the most sought-after medium in London and set her fees accordingly."

Daniel didn't bother to ask how Flora knew that. She liked to read the Society columns and was up on all the gossip, even though she had no interest whatsoever in joining the ranks of the ton, which she could easily do if she only allowed her father to arrange a suitable marriage for her. Given that Flora was nearing thirty, her choices would probably be limited to widowed, middle-aged men, but if she were interested in climbing the ladder of social prominence, she could do quite well. It wasn't lost on Daniel that he was a widowed, middle-aged man, albeit without a title or an enviable fortune. Whether Flora married or not, she would be well provided for since after her brother's death, there was no one left for her father to leave his wealth to. Among other things, Flora would inherit Ardith Hall, a medieval monstrosity that she desired about as much as she hoped to be stricken with the plague.

"So, you think Constantine murdered Alicia so he could claim her inheritance before she had a chance to bequeath it to someone else?" Daniel reiterated.

"It's as good a motive as any."

Daniel grinned. "I would have to agree."

Flora smiled back. "If there's one thing I learned from my father, it's that there's always a financial trail to follow. And the thing I learned from my mother is that the love of money is the root of all evil."

"I think your mother quite enjoys having money," Daniel pointed out.

"She does, but having been married to my father for more than thirty years, she also knows how corrosive greed can be."

"Are you saying that your father is greedy?"

"Mother prefers to call it ambitious. And I bet you anything Constantine Moore had ambitions of his own."

Daniel nodded. "I wonder if Katherine said much the same thing to Jason."

"I doubt it," Flora replied airily.

"You don't think Katherine Redmond recognizes greed?"

"Oh, she does. Katherine was trained by her horrid father to identify all the deadly sins, but she has been somewhat preoccupied these past few weeks."

Daniel was about to ask for an explanation when Flora put a finger to her mouth. "My lips are sealed," she said.

"Is it Mary?" Daniel asked warily.

Whenever problems arose in the Redmond household, they could usually be traced back to Mary, who, in Daniel's opinion, was more feckless and reckless than any woman who could call Jason Redmond her benefactor had a right to be. Of course, Mary didn't wish for a benefactor, nor did she wish to be reminded of all the things Jason had done for her and Micah. *The ungrateful minx*, Daniel thought with a shake of the head. It was tragic to lose one's parents and brother, but if one got Jason Redmond in the bargain, things weren't all that bad.

Of course, now Mary had lost her husband as well, and what a scoundrel he had turned out to be. Thankfully, she was back on English soil and safe with the Redmonds, instead of in Boston, where she would be hunted by her late husband's associates in the hope that they could recover the funds that ne'er-do-well had appropriated from the gang he'd worked for.

"She's a fiery Irish lass," Flora said, as if reading Daniel's mind. "And I admire her all the more for her spirit."

"Having spirit is all well and good," Daniel replied, "but biting the hand that feeds you speaks to ingratitude and disrespect."

Flora chuckled. "Jason loves a good cause, and Mary and Liam make him feel less guilty about all that money he inherited from his draconian grandfather. For all his democratic leanings, Jason is still a nobleman who's not averse to using his status and wealth to get what he wants."

"You have him all wrong, Flora," Daniel said loyally. If not for Jason, Daniel and Flora wouldn't be sitting in this cozy parlor, gossiping like an old married couple.

"I admire Jason Redmond, Daniel, but not quite as much as you do. He's an honorable man, but he is a man, and all men have faults. And

Jason has his own ambitions, even if they are not always material in nature."

"Dinner," Grace announced as she entered the parlor and interrupted their conversation. Her cheeks were pink from the heat of the range, and she smelled of freshly baked bread and roasted meat.

"Grace, won't you join us?" Daniel invited for what felt like the hundredth time.

It seemed wrong for Grace to eat in the kitchen by herself when he and Flora would welcome her company. By this stage, Grace was more family than domestic servant, but she refused every time, preferring to maintain the line between employer and employee.

"Thank you, Inspector, but I've already eaten my supper," Grace said.

"Tomorrow, then," Flora said, and Grace offered her a noncommittal smile.

Chapter 13

Saturday, June 19

It was a glorious summer morning, the birds singing their hearts out in a nearby hawthorn tree and the sky a brilliant blue. Shimmering drops of dew dotted the grass, and the air smelled clean and fresh, the usual stench of a London summer held at bay by a pleasant breeze. After yesterday's lack of progress, Daniel felt more driven since his conversation with Flora and looked forward to sharing her theories with Jason.

He had just stepped outside when Jason's brougham rounded the corner. Joe Marin tipped his hat with a muttered "Inspector" as the carriage pulled up and Daniel climbed inside. Jason looked considerably better than he had the previous day, and there was an air of calm serenity about him that hadn't been there before.

"Good morning," Jason said.

"Good morning. How are you feeling?"

"Like we need to make headway into this case," Jason said, echoing Daniel's sentiments. "Were you able to learn anything last night?"

Sitting side by side made for an awkward conversation, but unless they wanted to waste time, they had to speak while on the move, and Daniel was eager to get going.

"I'd like to speak to Constantine Moore again," he said.

Jason called out the address to Joe, and the carriage glided smoothly away from the curb and merged with the morning traffic.

Daniel relayed his conversation with Flora, leaving out her more personal observations about Jason, then filled Jason in on his interview with the Guilfords and described how Jane Guilford had come to invite Alicia to conduct a séance at Rex Long's residence.

"Sadie Goodall?" Jason asked.

"Do you know her?"

"I know of her. She was mentioned in the Society pages," Jason explained.

"In what context?"

"Sadie Goodall is a medium who gained popularity over the past few years."

"Was she Alicia Lysander's rival?"

"Perhaps," Jason replied thoughtfully. "Although it was my understanding that few mediums are of the same caliber as Alicia."

"Might Sadie Goodall have been an associate? Or was she a friend?" Daniel asked. "I got the impression that Alicia's social circle was woefully small, but surely the woman had at least one friend. Then again, making friends is hard when one is not blessed with a trusting nature."

"I don't think anyone is inherently mistrustful. The wariness is a product of their experiences."

"I expect being taken away from one's mother at a young age would make anyone wary," Daniel said, his thoughts unwittingly going to Charlotte, and Sarah's decision to remove herself from her daughter's life.

At least Alicia had known that it wasn't her mother's choice to leave her. Her British father had simply tired of his native mistress, which placed the blame squarely on his shoulders. It was a cruel thing to do, but he had probably thought he was doing what was best for his only child and didn't want to leave her in India when it was time to return to England.

"Do you know where we might find this Sadie Goodall?" Daniel asked.

"I seem to recall reading that she keeps a salon near Covent Garden. Perhaps Constantine can direct us. That was one important distinction between Sadie Goodall and Alicia Lysander. Alicia went to her clients' homes, which earned her their trust," Jason said.

"Why would going to them earn trust?"

"There's much skepticism when it comes to a person's psychic ability, and those who seek answers are more likely to be convinced of a medium's authenticity if they summon the spirit into a place they cannot alter to suit their needs."

"You mean there's less chance of pulling off a convincing parlor trick when they can't rig the table or have someone knock on the wall from the other side?"

"Precisely. All Alicia ever asked for was a darkened room and a single candle, and she arrived with nothing but her reticule."

"So her clients could clearly see that she wasn't bringing in anything that might be used to deceive them," Daniel mused.

He had not been invited to attend the séance during which Alicia had provided Jason with a vital clue that had helped them to find Charlotte. Alicia had thought Daniel might be too unstable and give in to impulses that might interfere with her ability to summon a spirit who could help them. Daniel still had questions, especially now that Alicia was gone, but he was glad he had not been present. In hindsight, he had to agree that Alicia had probably been right to exclude him. Would she have refused to perform the séance at the earl's house if she had known what the outcome would be? It was impossible to know, particularly since the attendees had been supposed strangers to her, but what if they weren't? What if someone in that room had given in to impulses of their own?

"Do you know how this Sadie Goodall works?" Daniel asked.

"I don't know anything about her methods."

"Then perhaps we should find out," Daniel said as they turned into Greek Street.

If Constantine Moore was surprised to see them again so soon, he didn't show it. He invited them into the parlor, and they sat around the intricately carved wooden table at the center, much as they had the day before. Constantine wasn't overtly hostile, but he was understandably wary when he realized that they weren't there to inform him of an arrest but to ask him more questions, the answers to which might implicate him in the death of his lover.

"Mr. Moore, did Alicia have a will?" Daniel inquired once he had answered Constantine's questions about the investigation.

"I don't know. Why do you ask?" Constantine looked nonplussed, as if the question of Alicia's estate had never crossed his mind.

"Because as far as we know, Alicia had no living relatives. Who inherits her assets?" Daniel asked bluntly.

"I suppose I do. Alicia kept an account at the Atrium Bank in the City."

"And the Atrium Bank just let her open an account?" Daniel asked. Few women held accounts in their own name, and if they did, it was because a male relative had guaranteed the account.

"The account had been cosigned by Captain Lysander. He had permitted Alicia to maintain an account of her own. When he passed, the bank turned a blind eye since they saw no added benefit to losing Alicia as a client."

"Do you know how much she kept in the account?" Daniel asked.

"No, but I have her bankbook."

"May we see it?"

"How is this relevant to your investigation?" Constantine bristled.

"Mr. Moore, greed is always a motive for murder," Jason replied, his tone as cutting as a newly sharpened knife.

Constantine shrugged. "I didn't hurt Alicia, and I have nothing to hide."

He left the room and returned with a jeweled box as stunning as a priceless reliquary. There was a discreet keyhole just beneath the lid, and Constantine extracted a small key from his waistcoat pocket and laid it on the table, choosing not to hand it to either Jason or Daniel in what was a small act of defiance. Jason didn't reach for the key, so Daniel picked it up and turned the box to face him. He inserted the key and lifted the lid, which was surprisingly heavy. The pleasant aroma of cedar drifted from the open box, and another scent that was spicy and foreign overlaid the smell of the wood.

The interior of the box was polished to a shine, the wood smooth and silky beneath Daniel's fingers. The opening was no bigger than a loaf of bread and contained a stack of papers that had been laid atop several pieces of jewelry that had clearly been brought from India. There was a thick gold necklace with a magnificent, jeweled pendant, and two bracelets in the shape of a cobra that would coil about the wrist toward the elbow, the eyes of the snakes bits of glowing ruby. There was also a gossamer silk scarf inlaid with elytra embroidery, the beetle wings used in the pattern iridescent in the morning light and so unlike anything Daniel had ever seen.

"What is this?" Daniel asked as he held up a gorgeous piece that was shaped like a brooch but did not have any means to pin it to a garment. The circular ornament depicted an unusual flower that was crafted of amethysts, emeralds, and bright yellow gold.

"It's a nose ring," Constantine said. "These jewels were gifts that Alicia's father had given to her mother while she was still in favor," he added angrily. "She left them for Alicia when she was evicted."

"These will be worth a few bob," Daniel said. "What do you intend to do with them, Mr. Moore?"

"I don't know. I forgot all about them until I saw them just now."

Jason leafed through the documents, then passed the stack to Daniel. There was a bankbook, several letters written in a foreign language, and a photograph of a beautiful dark-eyed girl, who stared directly into the camera as if she were frightened. The child was clearly of mixed race, but she wore a printed frock decorated with ruffles and a sash, white stockings, and black boots like any English child. Based on her clothing, Daniel thought the child was the daughter of a middle-class family and most likely an only child since the photograph would include her siblings if she had any.

"Is this Alicia?" Daniel asked.

Constantine peered at the photograph as if he'd never seen it before, then nodded. "Her father must have had this taken when they still lived in India."

"And these letters?"

"I think that's written in Hindustani," Constantine said.

"Do you know who they are from?" Daniel asked.

Constantine shook his head. "I've never seen them before, but I believe that's what Alicia's mother's family spoke, so perhaps they were written by her mother before she passed. May I see the photograph?"

Constantine accepted the photograph from Daniel and held it up to his face, his eyes misting with tears once he set it down on the table. "I can't believe she's gone. There's such a void…" His voice trailed off as he swallowed hard and angrily wiped away the tears that slid down his pale cheeks. "I know you think I had something to do with Alicia's death, but I would have never hurt her. Not even if she no longer loved me."

"Alicia kept a substantial amount in her account," Jason stated. "There's enough to keep you in comfort for years to come."

"I had no idea how much money there was. I knew Alicia kept the bankbook in the box, but I never opened it."

"You had the key," Jason pointed out.

"Yes. I knew where Alicia kept it, but that doesn't mean I ever used it. Alicia was a very private person, and she would be upset if I went snooping through her things."

"That doesn't mean she didn't tell you how much she had," Daniel said. "Or what else she owned. Surely her father and husband must have left her all their assets."

"I don't know what they left," Constantine cried. "We never spoke of it, and I never saw any deeds or titles to properties. I only knew what we had together, and this was it," he said, spreading his arms to encompass the room and the apartment beyond.

"These statues must be valuable," Daniel said, his gaze straying to the frightening woman with ten arms.

"I didn't kill her," Constantine bellowed, his eyes reflecting his desperation. "I don't want her money. I would give anything to have her back, even for a day."

"But she's gone, and someone gets it all," Daniel said.

Constantine shook his head in a way that was meant to convey that Daniel could never understand his pain.

"Do you know Sadie Goodall?" Jason asked, the question clearly taking Constantine by surprise.

"Sadie Goodall? What's she to do with any of this?"

"It would seem that Miss Goodall put Jane Guilford in touch with Alicia, so they must have known each other."

"They did. Sadie is a medium just like Alicia is. Was," Constantine corrected himself.

"Were they friends?" Jason inquired. If Sadie was a rival, she probably wouldn't have been too quick to send clients Alicia's way.

Constantine sighed heavily, his shoulders drooping as if he were exhausted, even though it was barely ten in the morning.

"Alicia didn't have friends. She gave up on forming meaningful bonds years ago. Most people thought her too intimidating and too different from what they found acceptable to welcome into their homes. She didn't seek out the company of other mediums, but she did like Sadie."

"Why?" Jason asked.

"I suppose it was because Sadie treated Alicia like she would any other woman and not someone who could help her gain more clients or teach her tricks of the trade. Sadie seemed genuine."

"And is Sadie psychic in the true sense?" Daniel asked.

"I don't know," Constantine said. "Only Alicia would know, and she never said." He paused, momentarily lost in thought. "I don't think Alicia's relationship with Sadie ever touched on the spiritual. I think Alicia craved the company of another woman who wouldn't judge her for the way she lived."

"When was the last time Alicia saw Sadie?" Jason inquired.

"Last week. Alicia invited Sadie to tea."

"Were you there?" Daniel asked.

"No. Alicia liked to have time to herself, so I sometimes went out in the afternoon to give her privacy."

"Where did you go when Sadie Goodall came to tea?" Jason asked.

"I went to the British Museum. There was a new exhibit I wanted to visit. I'm very fond of all things Egyptian. I've always hoped to visit and see all the wonders for myself."

"Was Miss Goodall still here when you returned?"

"No, she had already gone."

"And how was Alicia after Miss Goodall left?" Jason asked.

"She was fine. Her usual self. She asked me where I had been, and I told her about the exhibit. She said she'd have liked to have seen it and asked if I would mind going again."

"Did Alicia and Sadie meet often?" Daniel asked.

"About once a month. And I don't know what they talked about, if that's your next question."

"Actually, my next question is, did Mrs. Lysander have a solicitor?" Daniel asked.

Constantine stared at Daniel, dumbfounded. "Why would she need a solicitor?"

"There's no will," Jason said, his gaze going toward the stack of documents Daniel had replaced in the box.

"Alicia was twenty-seven years old, and she was never ill, not even a sniffle. She had years and years ahead of her." Constantine choked on the words and hurried from the room, seemingly unable to contain his grief any longer.

Leaving the box on the table, Daniel and Jason saw themselves out and climbed back into the brougham after Jason had instructed Joe to take them to Covent Garden.

Chapter 14

Sadie Goodall's salon was precisely what one would expect of a medium's workplace, except for the bell that jingled above the door when they entered the shop. There was a round table covered with a fringed green velvet cloth, a crystal ball positioned at the center, an ancient-looking deck of tarot cards, and a leather pouch that probably held dice or a set of runes. A narrow sideboard was covered with an embroidered cloth that looked like it might have been lifted from an altar and held the other tools of Sadie's trade. There were several jeweled bottles, a wooden board with letters and symbols carved into its oddly shaped surface, and a book on palmistry. The red-painted walls were devoid of adornment and reminiscent of a carnival tent, and the floorboards were bare, all the easier to tap on the wood in the dark.

Jason found it surprising that Alicia Lysander, who had prided herself on her authenticity and inborn ability to commune with the dead, would associate with someone who resorted to every trick known to spiritualists the world over, but he also realized he knew little of the woman Alicia Lysander had been. He had been exposed to her psychic persona, not the real individual, who'd worked hard to keep her distance from the rest of the world and fiercely protected her true self from anyone who had the power to hurt her. Jason couldn't help but wonder what it was about Constantine that had earned her confidence, and had Alicia really trusted him, or was he just a handsome, helpful man she had used to keep loneliness at bay?

A beaded curtain that covered a doorway set into the back wall clinked as it parted, and a woman entered the room. She wasn't quite what Jason had expected either. He had thought that Sadie Goodall would resemble Alicia, who, despite the eye-catching jewels in her box, had been a minimalist when it came to her appearance. Alicia, who had been tall and willowy, had usually worn high-necked black gowns, and her jewelry had been understated and elegant. Sadie Goodall had to be in her mid-forties and was the complete opposite of her friend. She was short and buxom, and her hair, which was gathered into a knot atop her head, was light and frothy, several pale tendrils escaping their restraints and curling around her flushed face. Sadie's eyes were a very pale blue, and her cheeks and lips were too pink to be natural. She wore a taffeta gown of dark red that was piped with black velvet and embellished with jet beads. Matching jet earrings dangled from her ears, and a choker of jet beads encircled her throat. The black beads had to be a nod to the dead, since jet jewelry was usually worn during the period of mourning, a custom introduced by Queen Victoria and eagerly copied by her female subjects.

"Good morning, gentlemen," Sadie said, and smiled in a way that was clearly meant to disarm. "Are you here to inquire about a séance?"

"We are," Daniel replied, "but about one that already happened."

"I beg your pardon?"

"I'm Inspector Haze of Scotland Yard, and this is my associate, Dr. Redmond."

Daniel held up his warrant card for Sadie to see, but she only glanced at it, her gaze going to Jason in a way that suggested she had heard the name. Jason always left the introductions to Daniel's discretion, since Daniel amended Jason's title based on the situation. His rank was useful when speaking to members of the nobility, but when dealing with the general public, Daniel chose to downplay Jason's social status for fear of intimidating the people he intended to question.

Sadie didn't say anything, but Jason suspected that Alicia had mentioned him to her friend.

"Shall we sit down?" he suggested.

Sadie reluctantly lowered herself into the chair Jason held out for her. Daniel sat directly across from her, with Jason taking the seat in between. Sadie looked from Daniel to Jason but still didn't say anything, seemingly waiting for Daniel to explain himself. After a dramatic pause, Daniel began.

"Miss Goodall, I believe you are acquainted with Alicia Lysander," he said. Jason noted the present tense and wondered if Daniel was testing Sadie or just wasn't ready to reveal his hand just yet.

"Yes, I am. Is Alicia all right?" Sadie squeaked.

You're the psychic, you tell us, seemed to hang in the air, but Daniel appeared to catch himself before he said what was so clearly in his mind. His opinion of Sadie Goodall wasn't hard to discern, especially for Jason, who knew how Daniel felt about the countless frauds who fed off grieving families by means of spiritualism. After Charlotte had been returned to him, he had grudgingly admitted that there were those rare few whose gift was genuine, but although he had refrained from publicly speaking out against them, Daniel still believed that their primary reason for facilitating posthumous reunions was greed rather than a selfless desire to help those in torment. Jason didn't quite agree, but as in most things, they each cleaved to their own opinion.

"Miss Goodall," Daniel said, his gaze firmly fixed on Sadie. "Alicia was attacked the night before last and died a short while later."

"No!" Sadie cried, her hand flying to her heaving bosom. "No. I don't believe you."

"Mrs. Lysander was on her way to my home when she passed," Jason explained. "I think she thought I might be able to help her."

"Was she badly hurt?" Sadie asked.

Badly enough to die of her injuries, Daniel's face seemed to say, but Jason replied before Daniel had a chance to speak.

"The postmortem showed that the cause of death was a brain bleed. She would have had a terrible headache and perhaps felt disoriented and uncoordinated, but she would not have been in excruciating pain."

Sadie Goodall nodded and stared at the green cloth, swallowing audibly as she tried to keep the tears at bay. Her reaction to the news seemed sincere, and Jason could see that she felt the loss of her friend keenly.

"Miss Goodall, we need your help," he said before Daniel could say something that would offend the woman. She was their only lead, and they couldn't afford to alienate her.

Daniel seemed to sense Jason's disapproval and gave him a look that silently invited him to take charge. Jason nodded and turned back to the medium.

"As far as we know, you were Alicia's only friend. Did she confide in you?"

"Alicia was a very private person, Dr. Redmond. We spoke about our work and pondered how best to convince the public that what we did was real and not just an elaborate hoax."

Daniel was looking pointedly at the deck of cards and the crystal ball that reflected his scowling countenance but made his face appear ghostly and distorted.

"I know what you think, Inspector," Sadie said, correctly interpreting Daniel's dour expression. "But there are those who need to see these items to feel reassured. Without physical evidence, they can't accept a woman who can sense an otherworldly presence or interpret the vibrations a spirit sends forth in order to decode a message from the other side. They need props, much as they need a backdrop during a theater performance in order to imagine the actors in another place."

Daniel nodded but didn't reply, silently inviting Jason to continue.

"Did Alicia ever mention any other acquaintances?" he asked.

"No. The only one she trusted was Constantine."

"Why?" Daniel interjected, giving voice to Jason's own question.

"Because he had proven himself."

"In what way?" Jason asked.

"Alicia never told me, and I never asked, but even though Constantine was her partner in all things, she still kept a part of herself away from him. That was simply her nature. Alicia did not like to be made vulnerable, and opening up to another person left her feeling completely exposed."

"Did Alicia tell you all this, or is this your own perception of her character?" Daniel asked.

"She did tell me some things about her past, but mostly it's my own opinion, Inspector," Sadie said.

"What about rivals? Was there anyone Alicia felt threatened by or even feared?" Jason asked.

Taking a shaky breath, Sadie looked away for a moment, as if considering her options. Daniel looked like he was about to speak, but Jason lifted his hand just enough to warn him not to interrupt.

"I don't know if I should say," Sadie said at last.

"Withholding evidence is a crime, Miss Goodall," Daniel informed her sternly.

"I don't have any evidence, only a feeling, and I don't want to drop anyone in it if they had nothing to do with Alicia's death."

"Miss Goodall, we have no interest in fitting anyone up for a crime they didn't commit, but we do need to know about any past threat in order to conduct a thorough investigation," Jason said. "Who are you thinking of?"

"Angel Flyte."

"Angel Flight?" Daniel scoffed.

"Flyte, with a y."

"Is this Angel another medium?" Jason asked.

Sadie nodded. "Angel arrived in London about six months ago and set up shop in Russell Street. A few weeks later, she leased a small theater and began to advertise her 'Touched by an Angel' evenings."

"And what might those be?" Daniel asked.

"They're a clever combination of mesmerism, magic, and good old business acumen. The theater can seat up to one hundred people, and Angel charges a shilling entry fee. No one knows who will come through, so every person in that audience is filled with trepidation and hope. Angel usually brings messages from the dead to four or five people every night, so there are those who keep coming back in the hope of receiving word from their dearly departed one more time."

"You seem to know an awful lot about how this Angel works," Daniel remarked.

"I attended a few of her shows."

"Know your enemy, eh?" he jibed.

"She's not my enemy, Inspector, but she is someone who has the potential to steal my clients, and by extension the income I rely on to survive."

"Have you formed an opinion on Angel's ability?" Jason asked.

Sadie's laugh was bitter and laced with envy. "She's a fraud through and through, but she's a clever fraud who understands her audience. It's not difficult to convince someone who's desperate to believe, and she allows members of the audience to come to her."

"How so?" Daniel asked.

Sadie cast a derisive look in his direction. "Let us say, for argument's sake, that you have lost a child, Inspector." Jason could almost feel something within Daniel shrivel up, but his expression of mild interest did not alter.

"Go on," he said.

"Angel cries out, 'Mama, Mama, are you there?' And several people react, some more violently than others. Then Angel moderates her voice to mimic either a boy or a girl and narrows down her subjects to a few people who've obviously lost a beloved child of that sex. Then she directs the message toward one of those people and says something predictably tragic, like 'I miss you' or 'I don't blame you' or 'Please, don't grieve for me. I'm happy here in the spirit world.' Well, you get the gist," Sadie said. "The person who received the message is overcome and will tell everyone they know that Angel Flyte brought them a message from their loved one. The other people in the audience believe that they just witnessed something completely authentic and will keep coming back until their loved ones come through. And the next night, Angel will try something different, like a message from a parent or a spouse. All she has to do is read the audience and moderate her delivery until she knows she's hit the mark."

Sadie Goodall appeared to be repulsed by Angel Flyte's methods but also a little envious. Reading an audience was a true gift for a medium, and Angel seemed to be exceptionally good at her chosen profession if she could fill the seats every night and get people to come back again and again. Not only did they continue to pay the entrance fee, but they clearly believed in her gift and told others about her ability to commune with the dead.

"Did Alicia Lysander feel threatened by this Angel Flyte?" Daniel asked.

"Alicia had nothing to fear from the likes of Angel, but about a fortnight ago, Angel called out Alicia during one of her performances."

"Called out how?" Jason asked. "Did she mention Alicia by name?"

"She did not, but she described her accurately enough to make it clear whom she meant. And then she all but called Alicia a poser."

"Surely there are a number of people who could have fit the bill," Daniel said.

"Few mediums are on Alicia's level or would dare to charge the fees Alicia charged for conducting a private séance."

"Did Alicia ever perform at public gatherings?" Jason asked.

"She hasn't for several years now, but she used to, when she first began to make a name for herself."

"And did she resort to similar tactics?" Daniel asked.

"I expect she did," Sadie replied. "Spirits don't appear on demand, especially to a large group of people. They're frightened and overwhelmed by the energy in the room. It's much easier to connect with someone who's passed in a quiet, dark room, where only those who knew them are present."

"So, Alicia used fraudulent means to attract clients?" Daniel asked.

"We all do what we must, Inspector Haze. Alicia was the real thing, but in order to prove that, she first needed people to come to her and trust her."

"Why would Angel resort to calling out another medium if she was doing well for herself?" Jason asked.

"My guess would be that the attendance had begun to drop, and she wanted to reignite the public's interest. A feud between two mediums would eventually make it into the papers, particularly if Angel put someone up to reporting it to the *Illustrated News* or some other populist rag."

"Did Alicia respond to the insult?" Jason asked.

"Alicia had no need to defend herself. She is…was the most highly respected medium in London and had the freedom to pick and choose her clientele. Angel was resorting to cheap tricks in order to steal Alicia's patrons."

"Does Angel Flyte stand to benefit from Alicia's death?" Daniel asked.

"I expect so. Especially if she makes it personal," Sadie replied.

"And how would she do that?"

"If Alicia were to send a message from beyond and share it through Angel, the public would be enthralled. Angel could spew all sorts of tripe, and no one would be the wiser. Alicia coming through to Angel would only reinforce their belief in Angel and get them to come in droves."

"Would Angel really do that?" Daniel asked, clearly astonished that someone would sink so low.

"There's no law against it," Sadie said. "It's not slander. And if she says something perfectly innocuous, no one can accuse her of lying or impersonating Alicia."

"No, I don't suppose they could," Daniel agreed. "Where can we find this Angel of death?"

"At the Duke in Russell Street. There's a performance every night at seven."

"And what about Constantine Moore? How were things between him and Alicia of late?" Jason asked.

"Alicia never said anything outright, but I got the impression she was having doubts about him."

"What sort of doubts?" Daniel asked.

"The sort of doubts a woman frequently has when she fears her lover is drifting away."

"And was he?"

Sadie shook her head. "As I said, Alicia was a very private person. I can only tell you what I sensed rather than what she actually admitted to."

"There was nothing to bind Constantine to her. Alicia cohabitated with him without the benefit of marriage," Daniel pointed out.

Sadie bristled, clearly angered by what she perceived as an attempt to impugn Alicia's character. "Alicia wasn't someone who was bound by convention. You can hardly condemn her for having a lover when most men in this city avail themselves of whores, then lie down next to their unsuspecting wives."

"Not all men visit whores," Daniel replied.

"No, but enough to keep thousands of prostitutes busy from dusk till dawn," Sadie snapped.

Daniel visibly balked at Sadie's bluntness but didn't bother to argue. He knew her to be right, just as he knew that most men who visited prostitutes did not regard their transgressions as adultery, especially if they paid some woman to pleasure them in a doorway or an alleyway but did not engage in sexual congress.

"Alicia was a decent woman," Sadie said. "No matter her mistakes."

"What mistakes are those?" Jason asked.

"Marrying the wrong man, for one."

"It is my understanding that Mrs. Lysander had been widowed for some years," Daniel said.

"She was, but some relationships leave lifelong scars."

Sadie Goodall looked from Daniel to Jason, and Jason thought he sensed her uncertainty. She was holding something back and didn't know if she could trust them.

"Miss Goodall, I had the greatest respect for Mrs. Lysander and would not do anything to dishonor her in death. Please, if you know anything, anything at all," he implored.

Sadie Goodall exhaled loudly through her nostrils. "Alicia mentioned a lawyer. She said if I ever needed someone who'd discreetly look after my affairs, he was trustworthy."

"Do you remember this lawyer's name?" Daniel asked.

"Pritchard. Emile Pritchard in Marsham Street."

"Thank you, Miss Goodall. You've been a great help," Jason said.

"Have I?" Sadie Goodall asked, her gaze reflecting her doubt. "I should have warned her."

"Did you think Alicia Lysander was in danger?" Daniel was quick to ask.

Sadie nodded. "I saw a shadow around her the last time we met."

"A shadow," Daniel said. "Does a shadow foretell impending death?" His tone was mocking, but Sadie Goodall chose to ignore it.

She smiled bitterly. "Let me put it in terms you will understand, Inspector. It means, 'Something wicked this way comes.'"

It was a quote from *Macbeth*, and Daniel fixed Sadie Goodall with a cold stare. "I wouldn't be too quick to paint yourself as a witch, Miss Goodall. We live in a modern and tolerant society, but some things still go against God and His Church."

"Yes, like postmortems," Sadie muttered under her breath.

"Good day to you," Jason said, and stood.

Daniel followed suit, and within moments they were outside, the bustle of Covent Garden market replacing the unnatural hush of Sadie Goodall's salon, and the smells that accosted one as if with a physical blow carrying away all memory of her pleasantly scented salon.

"Oh, God, that's pungent," Jason said as they passed too close to a butcher's stall, the stench of raw meat overlayed with something more rancid as the cuts of beef and lamb roasted in the midday sun.

"Let's find a hansom and go see this lawyer," Daniel suggested.

Jason nodded and quickened his step, careful not to slip on bits of rotten fruit that had been left to bake on the pavement and mindful of the children who darted between stalls and among the harried shoppers, picking purses and relieving shoppers of whatever valuables were easiest to nick.

Chapter 15

The offices of Pritchard and Pritchard were just what one would expect of a prosperous legal practice. The address was respectable, the sign was discreet, and the rent was probably high. The waiting room was painted a pale green and furnished with handsome dark wood pieces that were arranged around a thick Turkish rug woven in muted colors, the traditional décor meant to convey solidity, prosperity, and dependability. And the pastoral paintings on the wall reminded the clients that the lawyers also had good taste and an eye for art.

A young, skeletally thin clerk sat behind the reception desk, his complexion so pale, Jason had to wonder if the poor man ever saw the sun. His reddish hair was parted in the center and heavily pomaded, his moustache resembled a bristle brush, and his round wire-rimmed spectacles gleamed in the light filtering through the window behind the desk.

"Good morning, gentlemen. I don't believe you have an appointment," the clerk said, looking pointedly at the book before him.

Daniel produced his warrant card and held it in front of the man's nose, which twitched as if he were a rat. "We'd like to see Emile Pritchard. Right away, if possible."

"Emile?" The young man asked confusedly, then seemed to realize Daniel's mistake and sneered in a way that was highly unprofessional. "You must mean M.L., Inspector," he said. "Just a moment, please."

The clerk disappeared down the corridor, then returned a few moments later, the smirk still tugging at his fleshy lips. "This way, if you please."

He led them to the second door on the right, knocked, and threw the door open with considerably more showmanship than necessary. Jason and Daniel stepped into a well-appointed office that was almost a replica of the waiting room. Daniel's sharp intake of breath underscored Jason's own surprise and explained the reason behind the clerk's mocking attitude. He would not say anything outright and would probably deny any wrongdoing if accused of inappropriate behavior, but his opinion of M.L. Pritchard was obvious to anyone who cared to look.

"But you're a woman," Daniel sputtered when M.L. smiled in greeting.

"Well spotted. You must be the detective," M.L. replied without missing a beat.

She was dark-haired and dark-eyed and had strong eyebrows and a generous mouth that twitched upwards at Daniel's impolite remark. Dressed in a gown of deep blue satin with only tiny sapphire earbobs for adornment, M.L. looked rather severe, the impression compounded by her erect posture and angular facial features. Jason couldn't tell if she was irritated or amused by Daniel's befuddlement, but he imagined she had to deal with masculine disdain on a daily basis and was tired of having to defend herself.

"Thank you for agreeing to see us," Jason said when Daniel failed to say anything that would defuse the tension in the room. "We only need a few moments of your time."

M.L. gestured toward the guest chairs situated in front of her desk. "I am Mila Luka Pritchard," she said once they were seated. "But I prefer to go by M.L, for obvious reasons. How can I help you, gentlemen?"

Daniel studied the woman with ill-disguised suspicion, while Jason tried his best not to smile. Alicia Lysander had surprised him once again, and he wished he could commend her on finding a female lawyer to help her with her estate planning. He thought he had heard of a woman called to the bar in the United States, but he wasn't sure where things stood in England.

Evidently, Daniel's thoughts were running along the same lines because he asked, "Are you a practicing solicitor?"

"Women are not permitted at the bar in England, but I earned my law degree in Serbia, which is more progressive in some respects, if not in others."

"Serbia?" Daniel choked out.

"That's correct. That's where I met my husband, in a Serbian court. He was there to defend a client who got himself into something of a bother. Please do not fear, Inspector Haze, *Mr.* Pritchard's name is on all the relevant paperwork, but I consult with clients and prepare the necessary documentation."

Daniel seemed to still be processing this, so Jason decided to offer an explanation. "Mrs. Pritchard, we're here in regard to your client, Alicia Lysander. She died in suspicious circumstances, and it's imperative that we learn who stood to benefit from her death."

M.L. didn't bother to hide her shock, and it was obvious that she was deeply upset by the news.

"How?" she asked at last. "How did Alicia die?"

Jason explained the circumstances and watched as M.L. grappled with her emotions. She wasn't ashamed to feel shocked and sad, and Jason admired her for that, all the more so because she knew that any show of weakness would be held against her by male clients who were negatively predisposed to dealing with a woman.

"Alicia Lysander was a force of nature," M.L. said. "I admired her greatly, and I'm very sorry to hear about her passing."

"Then perhaps you can help us by not invoking the client lawyer privilege," Daniel replied.

M.L. nodded and stood. She was tall for a woman, and slender, and her movements when she walked over to a cabinet in the corner were as graceful as those of a dancer. She pulled out a slim file and returned to her seat, opening the file to extract a two-page document.

"What exactly do you need to know?" she asked Daniel.

"Who's Mrs. Lysander's beneficiary, and how much do they stand to get now that she's gone?"

"Mrs. Lysander inherited her father's house in Marylebone. She asked us to manage the property, and we have been letting it out ever since. The proceeds are deposited into a specially designated account at the Bank of England that my husband set up just for that purpose. Alicia was also her late husband's sole beneficiary. She asked us to sell off all his assets and deposit the money into that same account."

"Why would she do that?" Daniel asked.

"Probably because both men had caused her nothing but grief," M.L. replied matter-of-factly. "She didn't want any reminders of her time with them."

"Who's the beneficiary on the account?" Jason asked. Somehow, he didn't think it was Constantine Moore.

"The sole beneficiary is Chara Devi-Collins."

"And who's she when she's at home?" Daniel grumbled. "Some poor relation in India?"

"Chara is Alicia's daughter. She's five years old."

"Her daughter?" Daniel exclaimed.

"That is correct. It was Alicia's stipulation that Constantine Moore should not know of Chara's existence, nor should he be informed after Alicia's death. That was the reason for a separate bank account that he knew nothing about."

"The photo in Alicia's box," Jason said. "That must be Chara."

"But why would she leave a photo where Constantine could see it if she didn't want him to know about the child?" Daniel asked.

"Because Constantine assumed the photo was of Alicia," Jason replied. "Where's Chara now, Mrs. Pritchard?"

"Chara lives with her paternal aunt and uncle, Peter and Gwyneth Collins. Alicia visited Chara once a month and planned to tell her the truth once she turned sixteen."

"And what is the truth?" Daniel asked.

M.L. looked uncomfortable, but she could hardly refuse to answer the question. "Mrs. Lysander met Chara's father, Captain Collins, while she was in mourning for her husband. They began an affair that lasted several years and resulted in Chara's birth. Since Captain Collins was married already, he implored his childless older brother and his wife to take the baby and raise her as their own. Alicia agreed to the arrangement in order to spare Chara the stigma of an illegitimate birth."

"Why did she not tell Constantine of the child's existence?" Jason asked.

"Mrs. Lysander never explained her decision to me, but I expect it was because she didn't entirely trust Mr. Moore to abide by her wishes."

"Is Constantine Moore mentioned in the will?"

"Alicia stipulated that Mr. Moore be given her personal possessions and the amount she kept at Atrium Bank. The rest, and it is a very sizable sum, was to be kept in trust for Chara until she turns eighteen."

"Who would benefit if Chara died?" Jason asked.

M.L. flinched at his bluntness but replied quickly enough for Jason to believe that she had anticipated the question.

"The Collinses would get half, and Mrs. Lysander's maternal aunt would get the rest."

"Do the Collinses or the aunt know about the stipulations of the will?"

"The Collinses do. I don't know if Mrs. Lysander ever informed her aunt that she was the other beneficiary. I know that we did not."

"Is there any way in which Constantine Moore can somehow claim Chara's inheritance?" Daniel asked.

"No. The terms are ironclad, Inspector Haze, and in case you're worried, the will was drawn up and signed by my husband. Its validity cannot be argued in court. Besides, Mr. Moore was not married to Mrs. Lysander. He has no spousal claim on her assets."

"Can he claim paternity of Chara?" Jason asked.

Since the child had been born out of wedlock, there was no way to prove that Chara had actually been sired by Captain Collins, unless the child was the spitting image of her father, which she couldn't be since she favored her mother.

"I don't believe so, since he did not meet Mrs. Lysander until after Chara was born, but if he tried to invent a tale in which they had met earlier and had engaged in a sexual liaison, I suppose he can."

"Which is why Alicia never wanted him to know about the child," Jason concluded.

"Mr. Moore would have to wait thirteen years to attempt to lay claim to Chara's inheritance," M. L. pointed out.

"He's young. He has time," Daniel said gruffly.

"Is Captain Collins involved in Chara's life?" Jason inquired.

"Captain Collins died eighteen months ago when his ship went down in the Arabian Sea."

"So, the child has now lost both her biological parents," Jason said, then thought of another question he really should have asked. "Mrs. Pritchard, did Alicia ever express a desire to take Chara back?"

M.L.'s eyebrows lifted slightly, but Jason didn't think the question had surprised her.

"As a matter of fact, Alicia and I discussed this very topic a few weeks ago."

"Did you?" Daniel asked, casting a meaningful look in Jason's direction.

"And what was her stance?" Jason asked.

"Alicia didn't have much choice about giving Chara up, but the situation had changed, and she was wondering if it would be possible to have the child come live with her."

"Would her adoptive parents agree to that?"

"They love Chara and see her as their own. I don't think they would be happy to simply hand her over," M.L. said.

"Would Alicia have brought Chara home while Constantine was still there?" Daniel asked.

"That was the other consideration. As far as I know, Alicia wasn't about to make any hasty decisions, but she was thinking about making life-altering changes."

"And had she discussed these possible changes with either Constantine Moore or the Collinses?" Jason asked.

"I very much doubt it, but I can't say anything for certain," M.L. said. "Alicia was a law unto herself, and for all I know, she may have done."

"Chara's safety and financial interests must be made a priority," Jason said.

"I will inform Mr. and Mrs. Collins that Alicia has passed, and that Constantine Moore might attempt to make contact. Do not worry, we will keep Chara's inheritance safe, and the Collinses will see to Chara's well-being."

"I will need the Collinses' address," Daniel said.

"Of course," M.L. replied, and copied it out on a sheet of paper.

"Were there any other bequests?" Jason asked.

"Yes, Mrs. Lysander willed a small sum to Sadie Goodall. Miss Goodall did not know about the bequest, so would have no reason to harm Mrs. Lysander."

"Thank you, Mrs. Pritchard," Jason said.

"Kindly contact me care of Scotland Yard if there's any attempt to thwart Mrs. Lysander's final wishes," Daniel said.

"Of course. I will apprise my husband of the situation immediately."

Jason and Daniel thanked Mrs. Pritchard again and took their leave, walking past the sniggering clerk.

"Wipe that smirk off your face or I will see to it that you're not only dismissed but will never work in London again," Jason said as he passed.

The clerk's face reflected his shock, but he instantly rearranged his features into an expression of humility. "My sincerest apologies, my lord."

Jason didn't bother to respond.

Chapter 16

Tired and hungry, Jason and Daniel adjourned to a nearby chophouse to evaluate what they had learned. They had interviewed nearly a dozen people, and although they were nowhere near identifying a suspect, there were now several possible motives.

"We need to speak to Peter and Gwyneth Collins," Daniel said once they had placed their orders. "Chara is now a very wealthy little girl."

"The funds will not be released until Chara turns eighteen," Jason reminded him.

"The Collinses can contest the will. If they can cast doubt on the validity of the will, a sympathetic judge might rule that Chara's inheritance should be released to her adoptive parents."

"I don't think that's a pressing concern, and I can't see that anyone would resort to bashing Alicia over the head on such a slim possibility. But if Alicia had let it slip that she might want her daughter back, that might give Chara's adoptive parents a motive, especially if they truly love her and think of her as their own."

"And if Constantine got wind of this new development, he might want to murder Alicia in order to seize her assets before she cast him out," Daniel said.

"Constantine asked Alicia to marry him a number of times, but she refused," Jason mused. "Why? Marrying Constantine would enable her to bring Chara home, since the child would no longer be viewed as illegitimate, but Alicia held on to her unmarried status. Was it to protect herself, her assets, or her daughter?"

"How would remaining unmarried protect her daughter?" Daniel asked.

"If Alicia married Constantine and took her daughter back, Constantine would become Chara's father in the eyes of the law, and if Alicia died, he would have control of both the child and her fortune. With Chara's natural father gone, perhaps this was Alicia's way of keeping Chara safe, since there would be no one left to protect her interests."

"Except the Collinses," Daniel said.

"Except the Collinses, who no longer have to worry about losing either Chara or her sizable inheritance."

They refrained from discussing the case while the waiter brought their order and set the plates on the table with great flourish, then departed.

"We can't discount Constantine Moore," Daniel said as soon as they were alone again. "Even if he didn't know about the child, he still stood to gain by Alicia's death. If she had decided to leave him, he wouldn't get a farthing off her."

"Constantine is not to be dismissed, but we don't have any evidence that links him to the crime," Jason pointed out.

"We know he was in the area," Daniel said. "He went to the earl's residence to collect Alicia. He might have caught up with her in Upper Brook Street and bashed her over the head."

"Yes, he could have," Jason agreed with some reluctance. "But before we build a case against Constantine, we must find out if the Collinses have an alibi for the night of Alicia's murder."

Daniel nodded in agreement. "And what about this Angel Flyte?" He snorted with amusement. "Blimey, what a name."

"I doubt it's her actual name," Jason said, smiling despite himself.

"I didn't think it was," Daniel replied, somewhat defensively, "but that's a tad blasphemous, don't you think? Painting herself as an angel of God?"

"It's certainly memorable."

"Alicia was attacked between nine thirty and ten thirty. Angel Flyte would have finished her performance by eight, which would give her plenty of time to get to Grosvenor Square and lie in wait for Alicia."

"She might have had opportunity, but what would be her motive?" Jason inquired.

"Jealousy. Alicia Lysander was well respected and sought after, while this charlatan was selling messages from the dead for a shilling. Now, I grant you, shillings add up, but perhaps she had set her sights on Alicia's clients." Daniel grinned. "She wanted—as you once put it—a bigger slice of the pie."

"I very much doubt that the wealthy and influential individuals who sought out Alicia Lysander would put the same faith in Angel Flyte. They wouldn't trust a medium who conducted mass séances for a shilling a head. And if Alicia and Angel were not in direct competition with each other, what would Angel have to gain by Alicia's death?"

"Maybe Angel is not as analytical as you are, my friend," Daniel said.

"Sadie Goodall painted Angel as a savvy businesswoman who can read her clients at a moment's notice. That doesn't sound like someone who would risk murdering Alicia on the off chance that she might inherit some of her clients."

"Still, with Alicia Lysander gone, there will be a vacancy."

"Yes, perhaps," Jason mused. "Or perhaps there's something we're not seeing."

"Such as?"

"If Constantine Moore, Peter Collins, or Angel Flyte had decided to murder Alicia, they would have come up with a better plan than assaulting her on the street. They had no way of knowing that the séance would finish early, nor could they know that Alicia would decide to walk rather than wait for Constantine or accept the offer of the earl's carriage. Likewise, she could have asked Jones to find her a hansom rather than just walking out into the night. And I very much doubt that any of our suspects had known that the fog would be so dense, no one would see them in the act of attacking a woman."

Jason shook his head, now even more convinced of the validity of his theory. "I don't believe the attack was premeditated, which shifts our three suspects down the list. Something happened on the night of the séance that frightened someone enough to want to silence Alicia immediately. The killer used whatever they had to hand and became so panicked, they didn't even wait around to make certain that their victim was dead. This whole thing speaks to desperation and chance, not a well-thought-out plan."

Daniel sighed heavily. "You have a point there, but who does that leave us with?"

"Everyone who attended that séance."

"But they're all accounted for," Daniel replied. "Lady Cynthia ran upstairs and was tended to by Bernice Crumlish, and the rest of them were all together at the time of the attack. They can alibi each other, and the butler and the parlormaid both saw them out when they were ready to leave. There's no way one of them could have nipped out to Upper Brook Street, hit Alicia on the head, and returned to the earl's house without arousing suspicion."

"We don't know that Alicia was assaulted in Upper Brook Street, only that the cab driver picked her up there. She could have ambled some distance before she spotted a cab."

Jason set aside his cutlery and pulled out his pocket watch. "I'm afraid I must leave you. I'm giving a lecture at the College of Surgeons at four o'clock. What will you do?"

"I'm going to call on the Collinses, and then I must return to Scotland Yard. Ransome will want an update, and it's hours yet until Angel takes her flight."

"Shall we reconvene tomorrow?"

"Of course," Daniel replied.

They paid their bill, stepped outside, and parted ways, walking off in opposite directions.

Chapter 17

Peter and Gwyneth Collins resided in a modest house in Holborn. It was the sort of home and neighborhood that spoke to respectability but not position or wealth. These were ordinary people who presumably led ordinary lives. When Daniel used the knocker to announce his presence, a young maidservant opened the door and smiled at him winsomely. She was no older than eighteen and had the wholesome appearance of a girl fresh from the country.

"Can I help you, sir?"

Daniel showed the maidservant his warrant card and explained that he would like to speak to Mr. and Mrs. Collins.

"I'm afraid they're not at home, sir. They had plans to join Mrs. Collins's sister and her family for luncheon. They usually stay a while so that their little girls can play. The children only see each other twice a month, and they so enjoy their time together."

That was considerably more information than Daniel had expected, so he decided to press the maid a little further. "Can you tell me if your master and mistress were at home on Thursday evening? I'm investigating an incident they might have witnessed."

Daniel did not explain the nature of the incident or how he would know that the Collinses might have been present, but he didn't think the maidservant was astute enough to realize that she was being led.

"They had an early supper, and then Mr. Collins went out around seven."

"Where did he go?"

"He attends lectures at the Botanic Society. A fiend for anything that grows is Mr. Collins. You should see the garden, Inspector. It's a thing of beauty."

"And does he often go to these lectures?"

"Whenever one is given, I reckon," the maid said.

"And were you still up when he came home?" Daniel asked.

"No. I went up to my room at eight, but I did hear him come in around ten. I couldn't get to sleep," the maidservant explained.

"And how was he the next morning?"

"Right as rain. He didn't mention any incident. He did have minor cuts on his hands, though," she added. "And the trousers he'd worn the night before were dirty at the knees. He tripped and fell, the poor man. Said the fog was so thick, he couldn't see his hand in front of his face."

"Did he walk home?"

"Oh, no. It's too far to walk from Regent's Park to Holborn, sir, but he did walk to the nearest cab stand. Can you tell me what happened, Inspector?" the maid asked.

"A robbery took place near Regent's Park on Thursday night, around ten," Daniel replied.

The woman shook her head. "Mr. Collins was back by then, so I expect he didn't see anything. The master and mistress will be back by five. Shall I tell them you called, Inspector Haze?"

"No need. I will come back if I need any further information. Thank you. What is your name?" Daniel asked as if the question were an afterthought.

"Dorcas Day."

"Thank you, Miss Day."

"You're most welcome, Inspector." Dorcas gave him a pitying look. "Would you like a cup of tea, Inspector? I expect you're on the move all day. You must be gasping."

Daniel wasn't gasping, but an opportunity to see inside the Collinses' home was not to be missed.

"That's very kind of you, Miss Day. I would welcome a cup of tea."

"I can't serve you in the parlor, but you can come into the kitchen. I was about to have a cup myself. Been on my feet all day and could do with a few minutes' break."

Daniel could not see too much of the house, but Dorcas led him past the parlor, and he caught a glimpse of two photographs on the mantel.

"Is that Mr. and Mrs. Collins?" Daniel asked, pausing in the doorway.

"Yes. And Chara, their daughter."

"May I see?"

Dorcas looked conflicted but then shrugged. "I don't see the harm. You are a policeman, after all."

"Thank you."

"I'll just put the kettle on. Come through to the kitchen when you're finished in here."

She pointed the way and walked off, leaving Daniel alone in the parlor. He felt like a cad for abusing Dorcas's trust but couldn't pass up an opportunity to snoop. The parlor was a square room, the maroon wallpaper with a floral design making it look dark on such a bright day. The furnishings and carpet were in reasonable condition, and the curtains looked new. The Collinses were comfortable but clearly not wealthy or frivolous with their money. The two photographs stood side by side on the marble mantel, their subjects looking mildly reproachful, as if they could see what he was up to and were deeply disappointed in him.

The first photograph was of a couple in their twenties, presumably taken on Peter and Gwyneth's wedding day. They were an ordinary pair, both in appearance and dress. Gwyneth had dark hair and dark eyes, while Peter's hair was lighter, and his eyes were probably blue. Neither was smiling, but Daniel thought he saw something friendly in their faces, an openness and contentment that spoke to their joy on their wedding day. There was no way to tell if they were still simpatico, but there was nothing in their demeanor that led Daniel to believe that they were cold-blooded killers.

The second portrait was of Chara. It was the same picture he had seen in Alicia's box, and he lifted the frame and looked at the child more closely. Now that he could see her adoptive parents, he thought that Chara could probably pass as their own, since Gwyneth Collins had the same dark hair and eyes as Alicia. The child's skin tone was a shade

114

darker, but that could be the lack of proper lighting in the photo atelier where the portrait had been taken. Chara looked like a well-cared-for, contented child. It was difficult to imagine that Peter Collins would resort to murder to keep Alicia from taking his daughter away, but he had come home with bloodied hands and filthy trousers. Perhaps Alicia had pushed him, and he'd fallen, or maybe he really had tripped over something or someone as he was running away from the scene of the crime. The only way to be sure would be to check with the Royal Botanic Society and verify if there had been a meeting on Thursday night and if Peter Collins had attended.

If there had been a meeting and he had stayed until ten o'clock, it was unlikely he would have made it to Grosvenor Square in time to see Alicia leave, since the park was about two miles away. But if he had left early, then he could have been there when Alicia had departed.

"Tea's ready, Inspector," Dorcas called out, startling Daniel out of his reverie.

He joined her in the kitchen and drank a cup of tea before excusing himself and heading over to Regent's Park. As he walked, his thoughts returned to Chara and Alicia, which, in turn, made him think of Charlotte and Sarah. Daniel was grateful when he realized that although the pain was still there, it wasn't as sharp as it used to be, more a dull ache at the thought of all the years Sarah had willfully thrown away and the moments they would never share as a family. Daniel had grieved for Charlotte and the knowledge that she would grow up without a mother, but as the years passed, he had come to realize that Charlotte would not miss what she had never known. She had been just a baby when Sarah had died and had no memory of her mother.

Charlotte had missed Rebecca, who'd looked after her after Sarah died, but in the way of children, she had forgotten her nursemaid after a few months and was now devoted to Flora. Daniel had to admit that he couldn't ask for a better mother for Charlotte than Flora. He loved her intellect, resilience, and boundless energy. Flora doted on Charlotte, and Daniel was certain she wasn't indifferent to him. The three of them fit well together, and he could see them rubbing along well for years, their little family complete.

Years ago, when he had been young and idealistic, he had dreamed of having a large family, but after the tragic loss of Felix and Charlotte's abduction, he had come to understand that he simply could not bear any more pain. He thanked the Lord for Charlotte and prayed every day that she would be spared the horrors that could so easily befall a child. He would be content with only one child as long as she was safe and well and grew into adulthood and hopefully old age.

      A church bell tolled in the distance, and Daniel realized it was nearly three o'clock. He could make his way to the Duke and take in Angel Flyte's performance after he called at the Botanic Society and gave his report to Ransome, but he'd be damned if he missed another evening with Charlotte. Angel would have to wait, he decided as he approached Regent's Park. After his meeting with Ransome, he was going home.

Chapter 18

The Royal Botanic Society met at the Botanic Gardens, which occupied eighteen acres of the park and were dominated by a magnificent structure made almost entirely of glass. Daniel had never visited the gardens but had heard that there was a palm house, a waterlily house, and several other wings that were full of exotic flowers, trees, and plants that had been sourced from all over the world. During the summer months, the gardens hosted various events, and a banner advertising an upcoming flower show was strung across the main entrance.

Daniel entered the building and was greeted by a rosy-cheeked woman of late middle age, who invited him to pay the fee if he wanted to tour the gardens. He showed her his warrant card and asked if he might speak to whoever was in charge.

"We're in a state of flux just now," the woman said. "Mr. James Sowerby, who founded the gardens, is about to retire, and his son, Mr. William Sowerby, is in the process of taking over as secretary. I suppose he can spare you a few minutes if it's truly urgent, but he is very busy."

"It is urgent," Daniel assured her. "Please tell him I won't take too much of his time."

The woman, who was nearly as wide as she was tall, waddled off, but not before she asked a young man who happened to be walking past to cover her post until she returned. He accepted payment from a young couple, handed them their admission stubs, and wished them to enjoy their tour. The young man watched Daniel with undisguised curiosity but didn't ask him anything, so Daniel felt no need to explain his presence. He looked about and decided he was going to bring Flora and Charlotte to the gardens the next time he had a day off and the weather was fine. Flora would enjoy the exotic offerings, and Charlotte would love to explore the paths that dissected the manicured grounds.

It took nearly a quarter of an hour for the woman to come back, but when she did, she directed Daniel to an office at the end of a long glass-roofed corridor bathed in brilliant sunlight that warmed the corridor to tropical levels. Daniel felt sweat break out on his forehead and upper lip and wondered if anyone else noticed how warm it was. The door to the office stood open, and the man seated behind the desk looked up, smiled, and beckoned Daniel forward.

"I'm sorry to keep you waiting, Inspector," he said. "William Sowerby," he added, and extended his hand.

"Daniel Haze." Daniel shook the man's hand and accepted the proffered seat. "It's awfully hot in here," he said, taking off his hat.

"Greenhouse effect," Sowerby explained. "It gets rather warm during the summer, but in wintertime, it's absolute bliss." He leaned back in his chair and tilted his head to the side. "How can I help you, Inspector?"

Daniel saw no reason to tell him about Alicia's death and Peter Collins's connection to the victim. Instead, he said, "One of your members might be a witness in a case I'm currently investigating, and I need to verify his whereabouts."

William Sowerby looked like he was about to ask for more information, then clearly recalled that he was a busy man and decided to forgo a longer discussion. "Anything I can do," he said.

"Would you be able to confirm that Mr. Peter Collins attended a lecture here on Thursday?"

Mr. Sowerby didn't hesitate. "Yes, he did. Peter is one of our more dedicated members and never misses a presentation."

"What time did the lecture begin and end?"

"It went from seven to eight thirty."

"Do you normally hold meetings so late?" Daniel asked, thinking that most people dined between those hours and had to be very committed members indeed to attend a presentation so late in the evening.

"We usually meet around four o'clock, but Dr. Jacobs, who has just returned from South America and had agreed to give a talk about orchids, could only spare us those hours on Thursday night. Otherwise, we would have to wait until he returned from his next adventure."

"And were there many people at this lecture?"

"At least fifty."

"Yet you're certain that Mr. Collins was there."

"I am. We chatted briefly after the lecture. The man is mad for orchids and wanted to thank me for organizing the talk."

"What time did you two speak?"

"It would have to be around a quarter to nine, maybe even a little later since the talk ran over due to the number of questions from the audience."

"What time did everyone leave?"

"I locked up at nine. During the summer people tend to linger, but it was such a filthy night outside, everyone seemed eager to get home."

"So, you didn't see Mr. Collins again?"

"No."

Daniel nodded. "Thank you, Mr. Sowerby."

"Is that all, Inspector?" William Sowerby asked. He seemed surprised that Daniel didn't have further questions.

"It is. I won't take any more of your valuable time."

"Well, do come back and see us. We have a magnificent flower show coming up next week. You should bring the family."

"I intend to," Daniel said, and saw himself out.

He thanked the woman for her help when he passed the ticket counter and hastened outside, taking a deep breath of the flower-scented air once the greenhouse was behind him. The sun was still high, and the sky was clear, but a slight breeze had picked up and the temperature had dropped a few degrees as the evening hours approached. Daniel imagined that the gardens would be quite intimidating when a thick fog descended, and one couldn't see where one was going. If Mr. Collins had lost his way, he might have wandered around the grounds for some time, but there was nothing to suggest that he'd got lost. He had to know his way if he came to every lecture, like Mr. Sowerby had said.

Walking down a gravel path toward the park exit, Daniel decided he couldn't exclude Peter Collins from his inquiries just yet. If everyone had left the gardens by nine, then Collins had been unaccounted for until he'd arrived home at ten. It was a stretch to suppose that he'd got to Grosvenor Square and then to Holborn in an hour, but Daniel supposed it was possible if he had been able to find a cab quickly and had arrived home later than Dorcas thought. As far as Daniel knew, Peter Collins had had no way of knowing that the séance would end early or that Alicia wouldn't wait for Constantine, but it was possible that Alicia had mentioned where she would be on Thursday, and maybe he had decided to try his luck. Alicia wouldn't be frightened if she met Peter Collins in the street, and perhaps he had even offered to see her home, then hit her over the head when she turned her back to him. Would a man who loved flowers be capable of murder? Most certainly, if he thought he might lose his only child.

Despite his desire to solve the case and see Alicia's killer swing, Daniel hoped Peter Collins wasn't the culprit. He wanted Alicia's daughter to have parents who loved her and would steer her safely through childhood and the often-turbulent years of adolescence. And if they benefited from Chara's inheritance once she came of age, then they would deserve their reward. But, until he knew different, Peter Collins was still a suspect.

Unfortunately, Daniel was no closer to a resolution than he had been at this time yesterday. Ransome would either rage at him for his lack of progress in the investigation or stoically accept Daniel's report and send him on his way. It all depended on how Ransome's day had gone and what other cases had come into the Yard while Daniel had been busy pursuing his flimsy leads.

Daniel shrugged, even though there was no one to see him. He'd become used to Ransome's rants and didn't take them as much to heart as he used to. Ransome's bark was worse than his bite, and as Daniel's father used to say, "Rome wasn't built in a day," and an investigation wasn't solved overnight. Feeling marginally less anxious, Daniel turned his steps toward Scotland Yard.

Chapter 19

The duty room was the usual pandemonium it tended to be toward the evening. Two men whose breath was so heavily laced with spirits, they could burst into flames if they came near a candle were arguing viciously and trying to throw punches at each other while Constables Collins and Ramsey attempted to subdue them. It was a bit early in the day to be so intoxicated, but some people had nothing better to do than drink the hours away if they had coin to spare. The two would probably sleep it off in the cells, then be released in the morning, unless they were guilty of criminal damage and would have to face charges once they sobered up.

Daniel wove past the brawling men and headed down the corridor toward Ransome's office. The superintendent looked up when Daniel rapped on the open door.

"Come in and shut the door, Haze," he snapped, then hastily filed away the document he had been perusing and stuffed the folder in a drawer.

"Is everything all right, sir?" Daniel asked.

"No, it's not all right, Haze. Have you made any progress on the Lysander case?"

"Not as yet, sir, but I have identified several suspects," Daniel hurried to add when he saw Ransome's scowl.

"Which are?"

"Mrs. Lysander's partner Constantine Moore, a rival who had recently grown more competitive, and the adoptive father of Mrs. Lysander's daughter."

"She had a daughter, did she?" Ransome asked, clearly intrigued.

"The child was placed with her paternal aunt and uncle, but Mrs. Lysander seemed to be regretting her decision and might have taken the child back had she lived."

"And you think this man would have murdered her in cold blood to keep that from happening?"

"He was out on the night of the murder and did not return until ten. He had both motive and opportunity."

"And what do you have on Moore?" Ransome asked.

"Nothing concrete, but he stood to inherit a sizable portion of Mrs. Lysander's assets, and there was some suggestion that things were no longer rosy between them. If Alicia Lysander ended their partnership, Constantine Moore would walk away with nothing."

Ransome nodded. "That certainly puts him in the frame. And the rival?"

"Too soon to say, sir."

"His Grace, the Earl of Ongar, has made a complaint to Sir David."

"He went directly to the commissioner?" Daniel exclaimed, outraged by the injustice of this.

For one thing, the earl had absolutely no grounds for a complaint. All Daniel had done was pose a few questions to members of the earl's staff, and Jason had engaged in polite discourse with the man that had lasted no more than a quarter of an hour. For another, going over Ransome's head was bad form and completely uncalled for, but Daniel supposed a man of the earl's stature could do anything he wished.

"What was the nature of this complaint?" he asked.

"His Grace said that you harassed his family and staff and upset his sister, Lady Amelia. You are to have no further interaction with anyone either related to or employed by the earl."

"Lady Amelia did not look upset in the least," Daniel protested.

"Be that as it may, you're not to go anywhere near the family."

"Can he do that?" Daniel exploded.

The earl had rights by virtue of his rank, but as far as Daniel knew—and he did know because he was from Essex—Ongar was not a sizable earldom, and although locally important, its standing had little bearing on the rest of the country.

"He can," Ransome replied. "It's not how much one owns but who they know when it comes to throwing their weight about."

"Are you suggesting I abandon the case, sir?"

"You have until Monday. Two more days," Ransome reiterated, which really meant one day, since Daniel wasn't likely to get very far in his investigation on Sunday.

He was about to ask for an extension, but Ransome wore the expression of a man who would not entertain any arguments. "Do you have enough evidence to charge any of your suspects?"

"I do not, which is why I need more time."

"Who's the most likely suspect?"

"Constantine Moore, but all I have is circumstantial evidence. He had a plausible motive, and he was in the area."

"Doesn't mean he killed her. What about the others?"

"Same," Daniel replied. "I don't have anything concrete."

"Do you have a murder weapon?"

"No."

"Can you conclusively prove that she didn't fall and hit her head?" Ransome asked.

"It's not very likely that Mrs. Lysander's death was the result of an accident," Daniel replied, recalling Jason's explanation.

He supposed it made sense that Alicia couldn't have sustained an injury to the top of her head if she had fallen, but what if someone had dropped something? It had been foggy and dark, and they might not have seen Alicia passing beneath their window. It was unlikely that someone would drop a stone, but what if a brick had come loose, or someone had thrown out a bottle or knocked over a flowerpot that had stood on their windowsill? It was just as plausible as Peter Collins stalking Alicia after his orchid presentation or Constantine Moore coming upon her in the dark and suddenly deciding to finish her off. Constantine had lived with the woman. Surely he could have come up with a clever way to dispose of Alicia if he were so inclined.

Ransome must have seen the doubts play out across Daniel's face. "Then there's your answer, Haze," he said. "Either find evidence or move on. We cannot afford to waste time on cases that will not guarantee a solve."

"The story is bound to be in the papers tomorrow," Daniel pointed out. "People will want answers."

"The only real answer is that a medium who was forever hailed as infallible was not able to foretell her own demise. People will chew on that for a day or two, then move on."

By this point, Daniel knew Ransome well enough to understand his thought process. It was more important to appease the earl and protect the commissioner and his own position than solve the case. Alicia Lysander might have been well known, but she wasn't important enough to risk negative publicity and adverse consequences for Sir David, who might have to explain himself to the home secretary if the earl chose to take his complaint further up the chain.

Alicia Lysander's case would be filed away, along with other unsolved crimes, and the whole thing would be forgotten unless Daniel found cause to charge one of the suspects, which would add another notch to Ransome's already well-scored belt. Either result would satisfy him as long as he came out unscathed. Every case came down to politics and future opportunities, and the only way Ransome would give up his position as superintendent was if he were made commissioner.

"Was there something else?" Ransome demanded.

"No, sir. Goodnight."

"Goodnight."

Ransome stood, evidently ready to go home himself, but Daniel didn't wait to walk out with him. He strode down the corridor and hurried across the duty room, which was quieter now that the two brawlers had been dealt with. Theoretically, he could still make it to Convent Garden in time for Angel Flyte's performance, but he decided to go home.

Chapter 20

Jason's lecture was meant to last an hour, but by the time he finished taking questions from eager surgical students, it was nearly six o'clock. The hall finally emptied, and Jason collected his things and walked out with a doctor of his acquaintance, who offered him a ride home in his carriage since he was heading in the same direction. Jason was tempted to accept but realized he wasn't quite ready to go home. He trusted Daniel's judgment and agreed that there was no urgency when it came to Angel Flyte and they could speak to her tomorrow, but something inside him demanded that he see the performance for himself.

Sadie Goodall had painted Angel as a clever businesswoman who had a talent for working the crowd, but having met Alicia, Jason now knew that there were individuals who had been blessed—or maybe cursed was the more fitting term—with an extra sense. He had no reason to believe Sadie, who had to be envious of Angel's success, and wanted to evaluate the medium's talents for himself. She had to be doing something right if she managed to fill a theater designed for one hundred spectators every night. Admittedly, the public was ridiculously easy to dupe, but after the first few missteps, people would catch on if they were paying to see a fake. Angel had been delivering for months, so some of her messages had found their mark.

Bidding his colleague goodnight, Jason found a cab and directed the driver to take him to Covent Garden. The cab crawled along, stopping frequently to allow for evening traffic, but as the businessmen and laborers finally arrived at home after a long day at work, the traffic began to disperse, and the conveyance began to move at a good clip. Covent Garden was crowded with pedestrians, but the market was empty, the stalls dismantled, and the vendors all gone. There was the usual odor of rotting fruit, rancid meat, and sour milk, since it hadn't rained, and the cobbles were slimy with refuse. Ragged children darted across the market, filling their arms with whatever they could find, from broken crates that could be used for firewood to anything that was still edible, even if it was rotten. Jason looked away, saddened by his inability to help these poor wretches in any meaningful way.

He arrived at the theater at twenty to seven, purchased a ticket, and went inside. The interior of the theater was hardly more than a square room where ten rows of chairs, each made up of ten seats, faced the stage. There was no backdrop, no curtain, and no footlights, only bare boards and a black wooden rectangle positioned in the middle and toward the rear of the stage. Four sconces were mounted on the walls, two at the front near the stage and two toward the back. The gaslight filled the space with a mellow glow that illuminated the individuals who had arrived early and had taken seats in the front two rows, probably in the hope of gaining the medium's attention and receiving a message from their loved one.

Jason sat in the outermost seat in the tenth row. He wasn't there to be seen, only to observe, and he didn't care to sit too close to other members of the audience for fear of contagion. If even one person was already ill with cholera, everyone who sat close to them could become infected. As the rows began to fill, Jason was glad that he didn't stand out since there were several gentlemen and well-dressed ladies present. By ten to seven, most seats were taken, and a few stragglers hurried in, looking around until they spotted an unoccupied chair and claimed it.

There was an air of suppressed excitement, and the members of the audience spoke in low voices, some sharing stories of their friends who had received messages from the dead through Angel, who was without doubt the real thing. Jason shifted his chair a few inches toward the wall when a well-dressed couple sat down next to him. They didn't look unwell, but that didn't mean they weren't carrying the illness.

At three minutes to seven, a girl of about twelve, who was dressed in a plain brown dress and wore her fair hair in two plaits, came out through a side door and turned down the gas in the sconces, leaving the auditorium in near darkness. It was just as she approached the last lamp that the final arrival hurried through the door and looked frantically about the room for an empty seat. There were only two left, and the man, who, even in the dim light, could be easily identified as Constantine Moore, took the one closest to him and settled his top hat on his thigh with an exhalation of what had to be relief that he'd made it. Jason looked down when Constantine turned back and surveyed the room, then faced forward, his gaze fixed on the stage.

At precisely seven, a woman emerged from behind the black rectangle. She was no older than twenty-one and was dressed in a flowing white gown and white boots. Her fair hair cascaded down her back in gentle waves, and her face was so pale, she might have been an apparition herself. Jason couldn't make out the color of her eyes, but he thought they were light, and her upturned nose and gently rounded cheeks gave her a slightly childish appearance. She bore a resemblance to the girl who'd turned down the lights, and Jason thought the child was probably Angel's younger sister. So, a family business, then.

Angel spread her arms, and the loose sleeves of her gown swayed gently, like the wings of a bird or a Biblical angel. She was playing this for all it was worth, Jason mused as he settled back to watch the performance. Angel surveyed the audience, turning her face very slowly from right to left. When she finally spoke, her voice was gentle and soothing, and every person in the audience leaned forward in order to better hear her.

"Ladies and gentlemen, I am Angel, and I thank you for coming tonight. I hope you will leave feeling uplifted and reassured, secure in the knowledge that our life on earth is only part of the journey, and that the soul is truly eternal."

Angel's smile was ethereal as she gazed at the audience like a benevolent fairy. "I do need to explain a few things before we begin," she said, her expression now taking on an apologetic cast.

"I know you all long to hear from your loved ones, but I can only deliver messages for some of you. That doesn't mean your loved ones aren't near; it only means that some spirits have a more urgent message than others, and I must honor their desperate desire to be heard."

Angel waited until members of the audience nodded in understanding, then continued. "The spirits of loved ones who are very recently deceased are sometimes disoriented and confused, and their messages might not be as clear as those of souls that had passed some time before. Please bear with me. I will do everything in my power to make sure your dear one is understood, their soul soothed, and bolstered by your undying love."

"What utter bollocks," someone whispered, and was instantly shushed by their companion.

Angel peered out into the audience. "Are you ready to begin? We have but an hour, and I want to make sure to deliver messages to as many of you as I can." Everyone nodded in unison, even the man who had spoken. "Kindly keep quiet and be respectful of both the spirits and their loved ones who are here to receive their message. Then go home in love."

Closing her eyes, Angel tipped her head back and stood perfectly still. The audience drew in a collective breath as everyone waited for something to happen. When Angel spoke again, it was in the high-pitched voice of a child. "Mama. It's me, Sylvie. Mama!"

A woman in the third row cried out as if she had been shot, and her hand flew to her breast as she tried to contain her emotions.

"Sylvie, my love," the woman wailed. "I'm so sorry. I only turned away for a moment. I never meant to leave you alone."

"It wasn't your fault, Mama," the child replied. "I didn't feel any pain when I drowned. I'm happy now."

"Sylvie," the woman cried desperately as the man next to her tried to calm her. "Sylvie, I will love you always."

"Tell Tommy I miss him," the tiny voice said.

Sylvie's mother wailed with grief, while the man, presumably the child's father, choked out, "We love you, baby girl."

Jason wasn't sure how he felt about what he had just witnessed. On the one hand, Angel had called out the name of the spirit and Tommy, probably the girl's brother. She had clearly reached her intended audience, but it was possible that she somehow knew of Sylvie's passing and had played a part. Her sister, or someone who was even now backstage, might have chatted to members of the audience as they arrived or waited to pay for their ticket. All Angel needed was one or two tidbits of information to convince the audience that she was in contact with the dead.

Jason turned away from the stage, his gaze finding Constantine. He could only see him in profile, but it was enough to gauge Constantine's reaction. He sat perfectly still, his gaze glued to the stage and his mouth quivering with emotion. Constantine appeared to be deeply moved, and Jason wondered if it was an act or if he truly believed that he had just witnessed a parting of the veil as Sylvie absolved her mother of her death by drowning.

Sylvie's mother sobbed quietly into her husband's shoulder as Angel looked out benevolently over the audience. It had to be too dark for her to make out individual faces, but she appeared to be searching for someone. Jason shifted in his seat when he thought she was staring straight at him, but there was no way she could see him clearly from her place on stage. The row he sat in was in near darkness, and his chair was practically touching the wall.

Angel's voice turned husky, her expression one of unspeakable sorrow. "Jason," she moaned. "Jason, hear me."

A shiver raced up Jason's spine and settled in his neck as his mouth unwittingly fell open. He wanted to believe that there was another Jason in the audience, but he knew that voice. He'd heard it several times and would have recognized it anywhere. Jason almost called out a response, then got hold of himself. This was a hoax. It had to be. Angel had to know that Alicia was dead and was trying to trick him.

"Jason," Angel called again. "He's killed three times."

Jason waited, his shoulders stiff with tension as he leaned forward to hear Alicia's message from beyond. He wanted to ask who Alicia was referring to and who else had been killed, but all he got was another cryptic clue.

"The anchoress of Ashburn doesn't sleep alone," Angel cried out.

Jason had no clue what that meant and hoped that Alicia or Angel would elaborate, but the medium's tone suddenly changed to one of calm resolve.

"Constantine, you must let me go."

The voice died away, and Angel appeared to shake off her trance, looking over the audience for confirmation that the message had been successfully received.

"Ally," Constantine cried, his voice filled with anguish. "Ally, don't go." His voice cracked on the last word, and he seemed to sink lower into his seat, as if all the strength had seeped out of him.

"I'm sorry," Angel said softly. "This soul has very recently passed and doesn't have the strength to come through for very long."

She began to search the audience again, but Jason didn't want to hear any more. He got to his feet and headed for the door. He had just stepped outside when Constantine caught up with him.

"You have to find her killer," he implored. "Alicia spoke directly to you. She knew you were there, and she charged you with avenging her death." Constantine looked like he was about to cry, his bottom lip quivering as he tried to control his emotions. "Please, your lordship. Get justice for my Alicia."

Looking at the man, Jason couldn't believe that he had anything to do with Alicia's murder, but if he were honest, he was a bit emotional himself and not in any state to carry on a rational conversation.

"We will speak tomorrow," he promised, and Constantine nodded, his shoulders drooping as if he were too exhausted to formulate words.

Jason found a hansom and gave the cabbie his address. He longed to go home.

Chapter 21

The house was strangely quiet, the lamps in the drawing room unlit and the dining room showing no signs of recent use.

"Where is everyone?" Jason asked Dodson, who'd taken Jason's hat and walking stick, then followed him to the drawing room to inquire if Jason might need something before Dodson locked up and retired for the night.

"Her ladyship asked for a tray in her room. Mary is in the nursery with Liam, and Fanny is in the kitchen with Mrs. Dodson. Would you like Mrs. Dodson to fix you some dinner, my lord?"

Jason shook his head. He had been hungry earlier, but now he felt slightly queasy and would have liked a cup of strong, sweet tea but didn't want to put Mrs. Dodson to any trouble. He considered pouring himself a drink, but the thought of alcohol soured his stomach.

"May I have a glass of warm milk?"

"Of course, sir. Shall I have Fanny bring it upstairs?"

"Please."

Jason made his way upstairs and opened the door to the bedroom as quietly as he could, in case Katherine was asleep, but she was sitting up in bed, her spectacles perched on the end of her nose as she turned a page in her book.

"Jason!" she exclaimed. "I was beginning to worry. Did you get held up at the College of Surgeons, or is it to do with the investigation?"

"I went to see a spiritualist," Jason confessed as he shrugged off his coat and loosened his tie.

Katherine set aside her book, pushed up her glasses, and fixed him with an inquisitive stare. "And?"

Jason smiled ruefully. "I can't believe I'm about to say this aloud, but I think I've had a message from Alicia."

"Did you? What did she say? Do you know who attacked her?"

"No. I'm afraid I didn't understand the message," Jason confessed. "And I'm not one hundred percent certain it was really from Alicia."

"Who do you think it was from?"

"The medium. She calls herself Angel Flyte," Jason began, and Katherine rolled her eyes but didn't interrupt. "She could have somehow found out that Alicia is dead and faked the message for dramatic effect."

Katherine smiled at him. "If you really believed that, we wouldn't be having this conversation."

"No, we wouldn't," Jason agreed. Deep down, he was sure he'd heard Alicia Lysander's voice, and he felt in his bones that the message held some important clue.

"What was the message? Maybe I can help," Katherine said.

"Angel, or rather Alicia, said that her assailant had killed three times. And then she said that the anchoress of Ashburn doesn't sleep alone. What in blazes does that mean?"

Katherine perked up. "Really? She said that?"

Jason took off his shirt but paused before unbuttoning his trousers. "Does that mean something to you?"

He hastily pulled on his dressing gown when Fanny knocked on the door, a glass of milk on a silver salver.

"Thank you, Fanny."

"Goodnight, sir."

Jason took a sip of milk while he waited for Katherine to explain, but she appeared to be deep in thought.

"Do you know what an anchoress is?" she asked at last.

"Is it something to do with sailing?"

That was the only anchor Jason could think off, but he wasn't aware of any female who was in charge of anchoring a ship.

132

"Not even close," Katherine replied with an indulgent smile. "I don't think there were any anchorites in the United States."

"Anchorite? I thought we were talking about an anchoress."

"An anchorite is a sort of living saint. In the Middle Ages, a man, or more commonly a woman, would go into seclusion and live a life of devotion and prayer. Anchorites were given the rite of consecration, which meant that they were dead to the outside world. A few retained their autonomy, but the majority were walled into a small cell attached to a church, with only a small window into the church that enabled them to attend the services, and another to the outside, so they could receive basic goods."

"Walled in?" Jason asked, unsure he'd heard Katherine correctly. He couldn't even begin to comprehend this idea of a living death.

"It was entirely their choice," Katherine explained. "Someone brought them food and removed their soil buckets, but otherwise, they lived in complete isolation, devoid of any creature comforts. They slept on a pallet on the ground and did not even have a fire during the winter months."

"Someone actually chose to do this?" Jason asked, still unable to understand why anyone would want such a life for themselves. If one could even call such an existence a life. No wonder they had received the sacrament. For all intents and purposes, they had been dwelling in their own grave.

Katherine nodded. "They did. There were quite a few anchorites during the Middle Ages. Julian of Norwich was one of the better-known ones since she is believed to have written several texts while in seclusion. And there's even some evidence that an anchorite once lived in a cell attached to St. Martin's Church in Chipping Ongar."

"Ongar?"

"That's right. The ancestral holding of the Earl of Ongar."

"How do you know this?" Jason asked.

Katherine had never shown an interest in saints and martyrs, despite her strict religious upbringing. Jason assumed that her father, the Reverend Talbot, had drummed these facts into Katherine's head, but he couldn't imagine that his father-in-law would uphold practices that he would most likely deem Popish given that they had come into existence before the Reformation and therefore, to the reverend's mind, were constructs of the Catholic Church.

Even someone as rigid as the reverend wouldn't condone walling a woman into a cell, unless that woman had sinned against God or a man and was therefore deserving of her fate.

Smiling wistfully, Katherine said, "My mother was interested in history, particularly the Middle Ages. She told me and my sister about Julian and some other notable women of the time."

"Did she approve of this barbaric rite?" Jason asked.

"No, but she thought that some of these women were looking for an escape from a life that had become unbearable."

"Were the anchoresses generally middle-aged?"

"I don't believe there was an age requirement. If a young woman expressed a desire to become an anchoress, the church would probably welcome her decision."

"This is certainly a chapter of British history I wasn't aware of, but what does this have to do with Alicia and her message?"

"Ashburn Hall is the ancestral seat of the Earl of Ongar. It's in Essex, near the town of Chipping Ongar and not all that far from Birch Hill."

Jason sat down in an armchair and took another sip of his milk. He was still queasy, and the thought of someone being walled in alive, willing though they might have been, made him feel sick to his stomach.

"Was there an anchoress at Ashburn Hall?" he asked.

"Yes, there was. The hall was built on the ruins of St. Mary's Abbey, which was destroyed during the Dissolution of the Monasteries. The church was smashed to bits, anything of value taken by Cromwell's men, even the brass plaque that commemorated Sigrid of Ashburn, who was the anchoress in the fourteenth century and lived and died in a cell attached to the church. I think Alicia was trying to tell you that the other victims are buried next to Sigrid."

"And where would Sigrid be buried? In the church graveyard?"

Katherine shook her head once again. "In some cases, a grave was dug inside the cell before the anchoress was walled in. This was so that she could contemplate her own mortality."

"And the other cases?" Jason asked.

"The anchoress was expected to dig her own grave with her bare hands, taking handfuls of dirt out every day until the grave was ready to receive her. If Alicia said that Sigrid doesn't sleep alone, she could only have meant that the other two victims are buried in her cell."

"Well, now I've heard it all," Jason muttered.

He could imagine the horror of staring into one's own grave all too well, having witnessed men dig their own graves at Andersonville Prison, and he clearly recalled the pits that the soldiers had dug to bury everyone who had died during a particular battle. Everyone knew they would die one day and saw numerous graves during their lifetime. Such was the nature of life that as soon as a person was born, they were marking days until their death, but to dig one's own grave over a period of years had to be its own form of torture.

Jason supposed that if someone was that devoted to God, they saw their death as a pathway to eternal life, but he still couldn't begin to fathom the days that led up to that moment and all the hours that were spent in a cold, dark cell from which there was no escape. And then he recalled something that expelled all thoughts of an anchorite's life from his mind.

"In death you have *anchored* me to eternal life," Jason recited.

"What?"

"Lady Amelia mentioned that the earl's late wife, Daphne, had intoned that during the séance."

Katherine's eyes narrowed as she tried to decipher the meaning. "You said Lady Daphne died while abroad. So did her lady's maid."

"What if they died much closer to home?" Jason said, his mind leaping three steps ahead.

"Then Lady Daphne's message would threaten the killer with exposure."

"Exactly," Jason exclaimed. "And they might try to silence the one person who had the power to reveal their secret."

"And the only person who was present at the séance who could have something to gain from Lady Daphne's death would be the earl. But why would he murder his wife and then concoct such an elaborate story?" Katherine asked. "There are easier ways to murder someone. And why kill the maid?"

"Perhaps Crumlish knew something that could incriminate the earl," Jason theorized. "The better questions is, how do we go about proving any of this?" He sighed resignedly, since he knew already there was only one possible answer.

"Jason, St. Mary's stands on the earl's property, and there are members of staff who live at Ashburn Hall year-round."

"Presumably they sleep at night."

"My dear," Katherine began, but didn't bother to finish the sentence. "You will not rest until you bring Alicia's killer to justice, will you?"

"No," Jason said simply. He found that the queasiness he'd experienced earlier had abated, and he felt a reassuring sense of resolve. "Do you have any desire to visit your father, my love?"

"My father?" Katherine peered at him from behind the lenses of her spectacles. "What, this week?"

"I was thinking tomorrow."

"What?" Katherine exclaimed.

"If I suddenly pick up and travel to Essex on my own, I will be tipping off the killer before I have any physical proof of his crimes. However, if we visit your father, no one will suspect a thing, and I can slip away unnoticed after dark."

"Oh, dear," Katherine said, but a smile tugged at her lips. "I suppose it has been quite a long time since he's seen Lily."

"She really should spend more time with her loving grandsire," Jason replied, a tad facetiously.

Katherine sighed deeply. "All right. I'll tell Fanny in the morning, and if we leave immediately after breakfast, we can be in Birch Hill in time for a late lunch."

"Perfect," Jason replied. "I'll tell Joe to bring the shovels."

Jason set aside his empty glass and climbed into bed, reaching for his warm, pliant wife. If he was to spend tomorrow night digging, he may as well make the most of tonight.

Chapter 22

Sunday, June 20

Jason and Katherine were up with the sun, having resolved to get to Birch Hill for the Sunday service. The ride would take approximately two and a half hours, so if they left at seven, they would arrive just in time, pending any unforeseen complications. The weather looked fine, and there weren't likely to be too many conveyances on the roads, it being Sunday. Jason left Katherine to pack for a one-night stay at the vicarage, while he instructed Joe to take him to Daniel's house.

If Daniel was shocked to find Jason on his doorstep at six in the morning, he didn't show it. He belted his dressing gown a bit tighter, adjusted the spectacles that were a bit askew, and invited Jason into the parlor.

"Would you like a cup of tea?" Daniel asked. "Grace just fired up the range, so it's no bother."

"Thank you, but I can't stay. Katherine and I are going to Birch Hill," Jason replied. "We will be back tomorrow afternoon."

"You're leaving now?" Daniel exclaimed. "Has something happened? Is it the vicar?"

"As far as I know, my father-in-law is in fine health, but I do need an excuse to go to Essex."

"Why?"

Jason relayed the details of the séance and Katherine's interpretation of the message from Alicia..

"Have you ever heard about this Sigrid of Ashburn?" Jason asked.

"I don't know. I may have. Now that you mention it, the name sounds familiar." Daniel's gaze grew more focused. "Do you remember what Lady Amelia said?"

"About?"

"She mentioned that Lady Daphne was interested in the lives of martyrs and saints and held a great admiration for women who refused to be bullied into marriage. Having lived at Ashburn Hall, she would be familiar with Sigrid and her devotion to God."

"According to Katherine, Sigrid lived around five hundred years ago. What possible bearing could her decision to become an anchoress have on the Countess of Ongar?"

"Perhaps she saw her as some sort of inspirational role model."

Jason sighed. As someone who had doubted the existence of God on too many occasions to count, he found it unfathomable that someone would see the life of an anchoress as something to aspire to, but he had also met many individuals whose beliefs bordered on fanatical. Perhaps Lady Daphne had been so unhappy in her marriage that a tiny cell had seemed preferable to the prison she'd lived in with her husband. Jason had no right to judge a woman who was long dead and could no longer speak for herself, but he wasn't about to discount her possible connection to the anchoress.

"The earl made a complaint to Sir David. I'm not to go anywhere near the family or the servants, and Ransome gave me until Monday to solve the case. This is my one chance to bring the killer to justice, so I'm coming with you," Daniel exclaimed as he sprang to his feet. "Just give me a few minutes to get dressed. I can ride on the bench with Joe."

"Daniel, if we both hare off to Essex in the middle of an investigation, the earl might suspect that we're on to him. He's already lodged a complaint with Commissioner Hawkins. What do you think he'll do if he suspects we mean to dig deeper?"

"I take your meaning and appreciate the clever pun," Daniel said with an amused smile. "But what am I supposed to do?"

"Attend the Sunday service, as you normally would, then find a way to speak to Bernice Crumlish. Her mother was Lady Daphne's maid. She knew her mistress's secrets and presumably died to keep them from getting out."

"She might not have shared what she knew with her daughter."

"Maybe not, but Bernice Crumlish grew up in that house. She is bound to know something of the woman her mother served for years."

Daniel nodded. "All right. I will find an excuse to speak to Bernice, but it might have to wait until Monday. His Grace would not look kindly on me calling by on a Sunday, more so since I already stand accused of harassing the staff."

"Then perhaps you can speak to Constantine Moore. He was at Angel's performance last night. That's not a coincidence. At the very least, he knew about Angel's rivalry with Alicia. At worst, he was somehow involved in her death and craved absolution."

"And he just happened to know that Alicia would come through?" Daniel asked, his skepticism written all over his sleep-creased face.

"He did not look frightened, only heartbroken, but that doesn't mean he told us everything he knows."

"I will wait to hear from you before I report to Ransome on Monday," Daniel said. "Try not to lose your temper with the old man. I know how he enjoys goading you."

"My hope is that he will be distracted by his beautiful granddaughter," Jason replied with a smile. "Lily is the only one who can bring a smile to that curmudgeon's face."

Daniel nodded. "Little girls have a way of doing that, don't they?"

"And we do have some happy news," Jason added shyly. He wouldn't tell anyone else and would be happy to keep Katherine's pregnancy from his father-in-law until the child was safely delivered, but he couldn't keep his joy from Daniel.

"Oh, Jason. My heartfelt congratulations. I hope all goes well."

"Thank you. We're not telling anyone yet."

"Your secret is safe with me," Daniel replied as he walked Jason out, and Jason knew that it was, even from Flora.

By the time Jason and Katherine set off, the city was coming to life and the morning edition of the Sunday *Telegraph* was hitting the pavement. Jason exhaled heavily when he heard a small boy of about ten bellow, "Murder of a Medium. Read all about it."

"How do they know it was murder?" Katherine mouthed over Lily's capped head. Lily's nose was pressed to the window as she watched the city slip by, unfamiliar streets and people making for a fascinating spectacle.

"Because someone has told them," Jason replied. "And I think I know just who that was."

"Constantine wants justice," Katherine said. "Can you blame him?"

"No, but I can't help but wonder if that's all he wants."

Chapter 23

As he sat through an excruciatingly dull sermon on the pitfalls of vanity, Daniel's mind kept straying to Essex. He wondered if Jason would find evidence to support Alicia Lysander's clue but knew he wouldn't learn anything until Monday afternoon and couldn't afford to waste the day if he hoped to have something to present to Ransome on Monday. All Daniel could do was work his end of the case and try to dig up something useful. Digging seemed to be the order of the day, and he was getting into the spirit of things, if only figuratively.

Once the service was over, Daniel saw his little party home, and after a rather hurried lunch, he excused himself to Flora and Charlotte, who were planning a walk in the park after Charlotte's afternoon nap, and took himself off to Greek Street to speak to Constantine Moore. When he came to the door, Constantine looked like he hadn't slept in days and had spent all his time drinking, which, judging by the reek of spirits that emanated from him, was exactly what he had done since last night's message from beyond the grave. Constantine stared blearily at Daniel, his gaze not quite focused.

"Where's your maidservant?" Daniel asked.

"I gave her the day off," Constantine slurred. "What do you want? I told you everything I know."

"Perhaps not everything," Daniel replied as he pushed past Constantine and made his way to the drawing room. He removed his hat and settled in one of the armchairs.

Constantine folded himself into the chair opposite. Despite his rumpled appearance and bloodshot eyes, Daniel thought he was more aware than he let on.

"You were at Angel Flyte's performance last night," Daniel said.

Constantine nodded, and his eyes grew moist. "Alicia and I were together for nearly five years, and she had a message for *him*," he complained. "How do you think that made me feel?"

"I should think it would reassure you to know that Alicia is helping us investigate her own murder."

"I loved her," Constantine cried. "She barely acknowledged that. Just told me to move on, like we'd had some sordid fling."

"Sometimes, setting someone free is the greatest act of love," Daniel replied.

It wasn't until he'd spoken the words that he realized that Sarah had done just that. She had set him free, knowing that their life together would be a lifelong sentence neither one of them could ever escape, so she had staged her own execution. She had hurt her daughter, but perhaps she had set Charlotte free as well, giving her a chance at a life untainted by sorrow and endless blame.

"I don't want to move on," Constantine grumbled.

He sounded like a petulant child, but instead of irritation, Daniel felt sympathy for the man. Constantine was hurting, but whether he was an innocent bystander or had had a hand in his lover's death remained to be seen.

"Why were you there last night?" Daniel asked.

"I went on the off chance that Alicia might have a message for me."

"That's not what I asked, and you know it," Daniel snapped. "You never told us about Angel or her rivalry with Alicia, yet you just happened to be there on the night Angel passed on a message from your lover, and this morning, news of her murder is in the *Telegraph*. Did you sell the story to the papers?"

"Yes, I did," Constantine said defiantly. "I wanted the world to know that Alicia was murdered, and I wanted to force Scotland Yard's hand. I'm not as dumb as you imagine, Inspector Haze. I know how this works. Alicia was murdered after a séance at the residence of an earl. Who do you think your superintendent is more concerned with, a woman he probably thought was a fraud or a nobleman who will use his influence to shut down the investigation at the first hint of scandal?"

"I take your point," Daniel replied, acknowledging the validity of Constantine's logic. "And I don't blame you for wanting to get the story out there. But I do wonder how well you know Angel Flyte."

"Angel and I met a few months ago. I went to her show, to size up the competition."

"Did Alicia ask you to do that?"

"No, but it was part of what I did for her. I kept my ear to the ground."

"And what was your impression?" Daniel asked. "Sadie Goodall thinks Angel is a hack."

"I believed Angel to be the real thing, like Alicia was. She is a conduit for the dead, and she proved that to me without doubt last night. Sadie was jealous of both Alicia and Angel. She gets her share of clients, but she wasn't blessed with the ability to speak to the dead."

"Did Alicia think she was?"

"No, but she was lonely and didn't see Sadie as a threat."

"Was she a threat?" Daniel asked, suddenly wondering if he and Jason had discounted Sadie's involvement far too soon.

"I don't believe so. Sadie had no reason to hurt Alicia, and I think she hoped to learn from her."

"What about Peter Collins? Did he have reason to want Alicia dead?"

Constantine looked blank. "Peter Collins? I never heard the name. Was Alicia in love with him?"

Constantine's pain was so raw, Daniel could almost taste his angst, but that didn't mean his grief wasn't a convincing act.

"No, she wasn't, but he is mentioned in her will. He's someone from her past." That wasn't strictly true, not in the sense Constantine had taken the news, but Daniel hoped to needle him enough to reveal something important.

"Alicia never mentioned him," Constantine muttered.

"Alicia kept things from you. Did you also keep things from her?" Daniel asked.

Constantine swallowed hard and nodded. "In the course of my research, I grew close with Angel. And I became fascinated with her gift."

"It's awfully convenient that the spirits come to her between seven and eight o'clock in the evening and pass on messages to individuals who just happen to be in the audience."

Constantine looked affronted. "I can't expect you to understand how a conduit works, Inspector Haze, but given that you have benefited from Alicia's ability, I would ask you not to disparage what Angel does for people who're desperate for one more moment with those they have lost."

"All right," Daniel conceded. "I will accept your assessment of Angel's ability, but I would like to know more about your personal relationship."

Constantine looked guilty as hell and hung his head in what had to be shame.

"Are you conducting an affair with Angel Flyte?" Daniel pressed.

Constantine nodded, then raised his head to meet Daniel's gaze. "I loved Alicia. I asked her to marry me a dozen times, but she always refused. I got the sense that she was keeping something from me and thought she was seeing someone on the side. I followed her one day," Constantine confessed. "I hid behind a tree and watched as Alicia came out into the garden with a little girl. Even if the child didn't look just like her, I would have known. The look on Alicia's face…" He shook his head. "She never looked at me like that."

"Surely you weren't jealous of a mother's love for her child."

"She didn't trust me enough to tell me the truth, and she refused to marry me because she didn't want me to lay claim to what she surely set aside for her daughter."

"You have no claim on Chara's inheritance," Daniel warned him.

"Is that her name? I always did wonder, especially after I saw the photograph in Alicia's box." Constantine faced Daniel, looking him squarely in the eye. "I never wanted Alicia's money. I wanted her love, but I could tell she was moving away from me, putting up walls."

"It never hurts to have money."

Constantine laughed bitterly. "I have money, Inspector. My father is Atticus Moore of Moore Iron Works. We've been estranged these past few years, but he's never stopped trying to bring me back into the fold. All I have to do is agree to work in the family business and I will be set for life."

"Why don't you agree?" Daniel asked.

He had heard of Moore Iron Works, of course. One couldn't walk ten steps without coming across an object manufactured by the Moores. Trains, ships, carriages, fences and gates, and everything in between was fitted with Moore parts. If Constantine was telling the truth, then he was an heir to a great fortune, greater even than that of the Earl of Ongar, whose estate couldn't be as profitable as owning a part of the future.

"I met Alicia when she conducted a séance at my parents' house. They wanted to contact my sister, who had died of consumption. I fell in love the moment I saw Alicia, and I longed to be part of her world, her life. It took months to get close to her, but once I did, I never wanted to leave. I was happy to be her assistant, and her protector. But I failed. I failed to keep her safe," Constantine said quietly.

"So, why didn't you tell Alicia the truth about your affair with Angel?"

"I had hoped that things between us would improve. I would have left Angel in a heartbeat if Alicia had agreed to marry me. Nothing would have made me happier than having a child of our own. And I would have happily accepted her daughter. I would have legally adopted her if that was what Alicia wanted."

"You do realize this gives Angel Flyte a motive for murder," Daniel said.

"Angel felt threatened by Alicia; that was true, but she would never hurt anyone. Angel has the greatest respect for life, just as she has a deep understanding of death. She knows it's not for her to decide when someone is called to the Lord." Constantine looked utterly wretched as he said, "I met Angel after the show on Thursday. I was with her until it was time to collect Alicia from the earl's house. I was a few minutes late."

"How convenient," Daniel said sourly. "So, you and Angel mean to alibi each other?"

"I don't care if you believe me, Inspector Haze," Constantine said. "I know I did not hurt Alicia. That's enough for me."

"I wonder if you would say that as you stand on the scaffold, about to be hanged for murder."

"I didn't do it," Constantine insisted. "If I did, Alicia could have told Lord Redmond so last night, but she didn't."

"She said, 'He has murdered three times.' She could have meant you."

"She also spoke of the anchoress of Ashburn," Constantine reminded him. "Perhaps you should decipher that clue before you lay the blame at my door."

"Don't leave town," Daniel ordered as he stood to leave. "If you are guilty, I will find you."

It was an empty threat. Constantine could be on a ship to America or on a train to Vienna or Munich by the end of the day, but in his bones, Daniel didn't believe Constantine was guilty. There was something else at play here, and he hoped that Jason would be able to provide the missing pieces of the puzzle. In the meantime, he wanted a word with Angel Flyte.

Chapter 24

Covent Garden was blissfully quiet on a Sunday afternoon. The market was closed, as were the theaters and gaming establishments that had the decency to close on the Lord's Day. A few pedestrians strolled past, but otherwise, Russell Street was nearly empty. The doors to the theater were locked, but Daniel was able to learn from a shopkeeper just down the street that Angel kept rooms above a confectioner's shop, whose bay window offered the most tantalizing display of marzipan, chocolates, and cakes. The shop was open, and several people stood in line, waiting to buy a Sunday treat.

Tearing his gaze away from the window, Daniel pushed open a side door and made his way up a creaking staircase that led to the upper floor. There was only one door, so he knocked and hoped Angel was in. A girl of about eleven or twelve opened the door and peered at Daniel.

"Hello, I'm Inspector Haze of Scotland Yard. Is Angel at home?" he asked in what he hoped was a nonthreatening tone.

"Mam," the girl called, and stepped away from the door.

The woman who came to the door had to be Angel, since she fit the description Jason had provided, but today she was dressed in a modest gown of pale blue muslin, and her hair was pulled back into a knot. Her delicate neck was long and pale, and she had the rounded cheeks and snub nose of a child, but on closer inspection, Daniel realized that she had to be at least twenty-five, not twenty-one.

"You're here about Alicia's death," Angel said. "Come in."

Daniel followed her down a blue-painted corridor to a parlor that overlooked the street. The room was clean and cozy, but the apartment was small, and the furnishings had seen better days. Someone who made a profit every night could surely afford something better than this, Daniel mused as he accepted a seat in a worn armchair. The armrests were protected by yellowed lace antimacassars, and the rug looked threadbare in places.

"One day, when I have earned enough, I will simply disappear," Angel said, having seemingly read Daniel's mind. "It's easier to travel light."

Daniel could understand the desire to disappear and start somewhere new. He had done that when he was a young man and had come to London, which had seemed magical and threatening in equal parts. He thought Angel might go someplace else, somewhere where the air was fresh, and the sea pounded the cliffs while gulls screamed overhead. He had no clue where that idea had come from, but it seemed to fit.

"I want to live in Cornwall," Angel said, as if reading his thoughts. "I want to be near the sea."

Maybe I'm becoming clairvoyant myself, Daniel thought wryly. "My associate was very impressed with your gift," he said. "How did you know he was in the audience?"

"I didn't. I had never heard of him until last night."

"Were you always psychic?" Daniel was genuinely curious about this woman, whose demeanor was as calm as a tranquil lake.

"No. I didn't experience my first encounter with the dead until I was fourteen. It happened a week after the birth of my daughter."

"Does childbirth bring on psychic ability?" Daniel asked.

"I don't think so, but sometimes trauma does."

Angel did not elaborate, but Daniel saw a shadow pass over her eyes and assumed that Angel's path to motherhood had not been a loving one.

"Constantine was with me the night Alicia was attacked. He couldn't have done it."

"So he said. Might you have a message for me as well?" Daniel asked, all the while wondering if Angel could turn her ability on and off like gaslight.

"I can try, but I don't feel anything at the moment."

"What do you normally feel?"

"A sort of vibration."

"So, the spirits take Sundays off?" Daniel quipped.

"They do not know what day it is," Angel replied, her expression somber. "There's no such thing as time in the spirit world."

"What is there?"

"Emptiness and quiet."

"That sounds lonely and frightening."

"It's really not," Angel replied. "It's the opposite of urgency and anxiety. It's very peaceful, most of the time."

"When is it not peaceful?" Daniel asked. He found that he was fascinated by this idea of an afterlife and wanted to learn as much as he could. Alicia had not been as forthcoming, but Angel seemed happy to talk about it.

"When a spirit feels their loved ones' grief and longing, they can't rest. So they try to make contact, to assure their loved ones that they are happy and well and those they left behind need to move on. It's the nature of life and death, and to grieve endlessly for someone who can no longer feel pain is futile."

"Sometimes the pain is not for someone who's lost but for themselves. They cannot move forward without the person they lost."

"There are people who are genuinely broken, Inspector, and then there are those who are self-indulgent and like to wallow in their grief. It's a way to gain sympathy and attention."

"That's rather a harsh point of view, wouldn't you say?" Daniel asked, wondering if she was referring to him.

"Not at all. Everyone has an agenda, and some people's agenda is to feed on the positive energy of others." Angel cocked her head to the side and studied Daniel. "My daughter and I had plans to go for a walk this afternoon, so if you'd like to try to make contact, we should get started."

"All right. What do you need from me?" Daniel asked, his nerve endings tingling with anticipation. He was nervous and worried both that Alicia would come through and that she wouldn't. He'd never experienced a visitation, and the prospect was alarming.

"I need you to open your mind and try not to block me, but first I need to prepare."

Angel stood and walked over to the window, where she drew the curtains, plunging the room into darkness. She called out to her daughter not to disturb them, then shut the door and returned to her seat. All Daniel could make out in the darkness was the whites of her eyes and the gleam of her teeth. It was extremely unnerving, but he closed his eyes and tried to clear his mind of all negative thoughts, hoping to open himself up to the experience. His hands trembled, and the roast he'd eaten suddenly felt heavy in his belly. The room seemed stuffy and the darkness oppressive, but he was as ready to receive a message from the other side as he'd ever be.

The silence stretched on, the air becoming dense with their combined tension. Or maybe it was just his tension because Angel seemed calm despite being closeted in a dark room with a man she'd just met. Daniel shut his eyes and waited, but his thoughts refused to give him a moment of peace as they warned him that she was a fake and he was a dupe for allowing this to happen. She would probably feed him some nonsense about Constantine being innocent and then claim that it had been a message from Alicia Lysander.

Daniel started with surprise when Angel finally spoke, her voice low and urgent.

"Danny," Angel intoned. "Oh, Danny."

He felt gooseflesh rise on the back of his neck when he recognized the voice, and his first instinct was to run for the door and yank it open until light from the adjacent room dispelled the darkness and he no longer felt so lost and vulnerable. He inhaled deeply, forcing himself to relax. He was never going to get another opportunity, and he had to take it, no matter how unsettled it made him feel.

"Yes?" Daniel croaked.

"Danny, I'm so sorry. It was cruel what I did, and foolish, but I'm at peace. I'm with my boy."

"Sarah," Daniel cried. "Sarah, I miss you, and Felix."

"Don't let her go, Danny," Sarah whispered.

"Charlotte is safe. She's well," Daniel replied. He couldn't believe he was speaking to Sarah and wished Felix would join her, but there was no sign of his son. Did children age in the afterlife, or did they remain the age they had been when they died? Felix had been three. Did he even remember the father who had been so frequently absent?

"Danny, don't let Flora go. Build a new family."

"Sarah…" Daniel whispered, but he found that he didn't know what to say. What was there left between them? Anger, recrimination, guilt, but he no longer felt love, only an echo of the feelings they had once shared.

"It's time, Danny," Sarah said, and Daniel thought her voice was fading.

Angel stirred, her hand going to her brow. "She's gone," she said, her voice low. "Her presence was very strong."

"She's been dead a while," Daniel said, still reeling from what he had just experienced. "Did you see her?"

"No, but I sensed her. She felt…" Angel paused. "Whole," she said at last.

"And Alicia?"

"She wasn't there. Perhaps she has nothing more to add or didn't think you were the right person to receive her message."

Angel stood and walked to the window, opening the curtain slowly to gradually let in the light. Daniel blinked as his eyes adjusted, and he looked at Angel, who was watching him.

"Was that real? Please, tell me."

"It was. I never knew your wife, but I do now. She was an unhappy woman, wasn't she? It's like I told you, Inspector, not all people can manage to go on. Some don't want to."

"She left me and our daughter."

"It was for the best. Now go forth and live," Angel said. "You heard her. It's time."

Daniel nodded. He still felt as if he were in a trance, but the strangeness of the experience was beginning to pass, and he wanted nothing more than to leave this dingy apartment and get out into the light.

"Thank you."

Angel nodded. "Now, I think it's time for that walk."

Chapter 25

Daniel thought he needed a walk too. He couldn't begin to think of going home until he'd had time to process what had just happened. Despite having a good breakfast and a hearty luncheon, he felt weak and shaky, his entire body vibrating with the shock he'd just received. He wanted to deny it, to call Angel a liar and a fraud, but deep inside he knew she was neither of those things.

He didn't believe Sadie Goodall's assessment of her was correct in the least. Or maybe it was precisely right, and she didn't want to admit that this strange young woman had talents Sadie could only dream of. Angel had had no need to fear Alicia. She had an ability that would see her and her daughter safe and fed for the rest of her days. Unless she sent the right message to the wrong man, as Alicia had clearly done.

Not having a destination in mind, Daniel walked the streets. Although he was aware of the carriages that drove past him and avoided bumping into pedestrians who were out for a Sunday stroll, his mind was on Sarah, the start of their life together and then its bitter end. They had known each other for so long, had loved each other, and had dreamed of a future in which they would grow old together as their children forged their own paths and made them proud, but now only half their family was left, facing a reality they had never expected.

Whole—that was a strange word to apply about someone who'd been dead for several years, but perhaps that was exactly the word Daniel had needed to hear. Sarah had not been whole in life, not since Felix had died, anyway, and if she could find peace in death, then perhaps she had done the only thing that had been still available to her. Strange that Sarah had made a reference to Flora, Daniel mused. He would think his wife would no longer bother herself with such worldly concerns, but maybe this was Sarah's way of letting him know that she wanted him to be happy. To be whole.

Daniel did not think he needed Sarah's permission to remarry. She had been the one to leave him, not the other way around, but he supposed knowing that she approved eased something in his chest. He no longer felt as if he was betraying her by moving on with his life and introducing a new mother to Charlotte. They both needed someone, and although they'd loved Rebecca Grainger and still missed her, Flora had fit into their tiny family as seamlessly as if she had always been the missing piece of the puzzle, and Daniel couldn't imagine how they would feel if Flora left them. Just the thought of losing her sent a bolt of panic to his heart.

Charlotte was growing up. Jason and Katherine were having another baby, and Alicia Lysander, who'd been such a force of nature, was suddenly gone. Life was changing, and not in the linear way one imagined while still young and naïve, where one step was naturally followed by another, and one continued to climb the ladder of personal and professional success. Life had a design all its own, twisting and turning in unexpected directions. It was time to stop fighting that ever-shifting flow and allow the current to carry him along to whatever future life had in store for him. And now Daniel knew precisely what that future was.

He found that he was no longer ambling dejectedly down the street, his limbs weak and trembling. His step was firm, his stride was long, and his intentions were as solid as the ground beneath his feet. It took him nearly two hours to get home. He unlocked the door and walked straight into the parlor, where Flora sat in his favorite armchair, Charlotte curled up in her lap. Chalotte's dark head rested against Flora's cream-colored blouse, and her gaze was fixed on the picture in the book Flora was reading. They both looked up when Daniel walked in, as if instinctively sensing that something was about to change.

Daniel tossed aside his bowler and got down on one knee. "Florence Tarrant, will you do me the honor of becoming my wife and a mother to Charlotte?" Daniel took a quivering breath and added those three all-important words that he hadn't uttered to anyone except Charlotte in years. "I love you."

Both Flora and Charlotte instantly sat up, two pairs of wide eyes looking at him with love and hope, and Daniel knew that the die had been cast. He was stunned by his impulsive declaration. He'd never been rash, but it felt wonderful to throw off the shackles of reason and follow his heart for once. All those years of thinking things through and weighing his options hadn't kept him from getting hurt, or protected those he loved. It was time to try a different approach. Throw caution to the wind and hope for the best.

"Yes," Flora said, her eyes filling with tears. "Oh, yes! I love you too. Both of you."

"Yes," Charlotte cried, and threw herself into Daniel's arms.

And suddenly, Daniel's world was complete.

Chapter 26

The day dragged on and on. After the church service, everyone wanted a word with the Redmonds, and they spent nearly an hour discussing their life in London, catching up on local news and fielding invitations from the Chadwicks, the Talbots, and the Tarrants, who wanted to hear all about Flora and how she got on with Charlotte and Daniel. By the time Jason and Katherine finally returned to the vicarage, it was time for Sunday lunch, during which the Reverend Talbot spouted the sort of misogynistic claptrap that set Jason's teeth on edge and generally did everything in his power to belittle Katherine and make her feel like she was somehow failing both him and God.

The only person the reverend didn't criticize was Lily, who, although clearly intimidated by all the new people and her grandfather's gruffness, still managed to charm him until the reverend was all but speechless and even offered to read her a story when she woke from her afternoon nap. Lily refused the story, probably sensing in that way children had that it was going to be something unbearably grim, but allowed the reverend to take her into the garden, where they spent some time smelling the flowers.

In the late afternoon, while Katherine and Lily stayed at the vicarage to spend time with the reverend, Jason excused himself to go check on Redmond Hall. The house was closed up, with only a full-time caretaker and a part-time gardener to look after the property, but Jason had decided that it would be good for the family to spend the rest of the summer in the country and thought that perhaps he could convince Daniel to send Charlotte and Flora away as well. They weren't safe in London since, as with any illness, the number of people infected with cholera was sure to rise rapidly during the summer months. Not everyone had the luxury of leaving the city, but when Jason had a country manor to retreat to, it was the only sensible thing to do.

Jason's secondary reason for visiting Redmond Hall was so that he could confer with Joe in private and decide what they would need for their midnight jaunt. Jason could hardly roll up to the ruins of St. Mary's in his brougham and leave the conveyance unattended in some lane while he and Joe searched for the anchoress's final resting place, shovels in hand. They would need horses, a change of clothes, an oil lamp, and possibly a lookout. Jason couldn't think of a better candidate for the job than Joe's nephew, Tom, who would need permission from his father if he were to join them in what even Jason had to admit was a harebrained scheme. But it was a lead he could hardly ignore, not when the suggestion had come from Alicia herself and had expressly mentioned the anchoress of Ashburn.

Had Alicia been familiar with the story of Sigrid of Ashburn before her death? Jason wondered as he walked down the lane where he had so often met Katherine while they were courting. Had Angel been aware of the anchorite's existence? If neither woman had ever heard of Sigrid, the information would be that much more valuable, but since Jason had no way of verifying the source of the clue, all he could do was rely on his faith in Alicia and hope that Angel hadn't somehow tricked him.

Jason, Joe, and Tom met in the hall kitchen, which to Tom's great disappointment was devoid of anything edible. He asked after Micah, and Jason thought it would be nice for the two boys to spend some time together once Micah came home from school. Micah would benefit from Tom's uncomplicated company, and it had been too long since any of them had enjoyed simple country pursuits and taken time out from what had become a very hectic existence.

Once they had agreed on a plan, Jason walked back to the vicarage. He didn't foresee any trouble getting away. His father-in-law was a creature of habit and usually retired promptly at nine, unless he had an invitation dine with either the Chadwicks or the Talbots, who included the vicar in their social circle, as was common among members of the British gentry. Tonight, the Reverend Talbot didn't have any plans other than to spend the evening with his London relations. If Jason left the vicarage at eleven, he should be able to get away unobserved, even by Davy Brody, since the Red Stag, which opened on Sundays these days, closed early out of respect for the Lord. Davy's bedroom faced the rear of the building, and Moll now had a home of her own some distance away from Birch Hill and her uncle.

Joe would bring the supplies as well as the horses they would need to ride to Ashburn. He would leave the brougham at the carriage house at Redmond Hall, where they would return to wash and change before Jason sneaked back to the vicarage, hopefully unobserved. He did not relish spending the evening with his father-in-law, but to retire early would be rude and unfair to Katherine. He would just have to find a way to get through it without giving away the real reason for this impromptu visit. Perhaps he could take Katherine for a walk once Lily went to bed.

Katie would enjoy the fresh country air and a half hour of solitude, and Jason could fill her in on his plans without fear of being overheard by either the reverend or his maidservant, Lucy Timmins, who came from a neighboring farm and was sure to enjoy a nice gossip with the other village ladies after Katherine and Jason had left. He could hardly blame the woman. There was no other form of entertainment for the women of Birch Hill, who were not permitted inside the tavern and only saw one another on Sunday at church.

"I must admit," Katherine observed once they were finally alone in what used to be her bedroom at the vicarage, "this feels awfully strange. I never imagined I would be sharing my girlhood bed with a man," she said with an amused smile. "Especially an American who'd swept me off my feet with his roguish charm and whisked me away from this sleepy village."

"It is rather scandalous, isn't it?" Jason agreed as he maneuvered her toward the bed and kissed her tenderly. "And unexpectedly exciting."

"Jason, my father is next door," Katherine whispered, but didn't push him away.

"Which makes it that much more—"

Katherine cut him off with a kiss, and they tumbled onto the bed, suddenly overcome with desire. Perhaps it was being back in Birch Hill, where they had first met, or maybe it was Alicia's sudden death that had reminded them yet again how precious life was and how easily it could be snatched away. At the moment, they had it all, but exposure to a person infected with cholera, a terrible accident, or even a kinsman of someone Jason had helped send to the gallows bent on revenge could put an end to their domestic idyll and shatter the beautiful life they had built together.

Jason forced the fears from his mind and concentrated on pleasing his wife, but once Katherine finally fell asleep, the anxiety returned, and he wondered if what he was about to do was utterly mad. If discovered by a member of the earl's staff, he would have a lot of explaining to do, and possibly even face a charge of trespassing and disturbing the remains of a woman some had considered a living saint. And he would probably have to explain his actions to Rex Long, who might enjoy humiliating Jason and making comments that would besmirch his reputation.

Jason didn't give a damn for the earl's good opinion, but if he intended to remain in England and make a name for himself as a trustworthy surgeon, he had to tread carefully and avoid any unnecessary run-ins with individuals who had good reason to discredit him. If Rex Long was guilty of murder, painting Jason as some lowlife opportunist would go a long way toward his defense should the case ever come to trial, and derail Jason's plans for the future.

But it was too late to turn back now, and Jason wouldn't be able to rest until he knew what lay hidden in that lonely grave. He'd taken on better men than Rex Long, and he would see to it that he didn't come off too badly if his midnight lark came to light. Slipping out of bed, Jason dressed in baggy trousers, a linen shirt, an old coat, and a flat cap he'd found at Redmond Hall and brought back with him specifically for the purpose of digging up a grave. The clothes probably belonged to Dodson, but Jason had never seen him wear anything so casual and assumed the butler had no use for them. Careful not to disturb his sleeping wife or alert his father-in-law to the fact that he was leaving, Jason crept along the corridor and let himself out the front door.

The night beyond was clear and dark, the air sweet with the scents of grass, flowers, and pine. There was no billowing coal smoke or the odor of horseshit that had been baking in the sun since morning. Absent was the fishy stench of the Thames and the reek of wet mud that was dotted with bloated remains of fish and drowned animals who were slowly decomposing on the bank, their matted fur crawling with maggots. For a moment, Jason was transported to Newport, Rhode Island, where he'd spent several summers while at university. He could almost smell the Atlantic Ocean, and taste the lobsters and clams he'd eaten during those sunbaked days and cool New England nights. It had been a wonderful, carefree time before tragedy had turned his world upside down and somehow deposited him here, in this foreign yet welcoming place, the birthplace of his ancestors.

For the first time in a long while, Jason felt a pang of homesickness for the places he'd known and the people he'd loved. He knew he could never truly go back, and he didn't want to subject his family to an Atlantic crossing. Maybe someday he would take Katherine and Lily and the new child to New York and show them the places that had been special to him. He'd take them to Newport or Cape Cod and treat them to lobster salad and fried clams and watch from the beach as the sun dipped below the horizon. As he hurried down the lane, he tried to imagine what Daniel would make of New York and decided that he would probably find it too modern, and perhaps a little intimidating. Some people were always raring to go forward, while others preferred the comfort and safety of a life they knew and understood.

Jason's thoughts were interrupted by a low whistle, and then Joe materialized out of the darkness, the darker outline of Tom leading the horses behind him.

"Ready?" Joe asked.

Jason nodded and vaulted into the saddle. Joe gave Tom a leg up, then mounted up behind him. Just as they set off, the wispy clouds parted to reveal the sharp-edged crescent of the moon.

Chapter 27

They rode in silence, both Jason and Joe intently focused on getting to their destination as quickly as possible without alerting anyone to their presence. Galloping horses were of no consequence during the day, but at night, the urgent pounding of hooves on dry earth was sure to cause alarm since anyone within hearing distance would immediately assume that something was either terribly wrong or someone was trying to get away before they were caught.

Jason slowed to a canter once they neared Chipping Ongar, and Joe followed suit, the two men skirting the town and maintaining the slower pace until they sighted Ashburn Hall. The dark outline of the manor loomed through the trees, the house situated on a gentle rise and surrounded by vast lawns. Katherine, who'd visited Chipping Ongar and the surrounding area, had drawn Jason a crude map, providing the approximate location of St. Mary's. The church was about a quarter of a mile north of the manor, the ruin surrounded by woods, since no one had bothered to clear away the encroaching forest in the years since the building had been destroyed.

The night was full of sounds made by nocturnal creatures who went about their business despite the unwelcome presence of humans. Crickets chirped, an owl hooted, and tiny paws scratched against ancient tree trunks and half-buried stones as they scrambled through the undergrowth. There was the occasional snapping of a twig, the rustle of disturbed leaves, and the glare of eyes reflected in the moonlight. Jason turned every time he heard an unfamiliar sound, but Joe and Tom seemed to barely register the noise since they were accustomed to the rhythm of a nighttime forest.

The ruin looked eerie in the moonlight, the clouds racing across the sky and the slowly swaying branches of the nearby trees casting deep shadows on what remained of the medieval structure. The church was simple in its design, a squat stone building in the shape of a cross that was dominated by a hexagonal tower, part of which still stood and pointed at the night sky like a jagged finger. The windows had been narrow and rounded at the top, the glass long gone, and the floor within looked like some prehistoric monster had burrowed beneath it, raising the flagstones with its scaly back. Tufts of grass and broken pieces of masonry were strewn across what had once been the nave, and the thick stone walls created pockets of darkness where they hulked over the uneven ground.

Tom tied up the horses in a small clearing and sat with his back to a tree, facing the darkened manor house. He'd spot a moving light if someone was coming and alert his companions, hopefully in time for them to flee. Tom was disappointed to be left with nothing to do, but Jason explained that Tom's job was the most important of all, since he was there to save them from getting caught digging up an anchorite's final resting place. Tom wasn't convinced but didn't complain and took out the biscuits his mother had packed for him, gnawing on the corner with his front teeth.

"This must be it," Joe said as he and Jason rounded what was left of the building and peered into a rectangular opening in the western wall that was divided into six squares by an ancient iron grille.

Framing the window into the church was the crumbling outline of a cell, the walls having long since tumbled down since they had been constructed as an add-on to the original structure. Jason came closer and peered inside. The cell was no more than four by six feet, with another small opening in what remained of a side wall. Jason's breath caught in his throat, his chest tightening at the thought of spending years walled up in a stone box while simultaneously digging one's own grave. What sort of person would agree to this, especially a young woman who had her whole life before her? Was it a true calling or something infinitely more disturbing, such as a crippling fear of the world around them, or of medieval men who weren't governed by anything but their desires? Had these women hidden away to protect their fragile sanity and virtue, or had they been truly content and lived a life filled with prayer and holy communion? How old had Sigrid of Ashburn been when she was entombed in this tiny cell, and how old when she died? Had she ever regretted her decision, and was there a way back if she had?

"Is this where Sigrid is buried?" Jason asked as he stepped away from the window and paced along the outer wall of the cell, covering the distance in four strides.

The tightness in his chest refused to shift, so he looked up to the sky and took several long, steady breaths until the suffocating anxiety began to loosen its grip on his ribcage. Joe's face was tinted blue by the moonlight, his eyes dark sockets in the shadow of the ruin.

"This side faces the church, and the side walls are not long enough to accommodate a body unless she was really short. It would have to be there," Joe said, jutting his chin toward the spot where Jason was standing. "The only place to leave an open grave."

"Jesus, that's gruesome," exclaimed Tom, who'd come to investigate the cell, then immediately lowered his voice. "So, who filled in the grave, then, if there was no door?"

Joe grinned. "I expect they got some skinny lad, like you, to squeeze through the window and shovel some dirt over the poor woman."

Tom shuddered and hurried back to his post.

"Bring the shovels," Joe hissed after him.

Jason wanted nothing more than to get away from this ghoulish place with its macabre history, but they could hardly give up now.

Joe cast a practiced eye over the ground. "The last two bodies would be buried no more than three years ago."

He pulled out a box of lucifer matches from his pocket and lit one, holding it close to the earthen floor of the cell. Jason couldn't see anything that looked out of place, but Joe was a country boy who would realize the significance of things that looked quite ordinary to Jason. Joe stooped next to the border left of the outer wall and knelt inside the cell, then patted the floor with his hand, feeling the ground beneath the bracken.

"There's just earth under here. Whatever stones had fallen on this spot were moved aside recently," Joe said. "And the dirt's a bit darker."

"What does that mean, Uncle Joe?" asked Tom, who had returned with the shovels.

"It means that it could have been cleared and turned over in recent years. If there's any spot here worth investigating, it's this one right here," Joe said. "And we'd best get to it. It'll be hard going and take a long while to dig deep enough to find what we're searching for."

Jason looked toward the manor house. The windows were still dark, and the peaked roof looked black and solid against the night sky, but sounds carried on the wind, and if someone was awake, they just might hear the scraping of the shovel as it encountered buried stones or the thud of the earth as they dumped it over the side of the open grave.

"Tom, keep watch and mind the horses. And keep quiet, for God's sake," Joe said sternly. Tom nodded and melted into the darkness, trotting toward the clearing where they'd tied up the animals.

Jason would have liked to remove his snug-fitting coat. Despite the chill in the air, he was sweating, and the digging would surely make him ever warmer, but he couldn't risk someone spotting the white of his shirt. Joe wore a brown tunic over buckskin breeches and old boots. He pulled a blue kerchief from his pocket and tied it around his head to keep his hair from falling into his face and absorb the sweat from his brow. Jason wished he'd brought a kerchief as well, but the cap would have to do.

"Best if we dig by the moonlight," Joe said. "Our light would be clearly visible from the house, even if we set the lamp behind the stump of the wall."

The crescent moon gave off hardly any light, but one didn't need bright illumination to dig a hole in the ground. Joe used his shovel to push aside bracken and leaves, then, choosing a spot, drove the blade into the earth and began to dig. Jason left about three feet between them and went at it from the other side. It was extremely hard going, the rocky earth packed and crisscrossed with thick roots that had been growing unchecked for years. They worked in silence, too focused on their task to carry on a conversation. Jason's hope of finding anything waned as the hole grew deeper. It would take one man a long time to dig a proper grave, and if the earl was brazen enough to bury his wife on his land, he clearly wasn't overly worried about her remains being discovered, not when everyone thought the lady was abroad. He wouldn't have dug this far down, not unless he'd had help.

Joe stopped digging and looked at Jason, his face gleaming like a skull in the feeble moonlight. "Shall we call it a night, your lordship? I don't think there's anything here."

Jason nodded. Either Angel had passed on a message she had made up on the fly or they had the wrong spot. For all they knew,

Sigrid's remains had been moved from the cell and reburied in the graveyard, or maybe her bones rested beneath a tree or atop some hill. Perhaps her parents had claimed her body, or maybe she had been intombed inside the church. Was there a crypt? Even if there was, it would be impossible to access with all the debris that had toppled onto the floor of the church over the years. To even attempt it would be madness.

"Let's fill it back in," Jason said.

His shoulders and arms burned, and his neck was so stiff, he thought the tendons might snap. He wasn't accustomed to hours of physical labor and felt the strain in every bone and muscle in his body. All he wanted was to wash his hands and face with cool water, take off the filthy clothes, and climb into a soft, clean bed. But maybe after a good breakfast, he decided, when his stomach growled with hunger. He hadn't eaten much at dinner, put off by the fatty mutton resting atop a puddle of congealed fat. Katherine had also barely touched it, preferring to eat the soup and the vegetables that had accompanied the meal. They had become spoiled by Mrs. Dodson, whose culinary skills had reached new heights since moving to London, where she had access to the latest housekeeping manuals and the neighbors' cooks, who were happy to share their recipes when they met for tea and cake in Jason's basement kitchen.

Joe picked up a shovelful of dirt and tossed it into the gaping hole. Then another. And then he stopped.

"What is it?" Jason asked.

Joe peered into the hole, then set aside the shovel and got to his knees. He took out the box of matches and lit one, holding it as low as he could without falling in. "Have a look, sir. Is that a pebble or a…" He didn't finish the sentence but brought the light a little closer to the oddly shaped stone that protruded from the ground.

Jason jumped in and excavated the stone, holding it up to his face for a better view. It was even darker inside the grave, and Joe's match quickly flamed out, but Jason didn't need to see any more. It was enough to examine the outline with his fingers since he knew exactly what they had found. Suddenly desperate to climb out of the hole, Jason scrambled to the top and moved away from the grave, standing in a pool of moonlight. He held up the object to show Joe.

"This is a distal phalanx," he said. "A finger bone," Jason hurried to explain to Joe, who was staring at him as if he had just said something incomprehensible, which Jason supposed he had.

"How old is it?" Joe asked.

"I don't know, but unless someone lost a piece of their finger in this exact spot, there's at least one body buried down there."

Joe jumped in and began to dig, breathing heavily as it became more difficult to lift shovelfuls of dirt and toss them over the lip of the grave. Reluctantly, Jason joined him, his muscles screaming in protest as he lifted the shovel and his hands stinging where the wood of the handle scraped against the blisters that had formed on his palms. They must have gone down another two feet when Jason's shovel encountered something solid.

"Go easy, Joe," Jason said as he used the shovel to shift aside the layer of earth and squinted at the ground beneath his feet.

An earth-browned skull stared back, the eye sockets filled with dirt and the mouth open in what could have been a final scream. It was painstaking work to uncover the remains without splintering the fragile bones with the shovel, but at long last, the full skeleton emerged. Jason called to Tom to bring the lantern. There had to be clues buried along with the body. The flesh had decomposed, the fluids and what had been left of organic matter absorbed into the soil, but there had to be buttons, pieces of leather if the victim had worn shoes, and possibly even jewelry.

There were several thin sticks alongside the torso, and Jason was about to toss them aside when he realized that what he was looking at was whalebone from the victim's corset. So not Sigrid, then. He didn't know what an anchoress would have worn, but a whalebone corset was a fairly recent invention and would not have been worn in the Middle Ages.

Jason lifted out the skeleton bone by bone and laid it out on the grass, then returned to the grave and with his bare hands rooted in the earth. He hoped to find something that would definitively identify the victim. He would be able to learn more once he got the skeletal remains on the table, but he hated to leave a clue behind. It was as he pushed his hand into the ground where the feet had lain in the hope of finding what remained of the woman's footwear that his fingers closed around a bone.

"What is it, sir?" Joe asked.

"The big toe," Jason replied, and began to brush away the dirt with his hands. "There's another skeleton just underneath."

They worked in silence for what felt like hours, and by the time they finally finished, they had three skeletons lying side by side on the ground. Jason wished he could lie alongside them and take a rest, but there was no time to lose. Already the sky was lightening in the east, and the sun would shortly be up. The air had warmed, and droplets of dew quivered on the lush blades of grass that hadn't been disturbed by their efforts.

"Should we get going, sir?" Joe asked as he cast a worried look toward the manor house. The servants would be getting up soon and starting on their morning chores. And sooner or later, someone might look out the window and see two men inside the ruin, with three human skeletons laid out side by side on the other side of the cell wall.

Jason shook his head, too tired to formulate words. He had no intention of filling in the grave. As soon as the sun was up, he would send Tom to Brentwood for reinforcements, and maybe some sausage rolls. Jason was well known at the Brentwood Constabulary and was in no doubt that one of the detectives, perhaps even Chief Inspector Coleridge himself, would arrive on the scene as soon as his message was received.

Trembling with exhaustion and still sweating profusely, Jason sank to the ground, his back against the stone wall of the church as he took a gulp of water from the bottle Tom had handed him. He took off the cap, wiped his forehead with his sleeve, and watched silently as a bright dot appeared on the horizon, the rising sun turning the sky a brilliant pink as the shimmering orb ascended into the sky. The birds erupted into song, and somewhere, a rooster crowed, and despite his fatigue, Jason felt more alive than he had in ages and silently thanked Alicia for her help.

"Off with you," Joe said to Tom, who sat on his haunches, staring at the skeletons open-mouthed.

"Will you be able to tell how they died?" Tom asked Jason once Jason had given him the message Tom needed to deliver and made sure he'd memorized it.

"I hope so," Jason replied. "That all depends on the manner of death. It's impossible to tell if someone was stabbed or poisoned once the remains have skeletonized, but if there are broken bones or a bullet lodged in the skull, then the cause of death is more obvious."

"There are no bullets," Tom said, sounding disappointed.

"No, but there are other clues."

Tom looked like he had more questions, but there was no time to get into a discussion of the pathology of the deceased.

"Go on, Tom," Jason urged him. "You should get to Brentwood by the time the station opens up."

"Yes, sir," Tom replied.

Jason watched as Tom mounted up and cantered off, going slowly until he reached the road and was no longer in danger of getting his head taken off by a low-hanging branch. He quickly disappeared from view, leaving the two men to wait for his return.

Chapter 28

Monday, June 21

"I'll keep watch," Joe said. "Get some rest, your lordship."

Jason would have liked nothing more than to sleep until the policemen arrived, but first, he had to examine the remains. Now that the sun was fully up, there was enough light, and it was important that he learn as much as he could before the bones were taken away. He couldn't perform a postmortem on a skeleton, since there was no soft tissue or organs left, and it was imperative that he return to London today before the earl got wind of Jason's incursion onto his land and fled in order to avoid arrest.

Crouching next to the skeleton closest to him, Jason began his assessment, while Joe folded his coat into a makeshift pillow and curled up on the ground. He fell asleep instantly, snoring softly into the crook of his arm. Joe looked exhausted, his clothes filthy and his hands reddened with blisters, and Jason made a mental note to give him extra time off to rest once they returned to London and to compensate him generously for his help.

Jason worked slowly, mostly because his mind was sluggish and his body ached like the devil, but he also needed to make certain he didn't miss anything important. He examined each bone for nicks or damage from a bullet and evaluated every inch of the three skulls. When there was nothing more he could do, he shook Joe awake, then settled beneath a leafy tree, finally giving in to his weariness as he fell into a deep sleep.

Jason woke with a start when he heard the booming voice of Inspector Pullman, who looked happier than anyone had a right to on a Monday morning. Inspector Pullman stood next to CI Coleridge, while Constable Ingleby tried to peer from behind Sergeant Fleet, who towered over the skeletons. All four men appeared to be astounded by the discovery and were arguing about the best way to proceed. Inspector Pullman was advocating for the immediate arrest of the Earl of Ongar, while CI Coleridge was in favor of thoroughly examining the remains before jumping to conclusions and acting in haste. Like Ransome, he was concerned with the politics of the arrest and the impact the outcome might have on his career and the Brentwood Constabulary, especially if the charge turned out to be erroneous or if the accusation couldn't be proven in court.

"Well, well, well," CI Coleridge said once Jason managed to get to his feet and walk over to the knot of policemen. "If it isn't my favorite American."

"In the flesh," Jason managed to reply, but his mouth was so dry, he could barely speak.

Tom appeared from behind a tree and handed Jason a cup of water and a fresh roll. He looked alert and pleased with himself, and Jason thought he'd probably taken a nice nap in the police wagon on the way back to Chipping Ongar while the horse ambled behind the wagon. At least he'd remembered to buy something to eat and had managed to refill the water bottle.

Jason took a sip of water and sank his teeth into the bread, grateful for the sustenance.

"How do you suggest we proceed, your lordship?" CI Coleridge asked.

"I have already examined the remains, so I would ask you to load them up very carefully and remove them to the constabulary until further notice, along with the other items we have discovered inside the grave. The two modern sets of remains, which are the taller and broader skeletons, might be needed as evidence during the trial. I have set aside a number of objects that I will take back to London with me for the purpose of identification. The smaller skeleton belongs to Sigrid of Ashburn, who was an anchoress here in the Middle Ages and was buried in her cell."

"How can you be sure?" Inspector Pullman asked.

"We found nothing with her save dried-up bits of leather, which had to come from her shoes, and there was also a badly rotted wooden cross on what had to be a leather thong resting against her ribcage. She had no other jewelry or possessions, and given her diminutive size, I would say that this woman was severely malnourished in life, a deficiency that stunted her growth. Either that or she was walled in as a child and died shortly after."

"Sigrid of Ashburn was eighteen when she was walled in and died when she was twenty-one," Constable Ingleby announced. "I learned about her in school."

"Thank you, Constable," Jason said. "Good to know."

"I will arrest the Earl of Ongar if you are sure he's guilty," CI Coleridge said, returning to the matter at hand.

"The earl is currently in London, so if an arrest is made, it will have to be by Scotland Yard," Jason replied. "Which is why I must deliver the evidence to Superintendent Ransome today, before the earl gets wind of the case against him and flees the country to avoid arrest."

CI Coleridge nodded. "We will see to removing the remains. What should we do with the medieval skeleton?"

"I think perhaps she should be reburied," Jason said. "But not before the case is closed."

"As you say," CI Coleridge said. "All right, lads. Let's get these remains back to the station."

"I think we had better be going," Joe said, and pointed to three men walking toward them from the manor. Judging by his black suit, Jason thought the one leading the charge was the butler.

"We will take care of the earl's men," Inspector Pullman said, glaring at the approaching party.

Jason didn't need to be told twice. He was back in the saddle in moments, and he, Joe, and Tom set off for Birch Hill. It was going to be a long and painful ride, but despite the discomfort, Jason felt elated and couldn't wait to share his findings with Daniel.

Chapter 29

Daniel was still floating on a fluffy cloud of contentment when he set off on Monday morning. Grace had managed to find a bottle of champagne and had made a special pudding in honor of Daniel and Flora's engagement, and had even joined them at the table for once, along with Charlotte, who had been allowed to stay up late and eat with the adults. And later, once everyone had retired, Flora had slipped into Daniel's room and had kissed him soundly, giving him a taste of what to expect once they were married.

It truly had been a night to remember, and Daniel's heart drummed a cheery beat as he stepped out into the shimmering summer morning and drew in a deep breath of the dew-scented air. It was the same street in the same city populated with the same people who'd been there yesterday, but this morning, everything looked just a little bit brighter and smelled sweeter, and when Daniel set off, he was sure there was a spring in his step.

He looked forward to sharing his good news with Jason. He would ask Jason to be his best man and hoped that Jason would accept since he was the only person in Daniel's life who was worthy of the title. Both Daniel and Flora wanted to be married in Birch Hill, where they would be surrounded by family and friends and far away from the rapidly escalating contagion sweeping through London.

But as much as he wanted to spend the day with Flora and Charlotte and daydream about their wedding, he had a case to solve and couldn't afford to lose focus. And the first thing he had to do was invent an excuse to speak to Miss Crumlish in private without alerting the entire household to the fact that he needed to interview her again.

It had just gone nine o'clock by the time Daniel arrived in Grosvenor Square, but he didn't go up to the front door. Society ladies rarely left their beds before midmorning, so Crumlish would be busy with other tasks until her mistress summoned her when she woke. Daniel couldn't hang about on the off chance that Bernice Crumlish left the house. He needed a way to draw her out, but the only way he could do that was if someone passed her a note.

Daniel had prepared a short missive and put it in the pocket of his waistcoat, but the only way the note was getting to Crumlish was if

173

one of the maids gave it to her. Walking past the front door, Daniel walked the length of the house. There were no alleyways between the houses to allow him access to the back of the property, where he might approach one of the maids if she stepped outside. He could try the stables and see if one of the grooms might be willing to deliver a message, but that would look even more suspect than asking to speak to the woman outright. Bernice Crumlish might even lose her position if the housekeeper got it into her head that she was carrying on with one of the stable hands or making secret assignations with a policeman.

Daniel was still pondering his next move when a young woman with a basket over her arm came out by the tradesmen's entrance and headed toward him. She was clearly bound for the shops and would probably be gone for some time if she had a long list from the cook, but she was his only chance. Approaching her, Daniel recognized her as Sally Meeks, one of the kitchen maids he'd briefly spoken to on Friday.

"Miss Meeks," Daniel called out. "If I might have a word."

Sally balked at being called out that way, but then seemed to recognize Daniel, and the fear went out of her eyes, her shoulders relaxing marginally but not enough to signify that she would be willing to speak to him.

"Inspector Haze," Sally said, staring up at him from beneath the brim of her straw bonnet. "What are you doing here at this hour?"

"Miss Meeks, I need to speak to Bernice Crumlish, but I would rather not alert Mrs. Ascot or Mr. Jones."

"Why not?" Sally asked. She was a comely girl of about eighteen who was clearly too curious to simply accept whatever explanation Daniel offered.

"Miss Crumlish's earlier testimony has proved relevant to the case, but I would rather not single her out," Daniel explained. "I wouldn't want to jeopardize her position."

This was something Sally could understand, and she nodded sagely. "Mrs. Ascot would not look kindly on Bernice if she were working with the police."

"Would you be willing to pass on a message to her? I would rather we met discreetly, for her own sake, you understand."

"Of course," Sally said. "What shall I tell her?"

"Tell her I'll wait for her at the teahouse on the corner of Grosvenor and New Bond Streets. And please impress on her that she must be discreet."

Sally shook her head. "A teahouse is not discreet," she said, turning up her pert nose at Daniel. "Anyone might walk past, and if Mrs. Ascot hears that Bernice was meeting a man, and not on her afternoon off, she'd have her sacked right quick."

"What about by the Marble Arch?" Daniel asked.

Sally made a face. "I suppose that's better, but what if someone Bernice knows goes for a walk in the park?"

"Then she can say that I asked her for directions. No one can fault her for being polite."

"No, I suppose not," Sally replied. "All right. I'll tell her as soon as I get back. I won't be long."

Sally hurried off while Daniel strolled toward Hyde Park. It would take Sally at least an hour to get to the shops, make her purchases, and return to Grosvenor Square. And then it would take Bernice Crumlish time to get away. She might not come at all if she was worried about being seen speaking to a policeman or concerned that she might have to testify against the culprit should the case come to trial. Especially if said culprit proved to be her employer. Or Lady Cynthia might summon the maid and keep her busy for hours, leaving Daniel to wait in vain while Bernice delivered her mistress's breakfast and helped her get ready for the coming day.

Daniel looked up as he approached the Marble Arch, admiring the towering edifice. It put one in mind of a victory parade or a long-standing monument to achievement and longevity. He'd read that there were similar arches in Paris and Rome, the great cities of the world that had failed to fall despite centuries of power struggles, armed conflicts, and seismic shifts in government. Despite his appreciation of the arch, he could hardly just stand there until Miss Crumlish either came or it was time to give up and leave empty-handed.. Daniel walked on, strolling through the park for twenty minutes before turning back. He would see Miss Crumlish if she approached and would hurry to greet her, but if someone were watching, they'd think he was enjoying a morning constitutional and had run into an acquaintance.

There was no sign of the maid when Daniel reached the arch, so he turned around and walked away, this time covering half the distance before he turned back. As he approached the arch for the third time, he was gratified to see Miss Crumlish walking toward the arch, her head lowered, and her face hidden by the brim of her bonnet. She was clearly worried about being recognized, so Daniel stepped inside one of the side arches, where they were less likely to be spotted by someone Miss Crumlish knew. From a distance, they would look like any other couple seeking the deep shade of the arch to take a few moments' respite from the glaring summer sun.

Upon seeing him, Miss Crumlish walked into the arch but didn't stop. "Shall we walk?" she asked as she passed him.

Daniel had no choice but to follow her out. "I thought you might prefer the privacy of the arch."

Miss Crumlish looked up at him from beneath the brim of her bonnet. "Inspector, the very last thing I need is for someone to think that I came here for a romantic assignation. As long as we're in plain sight, no one can accuse me of doing anything improper, aside from secretly meeting a policeman, that is."

Dipping her head again so that passersby could only see the lower half of her face, she said, "I can only stay a few minutes. I told Mrs. Ascot I need new needles. She will be expecting me back within the hour."

"I'll get to the point, then," Daniel said. "Did your mother ever speak to you about her mistress?"

"My mother?" Bernice Crumlish gazed up at him again, clearly taken aback by the question. "You want to know about Lady Daphne? What does any of that matter now?"

Daniel didn't want to throw accusations around until he had proof, so he told Miss Crumlish as much as he reasonably could. "There's some suggestion that Lady Daphne's death wasn't quite natural."

"Suggestion by whom?"

"I must protect my source," Daniel said, hoping that his discretion would reassure Miss Crumlish that he would withhold her identity as well if someone were to ask him how he had come by the information she gave him.

Bernice walked in silence for a moment, then asked, her voice very quiet, "Are you suggesting that Lady Daphne was murdered?"

"There is that possibility."

"Based on what?" When Daniel failed to explain, Miss Crumlish said, "Inspector, Lady Daphne died in Italy. My poor mother with her. If what you're saying is true, then my mother…" She clearly couldn't bring herself to finish the sentence since the implications had frightened her. "No," Miss Crumlish said firmly. "It cannot be."

"Miss Crumlish, I need to rule out the possibility of foul play in order to ensure that the wrong person doesn't get the blame for Mrs. Lysander's death. Please, will you help me?"

The maid pulled her head into her shoulders, making herself look like a watchful crow. Her eyes darted from side to side, but the path was deserted, their conversation as private as it was likely to get.

"Lady Daphne was unhappy. She was bullied into marrying the earl, even though she feared him," Miss Crumlish whispered.

"Did your mother tell you anything else? Did the earl ever hurt his wife?"

"She never said anything like that."

"Why did they go abroad?"

Miss Crumlish stared down at the tips of her boots. She clearly knew something but didn't want to share it with Daniel for fear that it would get back to the earl and she would lose her position. Daniel couldn't say he blamed her. Someone like Rex Long could make sure that Miss Crumlish never worked again, setting her on a downward spiral that would inevitably end in penury and death. Helping Daniel with his inquiry could be the most dangerous thing Bernice Crumlish ever did, and it was obvious that she fully understood the risk.

"Miss Crumlish, Lady Cynthia might be in danger," Daniel said.

He felt awful for lying, but it wasn't impossible that Lady Cynthia could go the way of the earl's first wife if he was capable of violence, and Daniel had nothing else at his disposal with which to force Bernice's hand.

Bernice looked like she was going to cry. "Please, I don't want to get involved."

"I'm afraid you're already involved," Daniel said. He had no right to endanger Miss Crumlish, but neither could he allow a murderer to walk free, especially if said murderer had killed three times, as Alicia had warned Jason from beyond the grave.

"Lady Daphne was in love with another man," Bernice whispered.

"Who was he?"

Bernice bit her lip, but she had already said too much, and there was no going back. "Percy Guilford."

"Percy Guilford?" Daniel repeated. He had heard the name clearly, but he simply couldn't believe that the woman who had been described as holier-than-thou would permit herself to become involved with her husband's friend. "Did they have an affair?"

"Mum never said, but I always suspected that the reason His Grace decided to whisk his wife off to Italy was because he had realized that he had to do something to save his marriage."

Or rid himself of a wife who had betrayed him and had failed to provide him with an heir, Daniel thought.

"I have to go," Miss Crumlish whispered urgently. "Please, don't contact me again. I have said far too much already."

"Thank you," Daniel said, but Miss Crumlish didn't appear to hear him. She was already hurrying away.

Daniel checked the time. It was half past ten, and with any luck, Jason would be back in a few hours. They needed to compare notes before Daniel presented Ransome with what he thought was a plausible chain of events and requested permission to arrest the earl. Ransome would not be happy. In fact, he would probably be apoplectic since if the case against the earl fell apart, Ransome would have to eat some serious crow, but Daniel could hardly ignore the facts, or the suspects. While he waited for Jason to return, he would stop by Moore Iron Works and verify Constantine Moore's claim that he was the heir to the iron fortune, then have a word with Peter Collins, if only to rule him out.

Chapter 30

Jason nearly groaned aloud as the carriage jolted yet again, the wheels unbalanced by the ruts and depressions in the unpaved London-bound road. It would have been faster and more comfortable to take the train, but he didn't think it prudent to take public transport when traveling with a child and a pregnant wife. Both Katherine and Lily were vastly safer in the isolation of the brougham.

"You really must rest," Katherine said when she noticed his discomfort.

Jason's shoulders burned, his back ached, and his hands were covered with blisters that had burst and were now oozing sticky serum. His head tolled like a bell, and his eyelids felt so heavy, he thought he'd never be able to keep his eyes open for too long again. He was starving, since he hadn't had anything to eat since the sausage roll, and he would sell his tired soul for a pot of black coffee. The interior of the carriage was hot and stuffy, but to open the windows would allow in the dust kicked up the horses' hooves and the less-than-pleasant smells of the herds that seemed to graze ominously close to the road.

The pain and discomfort were well worth it, though. The evidence he and Joe had uncovered wasn't conclusive, but it went a long way toward filling in the blanks. The remains would be kept at the Brentwood police station until further notice, but Jason was satisfied with his examination and the conclusions he had drawn from the deceased and the physical evidence he and Joe had found buried with the bodies.

Eager as he was to confer with Daniel, Jason intended to take a long, hot bath, then enjoy a good meal followed by a quick nap. His stomach growled in support of this decision, and Katherine reached out and wrapped her fingers about his hand, her other arm around Lily, who had been lulled to sleep by the swaying of the carriage and appeared to be the only one who was content with her current situation. Katherine was pale, a sheen of sweat glistening on her forehead and upper lip. Jason thought she was probably suffering from motion sickness, but there wasn't too much he could do short of asking Joe to stop the carriage near a stretch of woods so that Katherine could rest in the shady freshness of the forest until the nausea passed. When he suggested as much, Katherine refused, saying that she would much rather get home as quickly as possible. Jason was in agreement. There was no point in prolonging the uncomfortable journey since the nausea would probably return as soon as they were moving again.

Jason's plans for a restful afternoon fell apart the moment he and Katherine walked through the door. The foyer smelled of cake and freshly brewed coffee, and unless Mrs. Dodson had turned clairvoyant overnight, they were about to come face to face with a coffee-loving visitor. Katherine took Lily upstairs while Jason followed the aroma to the drawing room. Daniel, who looked wonderfully comfortable, was enjoying a cup of coffee and one of Mrs. Dodson's jam tarts.

"Any more coffee in that pot?" Jason asked as he sank into a chair with an immense sigh of relief.

"I'll have Fanny bring a fresh pot and some sandwiches," Dodson announced from the doorway.

"Thank you, Dodson," Jason said.

The hot bath would have to wait, but at least he wouldn't go hungry or fall asleep mid-sentence.

"You look exhausted," Daniel said for the second time that week.

"I think I'm beginning to feel my age," Jason replied as he tried to get more comfortable.

"Did you discover anything?"

"Joe and I unearthed three sets of human remains."

"Good God," Daniel cried. "Were you able to identify them?"

"The remains were fully skeletonized, but we were able to recover enough evidence from the grave to hopefully identify the victims. The uppermost body was of a middle-aged woman who died in much the same way as Alicia. Blunt force trauma to the back of the head. She either died right away or was buried alive while she was unconscious."

"Blimey," Daniel muttered, obviously horrified by the prospect.

And who wouldn't be? Jason couldn't think of a worse way to go than being buried alive, and he'd encountered all manner of death in the past decade. After all this time, it was impossible to tell if Anne Crumlish had ever come to and tried to dig her way out, and Jason thought it was better not to know.

"What about the other two?" Daniel asked eagerly.

"The skeleton in between was that of a young woman. There were some strands of fair hair clinging to the scalp, and her betrothal and wedding rings were still on her finger. I expect those would be easily recognizable to people who knew her. There was also another small skeleton located between the pelvis and ribcage. I'd say the victim was about four months pregnant at the time of her death."

Jason would have preferred to forget the sight of that tiny skull and the delicate bones of the ribcage. He supposed it was a blessing that the child had died in utero and would not have felt any pain, but it still broke his heart, especially when his own tiny baby's heart now beat inside Katherine's womb, and he could already imagine cradling the child in his arms.

"How did she die?" Daniel asked.

"Fractured skull."

"So that's three women who were murdered in the same way."

"Yes. I would be greatly surprised if the victims weren't Anne Crumlish and Daphne Long, given that they were buried on the earl's estate, and the two women were never seen again after they supposedly traveled abroad."

"And the third victim?" Daniel inquired.

"The third female skeleton has to be Sigrid of Ashburn, the anchoress who lived in a cell built onto the wall of St. Mary's church. She would have died in the fourteenth century and been buried inside her cell. I didn't see any obvious cause of death, but I did notice multiple historic fractures, and the bones and teeth showed clear signs of malnutrition. Perhaps the poor woman had volunteered to be walled in alive to escape a life that had become unbearable. She couldn't go out, but neither could anyone come in. She was safe from whoever had hurt her."

"Walled in alive," Daniel said quietly. "I can't even begin to imagine what that must have been like."

"I imagined it all too well while I was there," Jason replied, and felt that awful tightness in his chest again.

His anxiety was alleviated by the welcome sight of Fanny, who brought in a heavily laden tray and set the contents on the table. There was coffee, cream and sugar, several cheese sandwiches, and a plate of warm jam tarts.

"According to Bernice Crumlish, Daphne Long was in love with Percy Guilford," Daniel said triumphantly once Jason had made himself a cup of coffee and bitten into a sandwich. "Which gives the earl a very solid motive indeed."

"Yes, it does," Jason agreed once he'd swallowed, "especially if the child was Guilford's."

"So, the earl and his lady were about to leave for their Italian holiday when something happened. Perhaps he found out that his wife had been unfaithful, or she confessed that the child she carried wasn't his. Passions flared, and Rex Long murdered his wife in the heat of the moment," Daniel said. "Anne Crumlish had to die if the earl intended to tell everyone that his wife died while abroad."

"That fits with what we know, but the two men are still friends, and Long's sister is married to the man who allegedly stole Long's wife," Jason pointed out.

"Is it possible that Long never knew who his wife's lover was?" Daniel asked. "I suppose that would explain how Long and Guilford remained friends, but how did the earl explain the fact that no one saw the two women leave?"

"Perhaps he told everyone that Daphne and her lady's maid had gone ahead while he followed with their luggage. And then came the news that they had died abroad. The earl returned to England, completed his period of mourning, and found a new wife," Jason replied.

"I think we have sufficient evidence to make a case against Rex Long," Daniel said. "And as of now, we really don't have any other suspects. It turns out that Constantine Moore is an heir to a great fortune. He's the son of Atticus Moore of Moore Iron Works."

"Is he really?" Jason exclaimed. "And what about Peter Collins?"

"Peter Collins had opportunity, since he was out on Thursday night and didn't get home until after ten o'clock, but after speaking to the Collinses, I don't believe they knew anything about Alicia's doubts concerning the child. Also, Peter Collins is about a head shorter than I am, which would have made it nearly impossible for him to hit Alicia over the head unless he managed to drop something heavy from above. Even if he knew where Alicia would be on Thursday evening, he had no way of knowing that the séance would finish early or that she wouldn't wait for Constantine and would go wandering about in the dark. He would have had to find an elevated place and a murder weapon and hope that Alicia passed directly beneath him in order to execute his plan. Seems unlikely. And from what I could tell, Angel Flyte didn't have a compelling reason to want Alicia dead."

"Given what Joe and I discovered, I think it's time we spoke to Rex Long."

Daniel sighed heavily. "And now I have to break the news to Ransome."

"Would you like me to come with you? I think my testimony will add weight to the accusations against the earl."

"Please," Daniel said.

"Give me half an hour to wash and change."

"Take as long as you need," Daniel replied generously, and reached for a jam tart. "I'll be right here."

Chapter 31

Ransome's expression remained inscrutable as he listened carefully to Jason and Daniel's account, his gaze straying to the jewelry that had been recovered from the grave. The newly cleaned rings, earbobs, and a silver locket that must have belonged to Anne Crumlish shone in the soft afternoon light and silently condemned the man who'd killed their owners. The necklace was simple, the flower-engraved oval locket the size of a large almond. The rings, however, were unique. Now that the dirt had been washed away and the design exposed, it was easy to see that they were probably very valuable and one of a kind.

The engagement ring was crafted of white gold or platinum, and the setting was in the shape of an eight-point star. Each of the eight sections was set with two diamonds and divided by elongated baguettes, the pattern fanning out from a halo of tiny diamonds that encircled the round brilliant at the center. The wedding ring was made of the same metal and came in two sections that were meant to fit around the engagement ring, adding an extra layer of tiny diamonds on each side of the band.

Ransome reached for the necklace and carefully opened the locket, staring at the photographs within. They were miraculously preserved, since no air or moisture had been able to breach the seal.

"Any idea who they are?" Ransome asked.

"Bernice Crumlish, and the man must be her father," Daniel said. He'd already seen the photographs and had identified the young girl as Bernice. "And the rings and earrings must belong to Lady Daphne."

"I want these positively identified. It shouldn't be too difficult to prove ownership given the distinctiveness of the design," Ransome said. "We can't afford to blunder on this one," he added once he'd set the items back on the table. He looked from Daniel to Jason. "Who would be best placed to help us?"

"Lady Daphne's parents," Daniel said, but Jason shook his head.

"It would cause them great pain to learn that their daughter was murdered, quite possibly by her husband," Jason said. "I think we should refrain from speaking to them until we're certain."

"I agree," Ransome said. "Who else is there?"

"Lady Daphne had a younger sister," Jason said, recalling what Lady Amelia had said about Imogen Salter. "The two had a close relationship."

"Do we know the sister's whereabouts?" Ransome asked.

"She is married to Lord Salter," Jason replied.

"Is she, indeed?" Ransome asked, seeming surprised. "Salter is one of Sir David's cronies. They meet at the Carlton Club. Salter must be considerably older than his wife," he mused. "He is of an age with my father-in-law."

"Lady Amelia did say the lady was pragmatic," Daniel said.

Ransome nodded. "Lord Salter is highly influential, but he prefers to operate behind the scenes. I have never met his wife, but I have heard that she's a force to be reckoned with."

Ransome replaced the rings and earrings in the linen pouch they had been stored in and handed it to Jason. "Let's see if we can get Lady Salter to confirm that these belonged to her sister. I will hold on to the locket for now. No sense drawing attention to Bernice Crumlish until we're sure about the rest."

"That's very considerate of you," Jason said, and Ransome inclined his head in acknowledgment. They needed to tread carefully before they turned Bernice Crumlish's life upside down.

Ransome pulled out his pocket watch and checked the time. It had to be nearly five o'clock. "Shall we reconvene tomorrow, gentlemen?"

"Of course, sir," Daniel said.

"Get some rest, Jason," Ransome said, his lips twitching as he tried to suppress a smile. "Never took you for a grave robber, but then your hidden talents never cease to surprise me."

Jason grinned and rolled his shoulders. "I don't think I'll be making a career of it, John. I hurt in places I didn't know I had."

Ransome grinned. "Goodnight, lads," he said, resorting to the kind of familiarity he normally avoided. "And well done."

Chapter 32

It was too late in the day to pay social calls, but it was the perfect time to find members of the upper crust at home. Having finished with the social obligations for the afternoon, they would be resting before dinner or preparing to go out if some sort of evening entertainment had been planned. Despite the quickly multiplying cases of cholera, the nobility behaved as if the spreading contagion had nothing to do with them and continued to socialize with those who were still in residence, although an increasing number of families were migrating to their country estates to escape the heat and the pestilence. The lower orders, who had nowhere to go, toiled on and armed themselves with hope and prayer, which did little to keep them safe in the face of a possible epidemic.

Some things never changed, Jason reflected as he approached the imposing Mayfair home of Lord Salter and his lady. If the wealthy could pay the poor to die for them, the poor would be making a good living. Another thing that didn't alter was that one had to breach the defenses of faithful underlings to get to the lords of the manor, and the Salters' butler was no different than most men of his ilk, who would sooner die than permit their master to be accosted by members of the police service. Therefore, Jason and Daniel had decided that Jason would call on the Salters on his own while Daniel waited for him in a nearby square.

"Forgive me, my lord, but their lordships are no longer receiving," the butler said, fixing Jason with a look that clearly said, *If you had any breeding, you'd know this.* "But do come back tomorrow. They will be at home to callers during the usual visiting hours."

Jason wasn't about to wait until Tuesday afternoon and then risk having to share his brief audience with Imogen Salter with other callers. He intended to speak to her this evening, and in private.

"This is not a social call, Mr—?"

"Lintern," the butler intoned.

"If you would be so kind as to inform your mistress that this is a matter of some urgency and extreme delicacy. It pertains to her sister, Lady Daphne."

Lintern's bushy eyebrows lifted in astonishment, but he tried to deter Jason once again. "Her ladyship is indisposed."

"Then lucky for her, I'm a doctor," Jason replied. "Announce me this minute or I will do it myself."

Utterly scandalized by such blatant breach of protocol, Lintern finally stepped aside and permitted Jason to step into the foyer, which was nearly as large as Jason's drawing room and put him in mind of a Grecian temple. Lintern disappeared, then came back looking smug, which could mean only one thing. He had tittle-tattled to Lord Salter and was awaiting reinforcements. The man himself appeared not two minutes later, clad in shirtsleeves and too red in the face for Jason not to feel professional concern.

"How dare you?" Lord Salter ground out. "You think you can use intimidation tactics to push past my butler and try to terrify my wife? Her sister is dead, so whatever it was you have come to say, say it to me and be gone from my presence before I have you thrown out."

Lord Salter had to be in his fifties, and although he looked fit and could still be described as imposing, if not handsome, he was not a man who could evict Jason on his own. Nor could he deter Jason from his mission.

"Forgive the intrusion, my lord," Jason said with as much deference as he could muster. "It is not my intention to either intimidate or terrify, but new information has come to light regarding Lady Daphne's death, and it's imperative that I speak to Lady Salter as soon as possible."

"I've heard about you," Lord Salter said, his eyes narrowing with suspicion. "You're that American muckraker who involves himself in the kind of sordid filth no self-respecting Englishman would care to touch."

"My position with the police service is authorized by Sir David Hawkins, who is a friend of yours, I believe. It is his willingness to involve himself in the kind of sordid filth no self-respecting Englishman would care to touch that has made this city safer than it has been in decades, and the only way he can do that is with the assistance of individuals who are not afraid to get their hands dirty, as I have done when I excavated what I believe to be your sister-in-law's grave."

"Daphne is buried in Italy," Lord Salter snapped, but Jason could see that he was as intrigued as he was peeved. "And what does Daphne's death have to do with you?"

"As I explained to your butler, I am a doctor, and I have just today examined the remains of a woman I believe to be Lady Daphne."

"And what is this belief based on?"

Jason pulled the linen pouch from his pocket and shook the two rings into his palm, then held them out to Lord Salter, who blanched and took a hasty step back.

"Where did you get these?"

"From the skeletal finger of the woman I believe to be Daphne Long. Do you recognize this ring?"

Salter nodded. "Come in," he said gruffly. "Lintern, ask Lady Salter to join us."

Lord Salter didn't apologize for his rudeness, nor did he ask a parlormaid who'd skittered past to take Jason's things, letting him know in no uncertain terms that he wouldn't be staying long. He led Jason into the drawing room, which was decorated entirely in white and gold. The room was airy and light and the décor unexpectedly modern while also antique in its appearance. The interior was like something out of a Roman villa or marble temple. Jason was invited to sit on the white settee, while Lord Salter took up a position by the fireplace, resting his elbow on the mantel and crossing his legs as if posing for a painting.

Imogen Salter looked apprehensive when she walked in, escorted by Lintern. She was half her husband's age and not the sort of woman others would call beautiful, but her gray gaze betrayed her intelligence, and she had a soft mouth, the kind that probably smiled often. Her patrician nose and razor-sharp cheekbones gave her face a rather harsh cast, and the frilly dressing gown she wore did little to hide a body that was too thin to be considered alluring.

"What is it? What's happened?" she asked, looking to her husband to explain.

"My dear, this is Lord Redmond. He has discovered something rather upsetting and would like to talk to you about it."

Lady Salter gave Jason a tentative smile. "Are you married to Katherine Redmond?"

"I am, my lady," Jason said.

"She's a lovely person, and she speaks reverently of you."

Jason smiled. In a world where many women barely tolerated their husbands, to be spoken of reverently was quite a compliment. "She had only good things to say about you as well."

"What is it that you have found?" Lady Imogen asked.

Jason took out the rings he'd put back in his pocket and held them out to Imogen, who gasped at the sight of the engagement ring.

"But these are Daphne's," she cried. "How do you come to have them?"

"I'm deeply sorry to cause you upset, my lady," Jason said, "but I recovered these from an unmarked grave on the Earl of Ongar's estate. There was another body buried on top, who I believe was your sister's lady's maid, Anne Crumlish."

"No," Imogen cried, her anguish heartbreaking to behold. "No, it can't be. Daphne died in Italy. Rex told us so."

"I believe your sister was murdered, and all the evidence points to her husband."

"But why? Why would Rex kill Daphne? He was mad for her."

"Perhaps that's why," Lord Salter interjected. "He could no longer bear her rejection."

"Will you tell me about your sister's relationship with her husband?" Jason asked softly. "Is it possible that she was in love with someone else?"

"Someone else?" Imogen stared at him, uncomprehending. "Like whom?"

"Percy Guilford was mentioned in connection with your sister," Jason replied.

"Mentioned by whom? Daphne regarded Percy as a friend, nothing more. Where would you get such tosh?"

Jason hated to point out the obvious, but this was his one chance to speak to someone who'd known Daphne intimately, so Imogen's feelings had to come second.

"From what I can tell, Daphne died from a blow to the head that was forceful enough to fracture her skull."

Imogen winced and her eyes brimmed with tears, but she didn't interrupt.

"Her husband lied about how she died and where she's buried. That alone is suspicious enough to cast doubt on his innocence. If we are to charge him with murder, we need to understand why he would assault his wife and then kill her maid to cover up his crime."

Tears slid down Imogen's gaunt cheeks, and her husband handed her his handkerchief, which she used to dab at her eyes and blow her nose.

"Daphne never liked Rex. She found him threatening," Imogen said once she felt composed enough to speak.

"Threatening how?"

Imogen shot a look at her husband, then replied, her voice firm, "Sexually. Daphne was repulsed by that side of marriage and wanted no part of it. She dreamed of joining a religious order, where she could devote her life to prayer and good works."

"But your father forced the marriage," Jason said.

Imogen nodded. "Rex was in love with Daphne, and I think he genuinely tried to make her happy, but Daphne rebuffed him at every turn. She closed her heart to him, as well as her body."

"My dear," Lord Salter interrupted, but Imogen held up her hand.

"Lord Redmond needs to know the truth. And I need to see my sister's killer punished." She turned back to Jason. "I'm not making excuses for Rex's behavior. He was unhappy, yes, but that doesn't justify what he did. Not by a long shot."

"Is it at all possible that Daphne had found a soulmate in Percival Guilford?"

Imogen shook her head. "Percy admired Daphne. He made no secret that he thought her beautiful. He compared her to Venus and Aphrodite and suggested that Rex have her sit for a portrait dressed as some mythical goddess, but Percy was always a charmer. He would never cuckhold Rex, even if Daphne was willing." Imogen smiled sadly. "In fact, Percy always had his eye on Jane Long, but after Daphne died, he had to wait to propose until the mourning period was over. They have only just recently married."

Imogen blew her nose again, then met Jason's eyes with her tearful gaze. "Where was she buried?"

"With Sigrid of Ashburn," Jason said. "All three bodies were within the cell."

Imogen nodded. "She would have liked that. Daphne admired Sigrid. She always said that if times were different, she would have liked to become an anchoress. I told her she was mad, and the life of an anchoress was worse than death, but she just smiled in that way she had and said that I could never understand true faith and devotion to God."

Imogen chuckled softly. "She was right. I never could, and I still don't. I always wanted to live, to explore, to travel to new places and meet new people, but Daphne wanted only to be left alone. The thought of having a child terrified her, especially after their firstborn died so horribly. She couldn't bear it."

"I'm sorry to tell you, but Daphne was with child when she died."

Imogen Salter looked shocked. "Was she really? She never told me she was expecting. Perhaps she wanted to pretend it wasn't happening. How far along was she?"

"About four months," Jason said.

Imogen nodded sadly. "Another innocent life lost. You said Daphne was buried inside the anchorite's cell," she said, her gaze thoughtful. "I suppose that means she was buried in consecrated ground. I hope Daphne and her baby are both in heaven. May they rest in peace."

"Amen," Lord Salter said with feeling. "Will you charge Rex with Daphne's murder?"

"We still don't have a clear motive, but yes. Given his lies, he had to have killed her."

"Thank you," Imogen said. "Thank you for searching for the truth. I know it won't bring my sister back, but it will help me and my parents to rest easier knowing that her killer no longer walks among us."

Imogen looked up at Jason as he stood to leave. "May I keep Daphne's things?"

"For now, they are still evidence, but once the case is closed, I will ask Superintendent Ransome if the rings can be returned to your family instead of to the earl."

"I appreciate that. Darling, please send our apologies. I can't go to Lady Earnshaw's supper tonight," Imogen told her husband as soon as Jason walked through the door.

"Of course, my dear. I quite understand," Lord Salter said soothingly.

Lintern cast an apologetic look in Jason's direction as he approached the front door. "Please accept my apologies, my lord. My behavior was unforgivable."

"You were only doing your job," Jason replied, and walked out into the lavender twilight.

It was too late to do anything more that evening, so Jason and Daniel wished each other a good night and parted company. Tomorrow, they would arrest the Earl of Ongar and charge him with murder. Tonight, they would spend time with their loved ones, grateful that they were safe and well.

Chapter 33

Tuesday, June 22

If it were up to Daniel, he would have rolled up to the earl's door in a police wagon, clapped the man in irons, and had two constables lead him out in full view of his neighbors, but Ransome had decided on a less conspicuous approach. The feelings of the aristocracy had to be protected, after all, and Ransome had to be shielded from blame should the accusation prove false, and the earl manage to talk his way out of a charge of murder. And it was because they couldn't go in trumpets blaring that they had to cool their heels until such a time as the earl was finally up and about and was dressed, had breakfasted, and was ready for the journey to Scotland Yard.

Daniel felt much as he imagined a caged tiger would, but Jason looked calm and well rested. Daniel had yet to tell him about his meeting with Angel and the message he had received from Sarah but couldn't seem to find the right moment to bring his personal life into the conversation. He wanted to share his happy news, but he owed it to Jason to tell him the whole truth of what had brought about his decision to propose to Flora and didn't want to have that conversation at Scotland Yard. It would have to wait until Rex Long had been charged and taken to the cells to await transport to prison.

An invisible rush seemed to pass through the duty room as the earl walked in, followed by Sergeant Meadows and Constable Putney, who had been dispatched to collect him. The earl was not cuffed, his right hand loosely closed about the ornate handle of his walking stick. He was dressed to the nines, his shiny top hat worn at a rakish angle, revealing one arched eyebrow. The earl's cleanly shaven face broke into a smile when he saw Jason, who waited to escort him to an interview room. Daniel had just stepped inside but witnessed the exchange through the open door and fervently hoped the earl would not use the walking stick as a weapon. It was sturdy enough to do serious damage if wielded like a club.

"Lord Redmond," Rex Long said jovially. "We meet again."

"Indeed, we do, Your Grace," Jason replied politely.

"I do wish it was under more pleasant circumstances," Long said. "Perhaps you can join me for supper at my club one of these days, or do you prefer to dine with your wife every night? Is that an American custom?"

"I'm not one for following customs, Your Grace," Jason replied smoothly. "Or revere men with titles."

"Very democratic of you, *my lord*," Rex Long drawled. "Do what suits one's needs at the moment, eh?"

"Something like that." Jason held out his hand. "If you have no objection, I will hold on to your walking stick until we're finished."

"If you feel it necessary," Long said dismissively. He handed the stick to Jason, then removed his hat and tossed it to him, as if Jason were his butler.

Jason deftly caught the hat and showed the earl into the room, where he hung the hat on the coat rack and dropped the walking stick into a stand in the corner. Rex Long took a seat across from Daniel and leaned back, surveying Daniel as if he were the one who'd been brought in for questioning. The amusement in Long's eyes and the twitching of his lips made Daniel want to slap the insolence from the man's smug face, but until he could prove Long's guilt, Daniel had to treat the earl with the respect due his rank.

Jason closed the door, effectively shutting out extraneous noise as well as John Ransome's in-person involvement in the interview. Ransome was desperate for news but would not confront the earl until he was sure of the man's guilt and could swoop in and take the credit for a successful solve that he would tout to the papers until his name was on the front page of every daily publication.

"Why am I here?" Rex Long asked, directing his question to Jason as if Daniel wasn't even in the room. "You have no evidence that proves I killed that psychic, so what's this all about?"

Daniel couldn't help but wonder if the earl was aware of the excavation that had taken place on his land only the day before. Was it possible that the staff had decided not to inform him of the remains that had been discovered, or was the earl simply trying to brazen it out?

"Are you certain we don't have proof?" Jason asked.

"I am. Because I didn't kill her," Long replied, his tone laced with exaggerated patience.

"But you have killed before," Jason said.

He reached into his pocket and withdrew the rings Imogen Salter had identified, setting them on the table and carefully watching Rex Long's reaction. The earl looked shaken, his earlier bravado dissipating like morning mist as the magnitude of his predicament seemed to finally sink in. He went white to the roots of his hair, then reached out and picked up the engagement ring, staring at the beautiful object that had the power to destroy him.

"Where did you find this?" Long asked hoarsely.

"Where do you think?" Daniel exclaimed, tired of being ignored and desperate to get to the crux of the matter. "I can promise you we didn't travel to Venice to dig up her ladyship's nonexistent grave, Your Grace," he added sarcastically.

The earl's penitent gaze and slack mouth told their own story. When he didn't deign to respond, Jason said, "These items were recovered from a mass grave on your estate. Lady Salter has positively identified these rings as belonging to her sister, Lady Daphne, who you claim died and was buried in Italy. I have no doubt that the locket that still hung around the neck of the other victim belonged to Anne Crumlish, Lady Daphne's lady's maid. We will ask her daughter to identify it before the locket is entered into evidence for the purposes of the trial."

Rex nodded slowly, his gaze glued to the two rings that lay innocently on the scarred wooden table. The interview seemingly at an end, Daniel stood and faced the earl. Daniel held his head high and pulled his shoulders back, as if he were going into battle, which in some respects he was. Once he uttered the words, there would be no going back.

"Rex Long, I hereby charge you with three counts of murder, as contrary to common law. You will be taken to Newgate Prison, where you will await trial. If found guilty, you will be taken to a place of execution, where you will be hanged."

Long didn't appear too impressed with Daniel's speech. "Sit down, Inspector," he said in a tone so patronizing, it set Daniel's teeth on edge. Daniel wanted to refuse, but Rex Long was innocent in the eyes of the law until he was proven guilty, and Daniel was duty-bound to hear the man out, if only to refute his claims.

Once Daniel was seated, Long said, "I did not kill my wife. Nor did I murder Anne Crumlish or Alicia Lysander."

"Then how do you explain the unmarked grave on your property or the lie you have been perpetuating since your wife's disappearance?" Daniel demanded.

Long took a while to answer, but once he began to speak, his voice was low and measured, and his gaze was fixed on Jason, once again reminding Daniel that he occupied the lowest position on the social register.

"My mother, God rest her soul, warned me not to marry a woman who didn't love me," Long said. "So did my sister, Amelia, but I was young and if not in love, then in lust with Daphne Burrows. I would have her, and no amount of warnings were going to stop me. I was certain that once Daphne was finally mine, I could make her love me. I was wrong," Long added after a dramatic pause. "Daphne wasn't ready to be a wife to any man, but she especially loathed me."

The earl looked down for a moment, and Daniel thought he was genuinely distraught and not just playing the part of the rejected lover.

"Did your wife tell you that?" Jason asked.

"Not in so many words," Long replied. All his aplomb had vanished, and he looked like a sad, dejected man, who couldn't quite figure out how he had ended up being questioned in connection with his wife's brutal murder. "Daphne refused to let me near her. She cried and begged me to leave her be. My wife was still a virgin when we returned from our wedding trip."

Daniel was shocked by Long's confession, but Jason's nod told him that Jason had suspected as much.

"Please, go on," Jason invited. "We want to hear your side."

Rex Long cast a dubious look in Jason's direction, but at this point, he had little choice but to continue. "After nearly six months of marriage, I was so angry and frustrated, I resorted to consummating the marriage by force and then continued to assert my husbandly rights until Daphne got with child. I was overjoyed. I thought an heir would make her face up to her responsibilities as my wife and the child's mother, but as I'm sure you already know, our son died. Daphne became convinced that God had punished her for her supposed impurity and locked me out of the bedroom. The only person she trusted was Anne Crumlish, who, although a woman of the world, had to support her mistress if she hoped to keep her job. I didn't blame her," Long said with a shrug. "I had it from Mrs. Ascot that Crumlish had her own child to support, which was an unusual arrangement for a lady's maid, but since her daughter was happy to work as an upstairs maid, there was no reason to refuse Crumlish the job."

"So, what happened?" Daniel asked, eager to get to Lady Daphne's death.

Rex Long sighed heavily. "Percy Guilford returned from Greece, where he had been carousing for the better part of a year. I invited him to stay at Ashburn Hall for a few days, and the die was cast."

"You knew," Daniel said, surprised that Long would admit to the affair, but he supposed it was futile to claim ignorance when his wife had been buried within a stone's throw from the manor house.

"I did. Daphne wasn't able to love me, but after she spent a few days with Percy, all that blather about living a life of purity died on her lips. To be frank, I didn't think my dearest friend would betray me, but Percy could never resist the lure of a beautiful woman, especially one who wanted no other man but him. I turned a blind eye to their affair. I thought that once Percy tired of Daphne, she might turn to me for solace, and I was right."

The earl shook his head in what had to be disbelief when he recalled that time in his life. "Daphne was heartbroken when Percy broke things off. She was so despondent, she agreed to a holiday in Italy. I thought it might be easier to try to fix the problems in our marriage without the added pressure of endless social engagements and prying questions from our families," Rex Long said. "And I wanted a son," he confessed, his abject misery there for them to see. "I am the last of my line, and I long for an heir. I won't deny that. That's why I married again as soon as it was decent. Cynthia is nothing like Daphne," Long said with a heartfelt smile. "She loves me."

"How long was it between the time Percy Guilford broke things off with Lady Daphne and your planned departure for Italy?" Jason asked.

Long appeared surprised by the question but answered without hesitation. "Nearly six months. It took some time to plan, and we wanted to go in the summer."

"What ultimately went wrong?" Jason asked diplomatically.

Daniel would have phrased the question more bluntly. He saw no reason to consider the man's feelings when three women were dead, but he had to defer to Jason, who seemed to inspire the earl's trust despite his role in the man's arrest.

"Percy came to see us off. In retrospect, allowing him to come was a dreadful mistake, but at the time, I thought it might be good for Daphne to see him one last time before we left and say a final goodbye. The two went for a walk after dinner and wound up by the ruin. They argued. Things became heated, and when Daphne came at Percy, he pushed her away. Daphne hit her head on a jagged stone," Long explained. "It was a terrible accident. Percy never meant to kill her."

Jason and Daniel exchanged looks, but it was Jason who voiced the question they both needed answered.

"If Daphne died as a result of an accident, why did you murder her maid and bury them both on your estate?"

Rex Long shook his head and met Jason's inquisitive gaze with a look that bordered on sincere. "It wasn't premeditated, Jason. Crumlish went to look for her mistress and found Percy weeping over her body. She began to scream and threatened to fetch the village constable. Percy lost control."

"That still doesn't explain why you claimed they died in Italy," Jason pointed out.

"Percy came to find me and explained what had happened. Daphne and Anne were already dead. There was no bringing them back, and I didn't think either Percy or I could survive the scandal or the revelations that would follow. We buried Daphne in a place she believed to be holy, next to a woman she had greatly admired, and then I told everyone that Daphne and Crumlish had gone on ahead with Percy, and I would meet them in time to board the steamer." Long sighed and continued, "If members of my staff didn't believe me, they chose to keep their suspicions to themselves, since there was little to gain by questioning my explanation. As we all know, people are motivated by self-interest, and losing their positions would have hurt them immeasurably." Long paused for a moment, then went on. "I had my coachman take me to the port, along with our luggage, and sailed away. I spent a month in Italy, where I took the time to grieve for Daphne and come to terms with my new life. When I returned, I told everyone that Daphne and Crumlish had died and were buried at Il Cimitero di San Michele."

Jason cocked his head to the side and studied Rex Long with an expression of barely contained disbelief.

"If I understood you correctly, Your Grace," he said, "you not only forgave Percy Guilford for killing your pregnant wife and helped him to bury her and her maidservant in an unmarked grave, but you then permitted a man who'd already killed twice to marry your sister."

Long looked like he'd been struck by a thunderbolt, his face twisting into a grimace of excruciating pain. "Daphne was with child?" he rasped.

"She was. About four months," Jason replied. "And according to you, that child was yours, not Percy's, since Daphne became pregnant about two months after they parted ways."

"Was it a boy?" Long whispered. His skin had turned a sickly shade of green, and he looked like he might be ill.

"It's impossible to say since the soft tissue has fully decomposed, but it might have been," Jason added cruelly. "Fifty-fifty chance."

"No," Long moaned, his eyes swimming with tears. "No. I had no idea Daphne was with child."

"Odd that she wouldn't tell you," Daniel commented, driving the knife in a little deeper.

Rex Long turned away then, staring at the wall behind him until he felt able to resume the interview. When he met Daniel's gaze, his eyes were hard, his hands clenched into fists on the tabletop. The situation had changed drastically for this man who had thought himself untouchable when he had first arrived, and they all knew it.

"Your late wife, whose spirit clearly couldn't rest, came through during the séance," Jason said. He was watching the earl intently, presumably searching for signs of guilt. "It upset your wife, who I presume knows nothing of what really happened but hadn't expected to be confronted by her predecessor, but it must have terrified you and Percival Guilford. Alicia Lysander had opened a Pandora's box neither of you could shut, and Alicia Lysander now knew enough to dig deeper until she uncovered the truth. She could go to the authorities with her tale or resort to blackmail and milk you for years to come. She had to die, and quickly, before she had a chance to tell anyone else what she had learned."

"I helped to cover up the murders of Daphne and Anne Crumlish, but I did not kill Alicia Lysander."

"There's only one other person who could have," Daniel chimed in. "And I need to hear you say it."

Rex Long nodded resignedly. "Once Daphne came through, Percy had no choice. I could see in Mrs. Lysander's eyes that she was frightened, and offered her the use of my carriage, but she refused. She wanted to leave as soon as possible and was willing to take her chances. I expect she thought she would meet up with Mr. Moore, but he was late, so she continued home on her own. That was her mistake. Had she remained, she would have been safe, at least for that night. But I'm sure Percy would have found a way to silence her eventually."

"Did Lord Guilford leave the house after Alicia had gone?" Jason asked.

No one had mentioned that Percival Guilford had left at any time after Alicia had departed. Surely someone must have seen him and could puncture a hole in his alibi, Daniel thought as he leaned closer to hear Long's answer.

"Percy said he felt unwell and excused himself. He was gone a good while and looked pale and sweaty when he returned. We all felt sorry for him and wondered if he had eaten something at supper that had caused him such an acute bout of indigestion. I expect Percy followed Mrs. Lysander and killed her before she'd had an opportunity to share what she had learned."

"Where is the cloakroom located?" Daniel asked.

"There is a washroom on the ground floor, between the library and the corridor that leads to the carriage house and the stables."

Jason nodded. "And in the stables, he would find a hammer, used when shoeing horses, which would be consistent with the injury Alicia Lysander sustained to the top of her head."

"I don't know what Percy used. We never discussed it," Long said.

"Did Lord Guilford tell you that he had attacked Alicia Lysander?" Jason asked.

"There was no need. I heard it from you the next day."

"I wager you were relieved," Daniel said.

Rex Long shook his head. "Alicia Lysander had kicked a hornet's nest, and I didn't care to get stung. But I did not kill her, and I wasn't glad she was dead," Long reiterated.

"So, what would you have done if your friend hadn't murdered this harbinger of doom?" Jason inquired.

"I would have paid her off."

"And if she didn't accept?"

"Everyone has their price, and if they don't, then there's something they treasure above all things that they wouldn't care to lose, such as a beloved spouse or a precious child."

"Point taken," Jason said.

Long nodded. "There's aways a way to silence someone, and I would have bought Anne Crumlish's cooperation if I had been given the chance. Sadly, Percy is more impulsive."

"Does Lady Jane know what her husband has done?" Jason asked, presumably referring to all three deaths and not just the murder of Alicia Lysander.

"Neither Jane nor Amelia has any idea what really happened. And if I could turn back time, I would do things very differently. Alas, we see things more clearly in hindsight."

Daniel would have liked nothing more than to charge the earl with being an accessory to all three murders and also with illegal burial, but if he had learned anything from John Ransome, it was that it was always more prudent to err on the side of caution since without proof, the earl's story was just that.

"I'm afraid I must invite you to enjoy our hospitality until we're ready to either charge or release you, Your Grace," Daniel said.

"I give you my word of honor that I will not flee if you allow me to go home," Long said.

"I'm afraid your word of honor doesn't carry much weight just now," Jason said, saving Daniel from having to express a similar sentiment. "You will have to remain in custody until we verify your account."

"You will come to regret that decision. Both of you," Long said.

"We're willing to live with the consequences," Jason replied. "Are you?"

"You can't touch me," the earl said. "You will only embarrass yourself and cause your flunky here to lose his position. Sir David will not stand for this kind of treatment of his friend."

"Sir David is a man of honor," Daniel retorted, but the earl's threat had hit a nerve. Sir David couldn't do anything to harm Jason, but what if the commissioner saw Daniel dismissed for his treatment of the earl? As Rex Long had pointed out, they couldn't touch him, not unless they had evidence.

"Constable Putney," Daniel called out once he'd opened the door. "Kindly take His Grace down to the cells and inform Sergeant Meadows that Percival Guilford is to be taken up immediately."

"Yes, sir."

Daniel knew Ransome would be expecting a full report before Percy Guilford was brought in, but he needed a word with Jason first.

"I don't believe him," Jason said as soon as the earl had gone, and Daniel had resumed his seat.

"Why not?"

"I've heard of close friendships and have enjoyed a few in my day, but there are limits to how much someone will risk on behalf of someone else. If Rex Long went along with Percy Guilford, it was because Guilford had something on him and wasn't afraid to use it."

"I don't know if I agree with you, Jason," Daniel replied. "Rex Long was trapped in a loveless marriage with a woman who had been unfaithful to him. She had neglected to tell him she was with child, possibly because she hoped the child would never be born, or because the child was really her lover's. Perhaps, at the time, Rex Long thought that Percy Guilford had done him a favor and had rid him of a wife who had become a liability. Anne Crumlish's death was unfortunate, but not enough to give any one of them lasting pangs of guilt. And like Anne, Alicia needed to be disposed of in order to protect the people who really matter."

"Perhaps," Jason conceded. "Long's testimony alleges that Percival Guilford committed three murders, but there's precious little physical evidence to support our case. The two sets of modern remains prove that the women died an unnatural death and were buried in secret, but they don't tell us who murdered them or if the deaths were intentional or accidental. And we have no proof that Percy Guilford murdered Alicia. Unless someone saw him enter the stables, pick up a hammer, follow Alicia into the night, and strike her over the head, his lawyer can easily get him off. He doesn't even need to be particularly clever."

Daniel sighed. Jason was right, and Daniel knew that he was standing perilously close to the precipice and one wrong step would send him over the edge. Perhaps he was already falling off the cliff that was the life he had built since Sarah's death, his treatment of the Earl of Ongar the decision that would cost him his reputation and livelihood. Jason didn't say anything; there was no need to drive his point home, but Daniel could see in his face that he was just as frustrated by their lack of progress and worried that they would never get justice for Alicia.

Jason would also feel responsible if Daniel got the sack, even if his downfall wasn't Jason's fault. Daniel suddenly wished that someone else had got this case, but it was too late for regrets. He had to see this through to the end, even though it was beginning to look like this would be the end of him rather than the men who'd murdered Alicia and had concealed the deaths of two women and an unborn child for years.

"Let's speak to Percival Guilford and see where that leaves us," Daniel said with more optimism than he felt. "Would you like to come with me to update Ransome?"

Jason sighed. "I could use a few minutes to clear my head, but I suppose I had better come."

"We need definitive proof," Ransome said once Daniel had relayed the details of the interview. "Lord Redmond is right. A skilled lawyer can get both men off and make us look like we don't know our arses from our elbows."

"But we know they are responsible," Daniel protested, unable to accept defeat without a fight.

"Maybe so, but unless we can prove their culpability beyond a reasonable doubt, we will come out of this looking like damn fools. Get me something I can use, Haze. An admission of guilt. A sighting of Percy Guilford the night Alicia Lysander was murdered. A member of the earl's household who witnessed something dodgy the night Lady Daphne and Anne Crumlish died. Surely someone must have noticed something or wondered why no one had seen the two women retire for the night or leave in the morning. Not as though they would have gone ahead to the port with night closing in."

Ransome looked truly desperate, and Daniel realized that his position was probably on the line as well. Sir David might have no choice but to appoint a new superintendent if the earl decided to pursue his grievance with the home secretary.

"Lady Daphne died three years ago, and even Bernice Crumlish believed that her mother had left for Italy with her mistress. I can't imagine that anyone would be willing to risk the earl's displeasure at this late stage," Jason said.

Ransome nodded. "That's what I'm afraid of. Everyone is keeping mum because they're worried about their own prospects."

"They have little to gain by biting the hand that feeds them," Jason agreed.

Ransome exhaled heavily, his breath hot on Daniel's face. "I think we might have dug our own graves on this one, Haze. Some cock-ups you can never come back from."

"We didn't cock up," Daniel snapped.

"No, but the law is a funny thing, Daniel. It doesn't much care about the truth, but it sure panders to those who have the power to bend it to their will."

"How I wish there was a way to trace a person's biological signature," Jason said, speaking almost to himself. "That would be all the proof we'd need."

Ransome chuckled. "You're a clever man, my lord, but just now you are off with the fairies, if you'll forgive me saying so."

Jason shrugged in response. "Advances in science will revolutionize policing, Superintendent. It's only a matter of time. It has already been proven that a person's fingerprints are unique."

"And how would you get the killer's fingerprints from a body?" Ransome asked.

"I don't know if fingerprints could be obtained from skin, but there has to be a way to lift fingerprints off hard surfaces, like the handle of a knife or the butt of a pistol, for instance. Or the handle of a shovel."

Ransome chuckled. "Well, I hope I live long enough to see these advances, but for now, we must work with what we've got." He pulled out his watch and consulted the time. "Take a break, gentlemen. You look like you need it."

"I'll be back in half an hour," Jason said, leaving Daniel to get luncheon on his own.

Daniel didn't think he could eat, so he made himself a mug of tea and settled in the break room, happy for the company of his fellow policemen. Given Jason's and Ransome's attitudes, he didn't think they were likely to get a result, and the prospect of the two men responsible for the deaths of three women going free made Daniel's gut burn as if he'd just drunk a cup of acid.

Chapter 34

Percy Guilford was all confused innocence when Sergeant Meadows escorted him into the interview room. Jason supposed that if he didn't know about the disturbed grave or the rings Imogen Salter had identified, he had no reason to worry. Perhaps he felt no cause for concern even if he was aware. There was no tangible proof of wrongdoing, and he knew it. Percy looked at them blankly when Daniel laid out the case against him, not even bothered enough by the accusations to muster a show of indignation.

"I don't know what you're talking about, old boy," he said dismissively.

"I think you do," Daniel countered. "You murdered three women."

"Utter tosh!" Percy scoffed, a smile of amusement tugging at his lips. "I'd be careful if I were you, Inspector. Throwing about baseless accusations can land one in prison."

Daniel ignored the thinly veiled threat. "So how do you explain Rex Long's allegation against you and the remains we found buried at the ruins of St. Mary?"

Guilford's eyes widened with feigned incomprehension. "I don't have to explain anything. I accepted Rex's account, same as everyone else. I had no idea Daphne was buried in Essex."

"So, you believe that Lady Daphne and Anne Crumlish were murdered by your lifelong friend, Rex Long?" Jason asked, impressed by the man's ability to retain his composure under pressure.

"I believe no such thing. I don't know what happened, but I trust Rex, always have done, and will not say a word against him," Percy said breezily. "Now, if we're done here, I have plans to lunch at White's, and I don't want to be late. Terribly rude to keep one's luncheon companion waiting."

"Who are you meeting?" Daniel asked.

"None of your affair, old chap," Percy Guilford said as he pushed away from the table and walked out without another word, leaving Jason and Daniel with a slew of unanswered questions, and simmering with anger.

"Can you believe that?" Daniel sputtered. "The gall of the man! And now we'll have to let Long go since we don't have anything on him save a grave we can't even prove he knew about since he can retract his statement at any time." Daniel threw up his hands. "We're right back where we started."

"Not quite," Jason said.

"If you have any suggestions, I'm happy to listen."

"Do not let Long go, and put a watch on White's."

"To what end?"

"To make certain Guilford doesn't flee." Jason grabbed his hat and made for the door.

"Where are you going?" Daniel called after him, but Jason had no time to explain.

It was a long shot, and Jason could be way off in his estimation, but if he peeled away the layers of denial and deception, there were several facts left. Daphne's and Anne's skulls had been fractured, and they had been buried in a secret grave on the Ongar estate. Rex Long had lied about what had happened to his wife and her maid. Alicia had been attacked shortly after the séance in which Daphne had come through and leveled an accusation at someone in the room. And Alicia had directed Jason toward Sigrid's resting place and had told him that the killer had killed three times. All these truths pointed to Rex Long and Percy Guilford, and even though Rex had admitted that Percy was the killer, he had done so safe in the knowledge that there was no physical evidence to convict Percy of the crimes. And Percy had refused to implicate Rex.

Daphne's and Anne's deaths and the subsequent coverup seemed to have bound the two men closer together rather than tear them asunder, and that was the one thing Jason couldn't square with the facts. Unless Rex Long was utterly devoid of any human feeling and didn't care about his sister's well-being, he had to have resented Percy Guilford for what he had done. Why then did he go to such lengths to protect him? One possibility was that the two men were more than friends and the love they felt for each other united them against the world, but Jason had met homosexual men before, and he did not get the impression that either Rex or Percy was anything other than a heterosexual man married to a woman he was seemingly fond of. Which left Jason with only one other supposition, that Rex had done what he had done to protect someone else, and the only person that bound Rex and Percy was Jane.

Lady Amelia had said that Jane had been in love with Percy since she was a child, but Percy had fallen for Daphne. If Jane had been aware of their relationship, it would have hurt her deeply. Jane and Percy were now married, which meant that Daphne had stood in the way of that emotional union—until she hadn't. Daphne had died, Rex had lied to avoid a scandal that would have destroyed everyone involved, and the whole thing had been swept under the carpet. A happy ending for all. Until now.

It was imperative that Jason got to Hanover Square before Percy Guilford had a chance to warn his wife to keep quiet, since the investigation had come dangerously close to exposing the lies and Daniel only needed one piece of proof that would stand up in court to tie it all together. Jason's only chance was to catch Jane unawares and hope that she made a misstep and led him to the truth.

Stepping from a cab, Jason approached the Guilfords' house, his heart rate accelerating ever so slightly as he lifted the heavy door knocker to announce his presence.

Chapter 35

The Guilfords' butler did not seem particularly alarmed by Jason's arrival. It was just past one o'clock, and a social call from a member of the aristocracy was nothing out of the ordinary, even if the butler had never laid eyes on Jason before. He showed Jason to the drawing room and announced him to the three ladies present. Jane looked sunny and radiant in a gown of yellow and white muslin. A few playful tendrils framed her lovely face, and a yellow ribbon held back her upswept curls. The other ladies, a mother and daughter, were visitors, and after introductions and the usual pleasantries were exchanged, they wished Jane a pleasant afternoon and left, presumably to pay a call on someone else. Jane and Jason were left alone together, and Jason hoped that another round of visitors wasn't about to darken the Guilfords' door.

"I'm afraid Percy is not here, my lord," Jane said, having assumed that Jason had come to see her husband. "Some horrid policeman came to fetch him. I expect it was in connection with that poor woman's death. Why would anyone think Percy had anything to do with that?" she mused, then seemed to recall her manners. "Would you care for some refreshment?"

"Thank you, no. I won't be staying long," Jason replied. "I only wanted to ask you a question."

"Oh? What about?" Jane asked, smiling at him beguilingly. She really was pretty, and very young. But beneath the smile, Jason could sense deep-seated apprehension, the sort one might feel if they had something to hide.

"Why did you murder Daphne?" he asked, his gaze boring into Jane as she absorbed the implication of what he was suggesting.

It was a gamble that could backfire spectacularly if Jason had got it wrong, but the shock and fear that sparked in Jane's eyes assured him that he had hit the mark. She drew back, her face turning the color of curdled milk as her eyes darted toward the door, no doubt thinking that if she called the butler and demanded that he evict Jason, they could all pretend this had never happened.

"We found her remains," Jason said before Jane could call out. "And the remains of her maid, Anne Crumlish. Mrs. Crumlish was innocent, Jane, as was Lady Daphne's unborn child."

"She was with child?" Jane's face turned even paler, her hand unwittingly going to her own abdomen. She wasn't showing yet, but just because she wasn't far along didn't mean she didn't have maternal feelings. "I didn't know," she whispered, and her eyes brimmed with tears. "I never meant to hurt Daphne," Jane cried.

"But you did, which brings me to my next question. Why did you invite a medium to conduct a séance when you knew that the truth might come out?" Jason pressed.

"How was I to know Daphne would come through?" Jane wailed. "We wanted to speak to Caroline. I had it on good authority that Mrs. Lysander always managed to connect with the right person. I had no reason to expect anything else."

Jane's agitation was obvious, and Jason knew it was cruel to take advantage of her distress, but he needed proof if he were to find out who had killed Alicia, and if Jane was guilty, then he felt no sympathy for her.

"Why, Jane?" he asked, pinning her with an accusing gaze. "Why did three people have to die?"

Jane began to cry in earnest, tears sliding down her face and dripping onto the yellow bodice, like raindrops on a flower. She was pretty even when she cried, and Jason could see how the two men in her life saw her as an innocent child that needed to be protected.

"I never meant for anyone to die," Jane said. "I was just so angry and frightened."

"Of what?"

"Of losing Percy. I couldn't bear to see the way he looked at her, like a faithful dog, desperate for any scrap of attention," Jane exclaimed, angry now. "I loved him, and I knew I could make him happy. And I have."

"Did Percy and Daphne have an affair?" Jason asked, now doubting everything Rex Long had said.

Jane shook her head. "Daphne would never be unfaithful. It wasn't in her. She was too devout to betray her marriage vows, even if she hated Rex, but that was what made her so desirable," Jane cried. "She was unattainable, like the saint she always longed to be, and Percy was lost, unable to move on from a desire he couldn't fulfill."

"What happened the night Daphne died?" Jason asked.

"I don't have to tell you," Jane said sulkily.

"But you do, because if you don't, your beloved Percy will hang for her murder."

That wasn't quite true, but Jane's only weakness appeared to be her love for Percy, and Jason didn't think she could bear to see him accused of a crime he hadn't committed. Jane looked terrified, her fingers pleating the fabric of her skirt.

"Rex and Daphne were due to leave early the following morning," she said, her voice low and urgent. "I don't know why Rex invited Percy to the house. Maybe he wanted to taunt him with the fact that Daphne had chosen him, or maybe he needed Daphne and Percy to say a final farewell." Jane's lips quivered as she tried to hold back the tears. "Percy looked so desperate, his eyes filled with longing as his gaze followed Daphne around the room, and I suddenly realized that he would never love me the way he loved her."

There was a sound of ripping fabric as Jane tore off the lace at her sleeve. She crumpled it into a ball and closed her fist around the delicate fabric. She didn't appear to realize what she was doing, all her emotional energy fixated on the night that had changed everything.

"What happened?" Jason asked softly when she remained silent. The question seemed to rouse Jane out of her reverie.

"I overheard Percy begging Daphne to meet him by the ruins, one last time, and I followed them. I don't know why I did it. I suppose I had hoped they would say goodbye and acknowledge that their love could never be, but when I saw them together, standing so close, their gazes locked, Percy's hand reaching for Daphne's and her not pulling it away, I suddenly realized that she might give in."

Jane looked at Jason as if willing him to understand. "I could see it in Daphne's face—she wanted Percy as much as he wanted her, and if not for fear of damnation, she would have let him take her right there. He cupped her cheek and leaned in to kiss her, and I thought, this is it. They will run away together and leave me and Rex to face the ultimate rejection and public humiliation." Jane shook her head. She was no longer crying, and there was an acceptance about her, as if she had just gone to confession and admitted to her sin. "I never meant to kill her. I only wanted to get her away from him."

"What did you do?" Jason asked.

"I flew at Daphne and shoved her with all my might. I was screaming and crying and begging her to let Percy go because I loved him," Jane said quietly. "Daphne fell backward and hit her head. There was so much blood, and she wasn't moving."

"And then?"

"I was terrified. I didn't know what to do. I cried and begged Daphne for forgiveness, but she couldn't hear me."

"And that was when Percy stepped in?"

Jane nodded. "I would hang for murder if anyone found out, so Percy hid Daphne's body behind the wall of the anchorite's cell and walked me back to the house. He made sure no one suspected anything and saw me to my room. Then he got Rex, and they came up with a plan that would keep us all safe. Rex sent Crumlish to look for her mistress, and Percy killed her once she was far away from the house."

According to Alicia's message, Percy had murdered three people, so perhaps Daphne had still been alive after the fall that had fractured her skull, the cavity filling with blood while Percy and Rex dug the grave that would ultimately kill her. Jason's only chance was to appeal to Jane's sense of self-preservation and her love for the brother who had protected her.

"Jane, I don't believe you killed Daphne. You knocked her unconscious, but she was still alive when she went into the grave. There's nothing you can do to save Percy. He murdered two women and an unborn child to keep you safe, but you can still help Rex. Unless you tell the truth, Rex will be implicated in the murders and go to prison, possibly even hang. That will be the end of your line, and even if it isn't, your family will never survive the scandal. You have a duty to make things right."

"No," Jane cried. "I won't let that happen." Then the full extent of what Jason had said sank in. "I didn't kill Daphne?" Jane asked, her voice shaking with hope.

"I don't believe so."

Jane took a deep breath and nodded. "What must I do?"

"You must provide me with a written confession. That's the only thing that will keep Rex's neck out of the noose. And yours." *And keep your baby from dying*, Jason wanted to add, but couldn't bear to be so cruel.

Jane inhaled sharply, then sprang to her feet. She rang the bellpull and asked the parlormaid who appeared for paper, ink, and a pen. Jason was on tenterhooks while Jane penned her confession, but once she signed it and handed it to him, he knew that the case was solved.

"Thank you. I will do everything in my power to help you."

"There's no need, my lord. I don't care to go on without Percy, and I don't want our child to live with the shame of what we had done. But I want to give Rex and Cynthia a chance. They deserve it."

Jason didn't try to dissuade her. Daphne might have been saved if she'd received medical care, but chances were she would have died anyway, and Jane had killed her in all the ways that mattered, just as Percy had killed Alicia without actually finishing her off. Jason saw no point in bringing Jane to Scotland Yard., She would be arrested and charged eventually. For now, he had what he needed.

Epilogue

It didn't take long for the papers to get hold of the story and for the furor that followed to bring the remaining members of the Long family even lower than they already were. Lady Amelia whisked Cynthia off to France to wait out the trial and the subsequent execution of her brother-in-law. The judge, who some thought was far too lenient, sentenced Jane to two years in prison, and gave Rex five for his part in the conspiracy. Despite her vow to die alongside her husband, Jane accepted her fate for the sake of her child and made no attempt to join Percy in the afterlife.

Lady Daphne was buried with all the respect due her by her parents and sister in their family vault in Highgate. Daphne's father, Lord Burrows, also paid for a funeral for Anne Crumlish, who was buried in another part of the cemetery. After the burial, Bernice Crumlish sailed to New York, where she intended to start a new life with the funds Rex Long had settled on her in recompense for her loss.

Jason left London as well, moving the family to Essex, where they planned to remain until the cholera epidemic abated and they could safely return. Although Jason felt guilty about taking a leave of absence from the hospital, it was more important that he protect his loved ones from contagion. Daniel, whose big news didn't come as much of a surprise to anyone, least of all Jason, refused to leave. He didn't visit Birch Hill for fear of bringing the illness with him, but Flora and Charlotte, who split their time between Harriet Elderman's house and Ardith Hall, were frequent visitors and spent many a happy afternoon with the Redmonds. Flora had decided on an autumn wedding, and she and Katherine were busy making plans, poring over dress patterns, and devising a menu for the wedding breakfast that would take place at Ardith Hall and hosted by Flora's parents.

Jason missed his work at the hospital and the frenetic pace of city life, but he appreciated the slower days and the peaceful nights that were his life in Essex and was grateful for the brief respite from the ugliness and death that stalked the streets of London. Katherine's pregnancy was progressing, Lily and Liam were thriving, and Mary and Micah were reunited once again, at least for the summer. Life was good, and Jason reminded himself that he had earned a break and relished the opportunity to spend time with his family.

He had promised himself that he wouldn't get involved in another case until he returned to London, but life had other plans, as it usually did. It was a week before the wedding, and the day after Daniel had finally arrived in Birch Hill to get ready for the big day that Micah and Tom exploded into the drawing room, where Jason had been taking afternoon tea with Katherine. The boys were pale, their breathing ragged as they looked from Jason to Katherine, uncertain if they should speak with Katherine in the room.

"What is it? What's wrong?" Jason asked, looking the boys over carefully to make certain neither was hurt.

They both looked fine, but something had clearly happened. "Let's talk in the study," Jason said, and shepherded the two boys out of the drawing room. He didn't want Katherine upset, since he had a feeling he was about to be on the receiving end of bad news.

"There's a body. In the woods," Micah cried as soon as Jason shut the door behind them. Micah had seen his share of bodies during the American Civil War, so it took a lot to rattle him, but he was clearly very upset.

"Who is it?" Jason asked. "Did you recognize the deceased?"

"We didn't see his face," Tom said. "He was tied to a tree, and someone put a sack over his head."

"You think this man was murdered?" Jason asked. He fervently hoped this was some silly prank and the person wasn't really dead, but he instinctively knew that his hope was in vain. Micah and Tom knew a dead body when they saw one.

The boys nodded in unison. "He was shot with an arrow, right through the heart," Tom exclaimed. "His coat is soaked with blood."

"Is there anything else you can tell me about the victim?" Jason asked as he moved toward the door.

"He's dressed like a gentleman," Micah said. "And I think he was young."

"And I didn't see a horse or a carriage, so he must have come on foot," Tom said. "Unless someone brought him there."

"Tom, fetch Inspector Haze and bring him to the woods. Micah, show me where you found the body. Not a word to anyone," Jason warned the boys just before they stepped into the corridor.

Jason hurried upstairs and grabbed his medical bag, just in case, but he didn't think he'd need it. It seemed he didn't have to return to London to investigate a case. Murder had come to Birch Hill once again.

The End

Please turn the page for an excerpt from

Murder in Bloody Weald

A Redmond and Haze Mystery Book 16

And if you can't get enough of Victorian murder mysteries,

Please check out my new series, Tate and Bell

An Excerpt from
Murder in Bloody Weald

Prologue

The late afternoon sun dappled the leaves of the massive trees, the shadowy spaces beneath the canopies pleasantly cool and the ground upturned by gnarled roots and covered by thick bracken. Bloody cranesbill, the flowers that had given the ancient wood its name, were no longer in bloom, but Bloody Weald seemed frozen in time, the trees that had taken root a thousand years before witnesses to centuries of violent conflict and home to outlaws and the travelers who came by every year and camped in nearby Bloody Mead.

This afternoon there was nothing sinister about the medieval forest. The birds were singing, the sun was shining, and school wasn't due to start until next week. Micah wished he didn't have to go back to Westbridge Academy, but if he hoped to become a doctor, he had to get an education. He had thought he wanted to be a detective, like Daniel Haze, but had decided that he would rather save lives than try to unravel the deaths of those already lost. He hadn't told his guardian yet but knew Jason Redmond would be overjoyed to hear that Micah wanted to follow in his footsteps and Jason would help him in any way he could. No orphaned child could be more blessed, and Micah thanked his lucky stars every day, secretly believing that his mam was looking out for him from heaven. He would make her proud, as well as the Captain—the name Micah still used for Jason Redmond, even though his days in the Union Army were far behind him.

Tom Marin walked next to Micah. He was chattering as usual, pointing out rare birds and deer tracks. Tom's father was a gamekeeper, so Tom spent most of his time outdoors, learning the ways of nature. He would take over for his father one day and raise his family in the tiny cottage that was tied to the Chadwick estate, which was some miles from Bloody Weald. Tom had no other aspirations, and Micah realized that this was probably the last occasion they would spend any considerable time together before life pulled them in different directions. Already they had grown apart, Micah looking to the future as Tom became more deeply rooted in village life. Still, it was nice to have this last summer.

Micah was tired and hungry and was looking forward to a cup of tea and a jam tart. Mrs. Dodson had promised to bake a batch today, and she always set aside a few extra tarts for Micah, who could easily eat four in one sitting. Micah was just about to invite Tom to share this bounty when Tom froze like a deer that had sensed a hunter's presence.

"What is it?" Micah asked. He stopped walking and turned to look at Tom, who was staring straight ahead, his eyes wide and his mouth hanging open.

Tom didn't say anything, just pointed toward something up ahead. Micah squinted, trying to see what had stopped his friend in his tracks. It took a moment, since the man's brown coat blended with his surroundings, and it was difficult to make out his face. The man was very still and appeared to be leaning against a tree, but there was something unnatural about his pose.

"Blimey," Tom said, his voice low. "What do you reckon that's all about?"

"I don't know, but something doesn't feel right," Micah said softly. "Let's tread carefully, yeah?"

Tom nodded, and they made their way forward, stopping every few paces to assess the situation. But by the time they got close enough to see the man clearly, they knew there was no need for stealth. He stood sagging against the tree, only a thick rope wound around his torso holding him up. A burlap sack loosely covered his head, and an arrow protruded from his chest. The front of his coat was soaked with dried blood, and a tall top hat lay upturned on the ground. His clothes were fashionable, the snowy cravat was expertly tied, and the tall leather boots shone with polish. A thick gold watch chain snaked from a button on his waistcoat toward his pocket.

Tom must have noticed it too because he said, "So not robbery, then."

"We have to get the Captain," Micah said. "He'll know what to do."

"Let's go," Tom said, and they took off at a run, their fishing poles slapping against their thighs and the fish Tom carried flapping as if it were still alive.

221

Micah had seen plenty of dead bodies when he had been a drummer boy during the American Civil War, but those men had been casualties of war who had died on a battlefield. This body was quite different. This man, whoever he was, had not been defending his country or following orders. He was a victim of cold-blooded murder.

Chapter 1

Monday, September 6, 1869

Jason Redmond set down his teacup and leaned against the back of the armchair, his gaze on his wife, who at nearly five months pregnant was the picture of blooming health. The only evidence of her condition was her slightly rounded face and fuller bosom, since her swelling abdomen was disguised by the voluminous skirts of her gown. Katherine planned to make her final public appearance next week, at Daniel Haze and Flora Tarrant's wedding, then she would follow Jason's orders, loosen her corset, and spend the remainder of the pregnancy in peace and comfort.

Not for the first time, Jason reflected on how fortunate they were to be able to leave London and spend the summer at Jason's ancestral estate at a time when so many in the city were ill with cholera. They hadn't resided at Redmond Hall in nearly two years, choosing instead to make their home in Knightsbridge, where Katherine could participate in charitable causes and help those in need, and Jason could volunteer at St. George's Hospital and lend his services to Scotland Yard. The Yard had its own staff surgeon, but Jason took on the more challenging cases, conducting autopsies on victims whose deaths weren't straightforward and whose postmortem results could help build a picture not only of their lives but also their final moments, which was sometimes vital to solving a crime.

"Can I pour you more tea?" Jason asked when Katherine set her cup down next to his.

Katherine smiled at him indulgently. Men weren't supposed to pour out. That was the woman's job, but Katherine was used to Jason's unconventional ways and no longer tried to guide him when it came to social conventions. She liked the fact that he was different, and when she called him *Yank*, Jason saw the affection in her eyes and the quirking of her mouth. They were truly blessed, and Jason was thankful every day that he had been granted a second chance at life after he had nearly died in Georgia toward the end of the American Civil War.

"Please," Katherine said, and rested her hand on her stomach, her face glowing with contentment.

Jason refreshed Katherine's tea, added a splash of milk, and placed two teacakes on her saucer, then passed the tea back to her.

"I've already had two cakes," Katherine protested.

"Have two more. It's hours yet until dinner, and you should eat something every few hours."

Katherine obediently took a bite of a dainty cake and set it down on the plate. "I'm absolutely fine, Jason. You needn't fuss."

"Spoken like a true Brit," Jason replied, and reached for the last teacake, which he popped into his mouth.

He knew Katherine was fine, but he still worried. So many things could go wrong, and a staggering number of women died either during or after childbirth. As did their children. The healthier and stronger Katherine was, the better chance that she would survive the delivery and recover normally in the weeks after. Jason tried not to think too much about their baby. He wanted to picture the infant and couldn't wait to hold it in his arms, but he had grown more superstitious than he liked to admit and didn't care to tempt fate. One day at a time, he reminded himself. One day at a time.

Jason was distracted from his thoughts by a commotion in the foyer and Dodson's reproachful tone. Micah and Tom exploded into the drawing room, Dodson on their heels, his expression apologetic.

"I'm sorry, my lord," he began, but Jason waved his apology away, immediately recognizing that something was wrong.

The boys were pale, their breathing ragged as they looked from Jason to Katherine, as though uncertain if they should speak until Katherine left the room.

"What is it? What's wrong?" Jason asked, looking the boys over carefully to make certain neither was hurt.

They both looked fine, but something had clearly happened, and it had to be serious since neither boy was easily frightened.

"Let's talk in the library," Jason said, and shepherded the boys out of the drawing room. He didn't want Katherine upset and needed to hear their account on his own before he shared the news with her.

"There's a body. In the woods," Micah cried as soon as Jason shut the door behind them. Micah was no stranger to violent death, and it took much to rattle him to such a degree.

"Did you recognize the deceased?" Jason asked.

"We didn't see his face," Tom said. "He was tied to a tree, and someone put a sack over his head."

"You think this man was murdered?"

Jason fervently hoped this was some silly prank and the person wasn't really dead, but he instinctively knew that his hope was in vain. Micah and Tom knew a dead body when they saw one, and Jason was certain they would have checked before running all the way back to summon him.

The boys nodded in unison.

"He was shot with an arrow, right through the heart," Tom exclaimed. "His coat was soaked with blood."

"Where did you find him?"

"We were walking back from our favorite fishing spot," Micah said. "We were hungry, so we took a shortcut through Bloody Weald."

Jason had passed through Bloody Weald only a handful of times, and mostly on horseback, since the road that cut through the wood wasn't wide enough for a carriage. The growth was dense, the silence almost menacing, especially after dark. Bloody Weald was part of both the Chadwick and Talbot estates but included public walking paths, since the people of Birch Hill and the surrounding villages had cut through the forest for centuries. It was a place of myth and legend, and there were some who claimed that King Arthur's Camelot had been located at Colchester and that Arthur and his knights had ridden frequently through the forest. Jason didn't really believe King Arthur had ever existed, but it was a nice story, and he could easily accept that the forest had seen its share of clashes and had offered shelter to people in search of a safe haven.

"Is there anything else you can tell me about the victim?" Jason asked as he studied the boys' anxious faces.

"He is dressed like a gentleman," Micah said. "And I think he is young."

"His watch was still in his waistcoat pocket, so he wasn't robbed," Tom added.

"How did he get there?" Jason asked. "Did you see a horse?"

The boys shook their heads.

"Was there anything near the victim?"

"No," Micah said. "We didn't see anything."

Jason nodded, his mind already weighing up the situation. The boys weren't skilled at assessing a crime scene, and they had been frightened by what they'd found. Whoever had killed the man could have left clues behind, but before Jason and Daniel searched the area, they had to identify the victim. There had to be a reason someone had put a bag over his head.

"Can you find your way back to where you saw this man?"

"Yes," Tom said.

Micah nodded.

"Okay. Tom, fetch Inspector Haze and bring him to the woods. Micah, lead me to the body. Not a word to anyone," Jason warned the boys just before opening the library door.

Jason hurried upstairs and grabbed his medical bag, just in case, but he didn't think he'd have need of it. If the man had been shot through the heart, chances were he was long dead, and there was even less chance that the death had been the result of an accident. It seemed Jason didn't have to return to London to investigate a case. Murder had come to Birch Hill once again, and it was up to him and Daniel to see justice done, since there was no longer a parish constable in the village and the Brentwood Police station was nearly an hour away.

"Lead the way," Jason said as he followed Micah outside. Micah nodded and took off at a trot.

Chapter 2

Daniel maneuvered the dogcart down the narrow path, then tied up the horse as close as he could to the place where Tom claimed he and Micah had found the body. By the time Tom led Daniel to the spot, Jason and Micah were already there, the two standing well back and staring at the corpse. Jason's medical bag was on the ground, near the tree, but Daniel could see right away that the victim was beyond earthly help. The head was covered with a burlap bag and tilted to the side, the hands hanging limp. The rope was wound twice around the man's chest, the knot behind the tree, where he couldn't have reached it even if he'd tried to free himself.

Tom had been accurate in his description. The man appeared to be young and fit, and well-to-do. The coat was made of fine broadcloth, and the boots must have cost more than Daniel earned in a month. The buttons of the waistcoat had the gleam of polished silver, and the watchchain was made of thick gold links. It could be goldplate, but Daniel suspected it was solid gold.

"I came as quickly as I could," Daniel said when both Jason and Micah turned at the sound of Daniel and Tom crashing through the forest. "Should we send for Inspector Pullman?"

As an inspector with Scotland Yard, Daniel did not have official jurisdiction in Essex since Essex had its own police service, and given that he was getting married in less than a week, the last thing he wanted was to become embroiled in what was clearly murder. Inspector Pullman, who had assisted Daniel many times while Daniel had served at the Brentwood Constabulary, was still green and needed time to gain experience, but he was competent enough. And if he needed help, he could always turn to his boss, Detective Inspector Coleridge, who had been something of a mentor to Daniel and had been happy to help when Jason and Daniel had found themselves on his patch.

Jason shook his head but didn't respond to Daniel's inquiry.

"What can you tell me?" Daniel asked, wondering why Jason was being so reticent.

"Rigor mortis has set in, and there is evidence of livor mortis in the fingers, since blood begins to pool in the lowest points of the body approximately six hours after death. I expect there's livor mortis in the feet as well, since the victim was left upright. I would put the time of death somewhere between ten a.m. and noon. The cause of death appears to be an arrow to the victim's heart. I think he was shot at fairly close range."

"Why do you think that?" Daniel asked.

"The forest is densely wooded, but the killer was able to aim straight for the heart. Had they been far away, a branch or a tree trunk might have got in the way."

"The killer had to be skilled with a bow and arrow," Daniel observed.

"Yes. I doubt this was a lucky shot. I searched the area before you arrived but saw nothing out of the ordinary. No other arrows, no broken branches or twigs."

"In other words, no evidence of someone crashing through the woods," Daniel surmised.

"Exactly. This wasn't someone who was in a panic, which would suggest that this was planned."

"So, you think the killer was lying in wait?" Daniel asked.

"It's possible, but they would have had to know that the victim would be coming this way."

"Or they might have followed him at a distance. Like a hunter stalking their prey," Tom suggested.

"Yes, they might have," Jason agreed, "but they would have to be stealthy to avoid detection."

"Maybe the victim realized he was being followed, and this is where the confrontation took place," Micah suggested.

Jason shook his head. "The killer would have to be a few yards away for the arrow to gain enough velocity to pierce skin and muscle. And since the victim was shot in the chest, he was likely walking toward the killer rather than away from them."

"Maybe they tied him first," Micah speculated, "and used him for target practice."

"The victim's hands are covered with blood, but his clothes are not in disarray, and there are no bruises on his hands or wrists. I think he clutched at the wound when he was shot but knew not to pull out the arrow because the tip would do more damage when extracted. I suspect the killer tied up the victim once he was already dead and put the bag on his head."

"To hide his identity?" Micah asked.

"Possibly. Or maybe to preserve his face for as long as possible before the birds and the animals got to him," Jason replied.

"Do you know who he is?" Daniel asked, his gaze going to the burlap sack.

He was surprised Jason had waited to remove the sack. It would have been the first thing Daniel would have done when arriving on the scene, and Jason's decision to wait made Daniel uneasy. Try as he might, he couldn't see anything through the dense weave, and the sack covered the man down to his cravat, so even his neck wasn't visible. Apprehension raced up Daniel's spine like a centipede and settled heavily on his breastbone. At this point, the need to know overrode every other instinct.

Jason turned to Micah and Tom, who were watching Jason intently, their eyes round with curiosity and shock. Daniel thought Jason would send the boys away, but then Jason turned back to Daniel.

"I didn't take off the sack, but I know who the victim is."

"How?" Daniel asked.

"I recognize the watch, and I have seen him wear that waistcoat."

Unable to bear the suspense any longer, Daniel approached the body and pulled off the sack. His breath escaped in a loud whoosh when he came face to face with the victim. He'd seen that face before, knew that gleaming hair, and had looked into the eyes that had either twinkled with amusement or been narrowed in mockery or anger. The bright blue irises were frozen in a blank stare of death, but the eyes were still beautiful. The man's generous mouth was slack, the golden stubble on his cheeks glinting in the late afternoon sun. Even in death, the victim looked like the subject of a medieval painting, his modern clothes the only thing that distinguished him from a Biblical saint. St. Sebastian came to mind, writhing in agony as his body was pierced with arrows, but the man before them was no saint. In fact, he was more closely related to the devil.

"Tristan Carmichael," Daniel said quietly.

He wasn't all that surprised to find that someone had finally taken justice into their own hands, as the Carmichaels had many enemies, but he was shocked by the method of the murder. He would have thought that Carmichael would get shot with a gun or shanked, but Daniel had never expected to find an arrow protruding from the man's chest. There had to be some hidden symbolism to Carmichael's death, even though the man before Daniel had been anything but a martyr, but at the moment, the only thing on Daniel's mind was his upcoming wedding and the wedding trip he and Flora planned to take. They were going to Scotland, where it was colder and the outbreak of cholera that had been raging in the South for months wasn't a threat.

Daniel had been looking forward to spending time with his bride, who had been tantalizingly close but just out of his reach these past few months. They would be truly alone for the first time, free to explore their feelings and bodies at leisure. Their wedding trip would be slow and luxurious, the weeks away devoid of the fear, pain, and never-ending ugliness that had punctuated Daniel's London life. Daniel thought of all the ways in which his precious happiness could be disrupted if he allowed himself to get involved in the investigation, and he unwittingly shook his head, desperate to push away a gnawing sense of inevitability.

"I think you and I need to take this one, Jason," Daniel said at last. "We have too much history with the Carmichaels to allow Inspector Pullman to head up the investigation."

Inspector Pullman, for all his good intentions, wasn't qualified to unpick the life and death of a man who'd been a viper in a nest that spanned both Essex and London and was expanding daily by means of opium, prostitution, smuggling, and intimidation.

More than anything, Daniel wanted to turn the investigation over to the Brentwood Constabulary and wash his hands of the Carmichaels, but this wasn't a case for the local police. This went much deeper and might lead to London, where Brentwood officers had no authority and Scotland Yard would need to get involved.

"We owe him nothing," Jason said.

"No, we don't, but we owe it to the community. This murder happened on our patch. It's important to figure out what happened and if this was an isolated incident or part of a bigger conflict that could put Birch Hill at the center of a turf war."

Jason sighed heavily. "Well, when you put it that way."

"Let's get him down," Daniel said. "Where do you want to move the body?"

"Redmond Hall. There's a disused shed behind the stables. It's cool, so the body will keep for several days."

"I came in a dogcart, so I'll be able to deliver the body to you."

"Thank you." Jason walked behind the tree and began to untie the rope. "This is an unusual knot," he said.

"It almost looks medieval," Micah piped up.

"How so?" Jason asked.

Micah shrugged. "I've seen something like it in a drawing."

"A drawing of what?"

"I think it was of a ship. This might be a nautical knot," Micah said eagerly.

Jason seemed to file the information away, and the two men worked to untie the rope and lower the body to the ground.

"Shall we pull out the arrow?" Daniel asked. The arrowhead was embedded deep inside the body and would probably mangle the flesh if pulled backward.

"Let's leave it for now," Jason said. "I'll remove it surgically once I get him on the table. And let's put up the top of the cart to shield the body from view. We don't want anyone to see you with Tristan

Carmichael's earthly remains. You know how gossip spreads around here."

Daniel nodded. Little of interest happened in Birch Hill, and the Carmichaels were both respected and feared since their influence stretched far and wide, as did the profits from their business dealings. There would be some who would jump to unwarranted conclusions that could result in Daniel arriving at church in a casket rather than his wedding finery.

Daniel nodded and bent down to grab the legs. Jason picked up Carmichael's torso, and together they carried the body to the cart. Rigor mortis prevented them from bending Tristan's legs, so they positioned the body against the seat and anchored it by planting Tristan's feet against the front panel. Then Daniel pulled up the leather top in case he should come across someone in the lane. The top did not conceal the body, but the shadow it cast made it more difficult to make out the passenger's face and upper body. Unless the driver of the oncoming vehicle slowed down and looked very closely, they would not notice the shaft of the arrow or make out the dried blood on Carmichael's brown coat.

Micah ran up behind them and handed Jason Tristan's top hat, which Jason plopped on Carmichael's head.

"See you at Redmond Hall," Daniel said once he had climbed in and taken up the reins.

Jason lifted a hand in farewell, and he and Micah headed back to collect his bag, the rope, and Tom.

Chapter 3

Once Daniel had brought the body and the boys had been dispatched to the kitchen to enjoy well-deserved tea and jam tarts, Jason and Daniel reconvened in the shed. Tristan Carmichael's body lay on the trestle table between them, and the late-afternoon light gilded his features, making him look as if he were merely asleep since Jason had shut the man's eyes. If not for the arrow protruding from Tristan's chest, Daniel would have expected him to awaken, sit up, and demand to know what he was doing in Jason's shed.

"Are you going to autopsy him?" Daniel asked once he'd managed to tear his gaze from Tristan's still face.

"The cause of death is obvious, and, in this case, I don't think I should open up the body without permission."

"Yes, I agree."

Tristan Carmichael was the only son of Lance Carmichael, who'd held Essex in a firm grip of vice for decades and wouldn't look kindly on Tristan's body undergoing an unauthorized postmortem in a shed by the stables. Such lack of respect might lead to repercussions neither Daniel nor Jason were prepared to risk, not because they were afraid for themselves, but because they feared for their loved ones.

Lance Carmichael's name elicited fear in everyone, from gentlemen, whose many sins Carmichael could divulge whenever he chose to, to working men, whose businesses and jobs could disappear on Carmichael's say-so, leaving their families to starve. Lance Carmichael was good to those who served him well and poured money into his many enterprises, but the threat was always there, and everyone knew of someone who'd stepped out of line and had paid the ultimate price in either reputation, fortune, or their very life.

The Carmichael network had grown exponentially since Tristan had been sent to London to oversee expansion into the city and had managed to quash or absorb several less-powerful gangs in order to take control of the East Side. Despite playing at being a gentleman and adopting the dress and manners of his betters, Tristan had been a remorseless criminal. The promise of grievous bodily harm or financial ruin had usually been enough to get him what he'd wanted, and as he had explained to Jason when Jason had questioned him in connection with the abduction of Charlotte Haze, the gangs operated according to their own code of honor. For the most part, this meant they did not go after each other's wives or children and limited their vengeance to those directly involved, but that could always change, depending on the offense, and an entire family could be exterminated.

"We need to inform Lance Carmichael of his son's death," Daniel said. "I expect he will tell the rest of the family and send someone to collect the body."

"I would rather his men did not come to my home, but I don't care to keep the body here any longer than necessary either. Perhaps I will deliver the body myself," Jason replied.

"What was Tristan doing here?" Daniel asked as he looked down at the corpse. "He was based in London, and even if he had come to visit his family, he wouldn't be anywhere near Bloody Weald."

"Perhaps he'd come to see someone else," Jason said.

"You mean Davy Brody?"

"Davy has a long history of working with the Carmichaels and sells their ale at the Red Stag. And at one time, Tristan was very fond of Moll Brody."

Tristan and Moll had enjoyed a brief courtship several years before, but their budding romance had come to an abrupt end when Lance had discovered that his son had been cozying up to a barmaid who was known to be generous with her affections. Moll wasn't the sort of woman Lance had wanted for his son, and shortly after the relationship had ended, Tristan had married a woman of his father's choosing. Last Daniel had heard, Tristan and his bride had welcomed a son, and by his own admission, Tristan also had an illegitimate son from a liaison he'd engaged in before his marriage. The boy would be about two or three now and lived with his mother, but Tristan had taken an interest in his son and made sure the child and his mother wanted for nothing.

"Moll would be a good place to start," Jason said.

"But Moll is married to Bruce Plimpton now," Daniel protested.

"I'm not suggesting that Moll and Tristan were still romantically involved, but Moll always knew everything that went on in the village and beyond. And she's married to a known associate of the Carmichaels. She might know what Tristan was doing in Birch Hill and whom he might have been meeting in the woods."

"You think he was meeting someone?" Daniel asked.

"Tristan Carmichael never struck me as someone who enjoyed nature. Why else would he go to Bloody Weald if not to meet with someone in secret?"

"Moll doesn't even live in Birch Hill anymore," Daniel reminded Jason.

"No, but she still has ties to the village and comes to visit her uncle on a regular basis."

"How do you know?" Daniel asked, genuinely curious.

Jason's interaction with the villagers was limited to the family's weekly outing to church and the occasional accident that required surgical intervention. He wasn't the sort to gossip with his patients, and Katherine Redmond wasn't one to engage in baseless tittle-tattle.

"Moll and Mary grew close while Mary lived with us in Birch Hill," Jason replied. "Moll still calls on Mary from time to time. I believe they saw each other several times over the summer."

Daniel nodded. That made perfect sense. Micah's sister, Mary, had never quite fit in in Birch Hill. Neither family nor a servant in Jason's home, Mary was the only Irish inhabitant in the village other than Micah, and her fiery nature as well as her child born out of wedlock had made her something of a pariah among the villagers. Moll, who had a reputation of her own to contend with, had befriended Mary, and the two young women had probably confided in each other, knowing they wouldn't be harshly judged. Daniel hadn't known that they had renewed their friendship since Mary had returned from America, but it made perfect sense that they would find comfort in each other's company once again.

"Do you think Mary might know something?" Daniel asked.

"I doubt it, but I will ask," Jason promised. "But first, I need to learn as much as possible from the body and the method of murder without conducting a postmortem."

"Is there anything unique about the arrow?" Daniel asked.

"I don't know very much about archery, but it looks fairly standard to me. The fletching is made of brownish feathers. Maybe pheasant or wild turkey. What do you think?"

Daniel ran his fingers over the fletching. "I expect some noblemen prefer to use distinctive fletching, but they would use arrows only when bow hunting on their own land, which is rare these days. I've never been invited to join a hunt, but I believe rifles are the weapons of choice."

"And what would they use for fletching if they did hunt with a bow?"

"Probably feathers from birds found on their estate, but they wouldn't make the arrows themselves."

"So, who would make the arrows for them?"

Daniel shrugged. "Perhaps their gamekeepers, or they would have the arrows custom made."

"Do you know of anyone in or around Birch Hill who hunts with a bow?" Jason asked.

"Bloody Weald lies at the edge of the Chadwick and Talbot estates, but there hasn't been a hunt organized by the Chadwicks since Colonel Chadwick died, and Tom would recognize the arrow if it was made by the Chadwicks' gamekeeper."

"What about Squire Talbot?"

"The squire used to join hunts organized by Colonel Chadwick, but the Talbots are still in half mourning for their daughter. According to my mother-in-law, they occasionally dine in company but don't accept invitations to any other social events. And Squire Talbot is not someone who has ever hunted for the pleasure of it."

"Would a bow and arrow be used for anything else?" Jason asked.

236

"Archery competitions."

"What about poaching?"

Daniel considered the question. "I suppose it's possible, but poachers usually come out at night, which would make it difficult to hunt with a bow, especially since most animals go to ground after sunset. Poachers are more likely to use traps, but I don't believe anyone in the area has reported a problem with poachers."

"I see," Jason said resignedly. "There isn't much to go on."

"No."

The light that streamed through the open door of the shed had softened, the rays slanting as the autumn sun began its descent toward the horizon. It was too late in the day to do anything but wish each other a good night and return to their respective homes.

"I will call on Lance Carmichael first thing tomorrow," Daniel said as he moved toward the door.

"I will have a word with Moll."

"She always did have a soft spot for you, but then Moll had a soft spot for anything in trousers," Daniel said.

"People are quick to jump to conclusions," Jason replied. "I don't know that Moll ever indulged her passions, but her flirtatious nature made her an easy mark."

Jason reached for a padlock that rested on a dusty shelf. The two men stepped outside, and Jason locked the shed behind them, putting the key in his pocket before they walked companionably toward the house in the gathering twilight.

Printed in Dunstable, United Kingdom